"I didn't mean to startle you. I came in late last night.

"In the storm..." Devon was talking too fast. Her voice kept bumping up against her galloping heart.

My God, what was this all about? She couldn't be frightened—Devon O'Rourke didn't scare easily. This was the man who'd been named as the father of her sister's child. In spite of the harshness of Eric's features, except for that brief flash of anger in his eyes, he didn't look at all like someone capable of violence. In fact, there was something about him that was almost...oh, good heavens, the word *sweet* was the one that came the most insistently to mind, with that endearing distraction, the juxtaposition of a fuzzy pink-hatted head and tiny waving fist against a naked, muscled masculine chest.... Her heart gave another lurch.

She could be in no danger here, not from this man.

Not right this minute, anyway.

Dear Reader,

July is a sizzling month both outside *and* in, and once again we've rounded up six exciting titles to keep your temperature rising. It all starts with the latest addition to Marilyn Pappano's HEARTBREAK CANYON miniseries, *Lawman's Redemption*, in which a brooding man needs help connecting with the lonely young girl who just might be his daughter—and he finds it in the form of a woman with similar scars in her romantic past. Don't miss this emotional, suspenseful read.

Eileen Wilks provides the next installment in our twelve-book miniseries, ROMANCING THE CROWN, with *Her Lord Protector.* Fireworks ensue when a Montebellan lord has to investigate a beautiful commoner who may be a friend—or a foe!—of the royal family. This miniseries just gets more and more intriguing. And Kathleen Creighton finishes up her latest installment of her INTO THE HEARTLAND miniseries with *The Black Sheep's Baby*. A freewheeling photojournalist who left town years ago returns—with a little pink bundle strapped to his chest, and a beautiful attorney in hot pursuit. In Marilyn Tracy's *Cowboy Under Cover,* a grief-stricken widow who has set up a haven for children in need of rescue finds herself with that same need—and her rescuer is a handsome federal marshal posing as a cowboy. Nina Bruhns is back with *Sweet Revenge,* the story of a straitlaced woman posing as her wild identical twin—and now missing—sister to learn of her fate, who in the process hooks up with the seductive detective who is also searching for her. And in *Bachelor in Blue Jeans* by Lauren Nichols, during a bachelor auction, a woman inexplicably bids on the man who once spurned her, and wins—or does she? This reunion romance will break your heart.

So get a cold drink, sit down, put your feet up and enjoy them all—and don't forget to come back next month for more of the most exciting romance reading around…only in Silhouette Intimate Moments.

Yours,

Leslie J. Wainger
Executive Senior Editor

Please address questions and book requests to:
Silhouette Reader Service
U.S.: 3010 Walden Ave., P.O. Box 1325, Buffalo, NY 14269
Canadian: P.O. Box 609, Fort Erie, Ont. L2A 5X3

The Black Sheep's Baby

KATHLEEN CREIGHTON

Silhouette

INTIMATE MOMENTS™

Published by Silhouette Books

America's Publisher of Contemporary Romance

SILHOUETTE BOOKS

ISBN 0-373-27231-6

THE BLACK SHEEP'S BABY

Copyright © 2002 by Kathleen Modrovich

Books by Kathleen Creighton

KATHLEEN CREIGHTON

has roots deep in the California soil but has relocated to South Carolina. As a child, she enjoyed listening to old timers' tales, and her fascination with the past only deepened as she grew older. Today, she says she is interested in everything—art, music, gardening, zoology, anthropology and history—but people are at the top of her list. She also has a lifelong passion for writing, and now combines her two loves in romance novels.

Prologue

She woke in the milky twilight that passed for darkness in the city, knowing she'd dreamed of Susan again. As always, she couldn't remember much about the dream—no details, not even a face. Just a voice—Susan's voice, childish and frail, calling to her. Calling her, pleading with her. *Help me…help me, Devon. Please…don't leave me. Help me….*

She threw back the covers and rose, paced barefoot to the window. She stared out across the glittering jeweled carpet that stretched all the way to the sea, squinting hard to hold back angry tears. How was I supposed to help you, she thought, when I didn't even know where you were? *You ran away, damn you. It's not my fault. It's not my fault!*

She held herself tightly as she shivered, and swallowed hard, once, then again. A tear ran warmly down her cold cheek.

Susan had been fourteen when she'd run away—almost a woman. But the voice in her dream was that of a little child.

Help me, Devon....

Dammit, Susan, she thought, angry and weary at the same time. I *am* helping, can't you see that? I'm sorry if I let you down, but I'm trying to make it up to you now, the only way I know. Isn't that enough?

She brushed at her cheek and jerked away from the window. The luminous numbers on the clock portion of the built-in entertainment center beside her bed glowed green-gold in the gray twilight—2:14 a.m. Way too early to even think about leaving for the airport. And yet she knew better than to try to go back to sleep. Calm, now, and resolute, she went to her walk-in closet and took her rolling over-nighter from its shelf. She lifted it onto the bed, unzipped it and began, carefully and methodically, to pack.

December 20—On I-80, Somewhere in Nebraska

His eyes wanted to close—insisted on doing so, in fact, in spite of his strenuous arguments against it. That, plus an inarguable need for fuel, forced him off the interstate.

He chose an exit somewhere east of Grand Island that promised half a dozen motels and at least that many restaurants. He bypassed all of them, though his stomach had been complaining for the last fifty miles, and pulled instead into a gas station where he could pay at the pump. While unleaded gasoline gushed into the tanks of his six-year-old Dodge, he stood with shoulders hunched and hands in his pockets, rocking himself in the bitter Nebraska wind and reflecting on how the California winters had spoiled him.

Just beyond the roof of the gas station's convenience store he could see a big green Holiday Inn sign, like a beacon summoning his exhausted mind and body into a safe harbor. But as much as he yearned for rest, as much as he knew he *needed* rest, he also knew that right now there was only one harbor in the world that would feel safe to him.

"We'll be there by tonight," he told his passenger, sound asleep in the back seat. "Five more hours…"

The fuel nozzle clicked off. He replaced it in its cradle, climbed back into his car and, after a moment's indecision, pulled across the parking lot and up to the drive-through window of the fast-food place next door. He ordered a double cheeseburger and a jumbo coffee and a short time later was back on the interstate, heading east toward evening.

In his rearview mirrors he could see, reaching toward him out of the west like menacing fingers, the dark purple clouds of the oncoming storm.

Chapter 1

It was the week before Christmas, and Lucy was sorting laundry.

She acknowledged that fact with a sense of mild astonishment—and not-so-mild vexation, for Lucy Rosewood Brown Lanagan was not a person to whom the adjective "mild" could normally be applied. At least, not often or for long.

"It's too quiet to be Christmas!" she declared loudly, though more to herself than to her sister-in-law, Chris, who was sitting at the kitchen table thumbing through magazines, looking for recipes.

"This looks good," Chris said without looking up. "Walnut squares…"

"Eric's allergic to walnuts."

Lucy said it without thinking, an automatic response—which she realized a moment later when Chris looked up and eagerly asked, "Oh, is he going to be here for Christmas this year?"

A familiar pain made Lucy's voice uncharacteristically light when she replied with a shrug, "Haven't heard from him." And a moment later asked, "What about Caitlyn?"

Chris's eyes jerked away, shifting back to the magazines spread out on the table in front of her as she said in a tone as artificially cheery as Lucy's, "She doesn't know for sure. Says she'll try her best to make it, at least for Christmas dinner." And a poignant little silence fell between the two women, fraught with empathy and unvoiced yearnings.

"It's too *quiet*—" Lucy began again, just as, with faultless timing, a door banged sharply and loud thumping noises started up out on the back porch.

Chris gave a gurgle of laughter. She and Lucy both looked toward the kitchen door as it burst open to admit their menfolk along with a gust of freezing wind. Lucy knew the smile in Chris's shining eyes was only a reflection of her own, though it gave her as much embarrassment as satisfaction nowadays to admit, even after more than thirty years, that the sight of her husband's face could still give her that seasick feeling under her ribs.

"Getting colder," the man himself announced as he ducked into the service room across the hall to wash up in the laundry tub. "That storm's on its way. Be here before morning."

"Forecast said midnight." Lucy's brother Wood zigzagged over to give his wife a hello kiss, peeling off gloves and ski cap on the way. "Pack it up, darlin'. I want to get back to the city before this thing hits."

"Edward Earl," Lucy said in a no-arguments voice—well aware that as his big sister she was the only person alive allowed to call him by his given name—"you've got plenty of time, you can stay and have some supper. I've got a roast in the oven and a Jell-O salad in the fridge, so you just go on in there and get washed up. Supper'll be on the table in ten minutes."

"I'd do as she says, if I were you," Mike said in a warning tone, grinning as he came into the kitchen, rolling down his shirtsleeves. He paused to give Lucy a peck on the cheek.

"Smells good. What've you two been up to?"

Though she wasn't the demonstrative sort, she gave him an elbow in the ribs to let him know her heart was doing a happy little skip-hop at his nearness.

"Looking up recipes. Everything all battened down out there?"

"Everything that can be... *More* recipes?" Mike was looking sideways over Chris's shoulder at the spread on the table. He cocked an eyebrow toward Lucy. "Who're you cooking for, the third division?" In an aside to Wood he added, "We had leftovers from last Christmas dinner for Easter." And then, probably because he knew very well how precarious Lucy's mood had been lately, coming up on this particular holiday season, he wrapped his arms around her and murmured next to her ear, "Honey, there's just gonna be the four of us. You don't need to go to so much trouble."

"Five," Chris said firmly, shuffling magazines into a stack as she stood up. And when nobody said anything for a second or two she lifted her head and looked her husband hard in the eyes. "Caitlyn's coming. She said she would."

"She said she'd *try*." Wood's voice, too, was gentle.

"She'll be here." Chris gathered up the pile of magazines and marched off to the parlor.

Wood muttered what sounded like, "I hope so," under his breath as he pulled out a chair and sat in it. And after a moment, "Sure does seem strange, doesn't it? Not having a houseful of kids around for the holidays? Doesn't seem like—"

Lucy interrupted him with a swipe at his shoulder. "Edward Earl, take off your coat before you sit down at the table!''

''Yes'm.'' He rose obediently, not trying to hide a grin.

''And hang it up, too—you know where it belongs.''

''Just like old times...'' he grumbled good-naturedly as he carried his chore clothes across the hall to the service room.

''Old times...'' Lucy muttered angrily, turning to the sink. It wasn't that she was angry, really, just that she could feel a familiar heaviness creeping around her heart, thinking about the season...the quietness. She hated that heaviness; it made her feel old and scared, panicky and depressed, all at once. *Old times. How I miss them... Mama, Daddy, Gwen. And the children. Where did the children go?*

Not to be put off, Wood was saying as he reclaimed his chair at the table, ''Speaking of 'old times,' I was thinking about how it used to be, you know? When we were kids.'' His wife came back in just then, and he craned to look up at her and reached for her hand. ''You should have been here, Chris.'' And then he laughed. ''I'm surprised you weren't, actually. Mom had this habit of inviting people. Anybody who didn't have anyplace else to go, Mom made 'em welcome here at our house. But even without the strays, we always had a crowd—remember, Luce? Aunts, uncles, cousins—whatever became of all those cousins, anyway? Does anybody ever see them anymore?''

''We mostly lost touch after Mama and Daddy died,'' Lucy said without turning from the sink where she was washing green beans. ''I get cards from some of them at Christmastime. You know, those letters everybody sends now that they've all got their own computers.''

''What I can't figure out,'' said Wood, lacing his fingers together behind his head and gazing around the kitchen, ''is where we used to put everybody. This room—this *house*—sure seems a lot smaller that it did when we were kids.''

"Everything seems smaller than it did when we were kids," Mike put in. He'd taken his usual place at the foot of the oval oak table and was indulging in a back-cracking stretch. "Something about perspective." Everybody paused to look at him alertly in case he meant to go on, since it wasn't Mike Lanagan's way to do much talking at times like this. Mostly, Lucy's husband liked to just watch and listen, like the reporter he'd been and still was, she knew, in his heart.

"What we *did,* was," she said when it had become apparent Mike had said all he was going to for the time being, answering Wood's question even though she knew he hadn't really expected an answer, "we put all the leaves in this table and the grown-ups squeezed in right here in the kitchen. The kids got to eat in the parlor. Dad would bring in two sawhorses and put planks on them, and Mom would put the oilcloth tablecloth from the kitchen table over that. The good linen tablecloth went on this table, along with the good china.''

Lucy turned on the faucet to run water over the beans. "Us kids got to eat on plastic or paper plates, like a picnic. I'm surprised you don't remember that, Earl. You always used to try to start food fights with your cousin Donnie— Donnie Hewitt, remember him? He could make milk come out of his nose, which is a talent I don't imagine benefited him much later in life.''

Wood passed an embarrassed hand over his eyes. His wife was gazing at him in wonderment. "That *was* a long time ago. I guess we've grown up some since then.'' There was a reminiscing silence, and then he added without any laughter at all, "I wonder sometimes, you know? About Mom and Dad—what they'd think if they could see the way we turned out.''

Lucy didn't say anything, but became intent on chopping up bacon to go on the green beans. She was thinking about Wood—Earl—and how he'd been just in high school when their parents were killed in that car accident in the middle of a bad thunderstorm. Thinking about it, even though it had been so many years ago, made her throat tighten up.

It's this season, she thought. She hoped she wasn't turning into one of those people who hate the holidays just on general principles.

Wood went on, after clearing his throat in the loud way men do when they're in danger of showing emotion. "They'd have to be surprised about old Rhett becoming president of the United States." Everybody laughed at that.

Lucy surprised everyone, herself most of all, when she turned, swiped the back of her hand across her nose and said fiercely, "They'd have been just as proud of you, Earl, becoming a teacher. Just think of all the lives you've—" Embarrassed, she broke it off and jerked back to the sink.

There was a long pause, and then Wood said softly, "Know who I think they'd've been proudest of, Lucy? *You*."

She made a sound like a startled horse. "Me!"

"Yeah, you. Keeping this place going all by yourself, after Rhett and I ran out on you. Think how many generations this farm has been in our family. All the way back to—"

"Great-great—I don't know how many greats—Grandmother Lucinda Rosewood, my namesake." Lucy picked it up, smiling around the ache inside her. "Who once foiled a Sioux raiding party when she set her barn and fields on fire, tied up her baby in her apron and climbed down the well and hid there—"

"While the fire burned all the way to the river!" everyone chimed in, laughing, on the refrain. It was an old Brown family story, well-loved and often told.

The laughter died and silence came. Wood broke it with a gruff, "You did—we all know it. It was you who kept it here for us all to come back to."

"For a little while, anyway," Lucy said. She plunked the kettle full of beans down on the stove and turned on the burner, making as much noise as she could to cover up the sounds of knowledge and sadness and inevitability in the room behind her. Just small rustling, shuffling sounds, because no one was about to say out loud what they all knew to be true, which was that, after Lucy, there wasn't going to be anyone left to keep the farm going. At least, not anyone in this family. The best they could hope for, Lucy knew, was that someone would buy the place who'd want to live in the big white farmhouse and keep cows and sweet-smelling hay in the great old barn. But the fact was, more than likely the farm was going to end up being swallowed by some agribusiness giant with offices in a high-rise in Chicago or Dallas or Kansas City, and the house and barn and all the other corrals and outbuildings would stand empty and abandoned like so many places she'd been seeing lately. Until, one by one, they were torn down, blown apart by a high plains wind, or fell in on themselves from the sheer burden of their loneliness.

Desperate to banish the images and feeling guilty for the sadness she'd brought upon them all, Lucy turned from the stove with a determined smile. "Hey," she said lightly, "who knows? Maybe one of the grandkids…"

Wood gave a hoot of laughter. "*Grandkids?* Whose? You guys having some we don't know about?"

Mike gave a wry snort and spread his hands wide as if to say, *Don't look at me.*

"Rhett's got grandkids. Lauren's two boys—"

"Who're way out there in Arizona on an Indian reservation. And I doubt Ethan and his rock star are going to be in any hurry to start producing rugrats." Wood was ticking them off on his fingers. "Ellie and her husband—and weren't the secret agent twins off in Borneo, or someplace, nabbing orangutan poachers?"

Mike cleared his throat. "That was last year. They're in Madagascar now."

"Ellie and Quinn are still in the honeymoon stages," Lucy said defensively. "So are Ethan and his Joanna, for that matter. There's plenty of time. Nobody's rushing anybody." She had a secret horror of becoming one of those mothers who're always hinting and nagging about grandchildren, as if their children's sole purpose in life was to provide them with some.

"And then there's our Caitlyn…" Wood said that on an exhalation, sitting back in his chair. He shook his head. "I honestly don't know if Caty'll ever get married, let alone have kids. She's too busy saving the world." Lucy thought that his eyes seemed sad, following his wife as she moved from place to place, quietly setting the table and that Chris seemed unusually pale, her face more than ever like a lovely porcelain mask.

"What's Caty doing these days?" she asked, glancing at Mike to see if he'd noticed anything out of the ordinary; if anything *was* amiss, he'd see it, and they would talk about it later.

"Who knows?" And Wood added, with a rare flash of impatience, "If she shows up for Christmas, you can ask her. Maybe you can get more out of her than we've been able to."

"Wood," Chris admonished softly.

"I guess that just leaves Eric." Wood was smiling, now, but too brightly. "You heard from him this year?"

Lucy shook her head. "It's early yet. He'll probably call." She opened the oven door and reached for the potholders, but Mike was already there, taking them from her and lifting the heavy roasting pan onto the counter.

"He'll call," he said in a low voice, catching her eyes and holding them across the sizzling, crackling pan, through a fog of garlic and spices and oven-roasted beef. "He always does."

Lucy held on to the quiet confidence in her husband's eyes and drew strength from it, as she had so many times before. And she smiled her special smile, just for him, to let him know she appreciated it.

"So, there you have it," Wood said, coming upright in his chair in hand-rubbing anticipation of dinner. "No pitter-patter of little feet any time soon. Personally, I'm in no hurry to become a grandparent. Hey—I don't feel old enough to be a grandparent. I feel like I just got grown-up myself. Frankly, I'm enjoying spending time with my wife." He reached for her hand as she slipped into the chair next to him. "Anyway, we keep pretty busy, between my classroom full of kids and Chris's physical therapy patients."

"It's not a matter of being *busy,*" Lucy said, in between carrying platters and bowls to the table. "Lord knows, we've always got plenty to do around here. It's just—" she broke off, frowning, to survey the table, then finished it as she seated herself. "It's just too *quiet,* that's all. Earl, will you please ask the blessing?"

He did, since she'd made the "request" in her no-arguments tone of voice, and then everyone was busy passing and serving and tasting and exclaiming about how good everything was. After that, conversation turned to the blizzard that was predicted to arrive later that night, and the new versus the old and familiar Christmas specials on TV.

It wasn't until later, when the taillights of Wood and Chris's car had gone bumping down the gravel driveway to flash bright and then wink out as they turned onto the paved road, that Lucy could finally turn into the comfort of her husband's arms. "I'm sorry," she whispered against his chest.

"Mmph," said Mike in a tender murmur. "What for?"

"I didn't expect to feel like this—not at Christmastime."

"Like what?"

It was a moment more before she could bring herself to say it. "Sad…" And then added quickly, afraid he might misunderstand, "About getting older, I mean. I always thought I'd be like Gwen, so full of laughter, right to the end."

"Gwen had her sad moments," Mike said into her hair.

"I suppose. I think—" she turned her head to one side so she could listen to his heartbeat and was silent for a moment, drawing strength from that. "I think it's because everything's changed, and I haven't. I still feel exactly the same as I did when I was young, and Mom and Dad and Gwen were alive and all the kids were home and it seemed like the house was always full of people and noise and laughter. I don't know how to explain…"

"You don't have to. You miss the kids. I miss 'em, too."

Lucy nodded. She and Mike held each other and listened to the silence together, and after a while she found that the silence didn't seem quite as lonely as before. "It *would* be nice to have some grandchildren," she said, with a laugh and a very small sigh. "To visit now and then."

Mike chuckled. "Maybe we could rent some."

She wasn't sure what it was that woke her. She lay for a moment, blinking and disoriented, listening to the howl of wind and the dogs' excited barking, watching patterns of light and shadows move across the walls.

"Mike—wake up! Someone's coming up to the house."

They'd fallen asleep watching television, as they often did, Mike stretched out on the couch with a book on his chest and his reading glasses askew, Lucy bundled in an afghan in Gwen's La-Z-Boy recliner. She righted the chair with a *ka-bump* and struggled out of the afghan, at the same time searching with her feet for her house shoes. "Mike! There's a car coming up the drive. Who on earth do you suppose—"

"Wha' time is it?" Scowling at his watch, he answered himself in tones of disbelief. "Almost *eleven?*" By that time Lucy was halfway across the kitchen.

She stopped in the service room long enough to grab a coat, which she was shrugging into as she stepped onto the back porch. The cold stabbed at her, making her gasp. The dogs were less frantic now that they'd achieved their purpose and the household had been properly roused. Lucy quieted what remained of the racket with a sharp command, then stood hugging herself as she watched the car lights drive past the front of the house and right around to the back door, the one everybody except strangers always used. *Not a stranger, then.*

She had begun to shiver violently, but it wasn't from the cold. She no longer felt the cold at all, in fact, only a strange numbness.

The car crunched to a stop near the bottom of the steps, just where Wood and Chris's car had been parked a few hours before. Lucy found that she was standing at the top of the steps, but when she would have started down, Mike's arms came from behind to encircle and hold her where she was. The car's headlights went dark. The door opened, while Max and Tippy, the two Border collies, circled close, wriggling and whining.

Lucy wondered how she could shake so hard and still stand. She wondered how she would stop herself from bursting into tears.

The driver—a man—stepped out of the car and slowly straightened. For one brief moment he lifted deep-set shadowed eyes toward them while his hands reached to touch the dogs' eager, searching muzzles, buried themselves in thick, silky fur. His face was gaunt, hard-boned, a stranger's face.

Lucy's breath caught in a sharp whimper. She could see that his lips were moving and knew he was speaking to the dogs, but she couldn't hear his voice for the rushing wind inside her own head. She felt Mike's arms around her, holding her so tightly she could scarcely breathe. She clung to his arms with icy fingers and tried to draw a breath, tried to speak—anything—just to say his name. But she couldn't. Not even in a whisper.

He was moving quickly now, almost at a run, not toward her, not toward the house, but around to the other side of the car. Then he was opening up the back door, and for what seemed to Lucy like a very long time he leaned into the car, bending over something inside. Suspense keened in her ears as she watched him take something bulky from the back seat and come back around the car, carrying it by a handle. Something covered with a blanket...

Mesmerized, Lucy stared at the blanketed *something* as her son carried it toward her up the steps, slowly, one at a time. It could not be what it seemed to be. It *couldn't*. But, two steps below her he halted, swinging the thing from his side to in front of him so that he held it in both of his hands, like an offering in a basket.

There was no mistaking it; it was an infant's car seat.

Lucy tore her eyes from it, then, to gaze into the face of the hollow-eyed stranger. He smiled, though she could tell it was an effort, his teeth showing white in a beard-shadowed face.

"Hi, Mom. Hi, Dad. Merry Christmas."

The breath she thought she'd lost came forth in a rush, but before she could make her lips form a reply, she heard Mike's voice saying calmly, "You'd better come inside, son. It's cold out here."

Then, somehow, they were all in the nice warm kitchen, and Eric was lifting the infant carrier onto the table. In a daze, Lucy reached out to touch, then carefully lift the soft pink-and-yellow-and-blue blanket that covered it.

"Her name's Emily," Eric said gruffly behind her.

Lucy said nothing at all. She was gazing down at the face of the sleeping baby, like a single perfect flower in a nest of thistledown.

"She's five weeks old," her son went on in the hard, cracking voice she didn't know. "And she's mine."

Chapter 2

Eric knew what their next question would be, and answered it before they could ask. "Her mother's dead. Died when Emily was born. I've been looking after her."

And while he was saying that his eyes were moving slowly around the room, seeing it all with a strange sense of déjà vu. Weird, he thought. *Not a thing's changed.*

Not that he'd really thought anything here would have changed, but what he hadn't been prepared for was that *he* hadn't. He'd thought he'd managed to grow up in the ten years or so he'd been on his own, but damned if he didn't feel exactly the same as when he'd last stood in this kitchen, just a kid, then, and all frustrated and misunderstood yearnings. It was as if time had stood still, as if he'd left home only hours ago, not years. He even felt the same itchy and indefinable sense of guilt.

Maybe it was the guilt that made it so hard to look at his mother just then. Because he didn't want to see any new lines around her eyes, unfamiliar streaks of gray in her hair. Didn't want to see the love, the joy, the anguish he'd caused her plainly written on her face. He imagined she'd be wanting to touch him. Of course she would. She'd never been overly demonstrative, Lucy hadn't, but she had her little ways. She'd be wanting to reach out to stroke his arm, hug him quick and tight, sniffle and cough and give him that fierce little frown she thought could hide the fact that she was crying.

It surprised him to realize that, deep down inside, it was what he wanted, too—to feel his mother's arms around him, soothing his fears away and mending his hurts the way she'd always done when he was a child. It was because he wanted it so badly that he wouldn't let himself get close enough to her to give her the chance.

Truth was, present feelings to the contrary, he knew he *had* changed. He was a long way from being that boy she remembered. He'd seen too much of all the bad stuff she'd tried so hard to protect him from. Yes, he'd come back to his childhood home in order to make his stand, but that had been instinct more than logical thinking, like a cornered animal looking for a tree to climb. In the final analysis he knew this was his battle and his alone, and when it came time for the showdown, he was going to have to fight it alone.

All of which he meant to explain to them, eventually. Tomorrow. Or was it today, already? He'd lost track of time. Right now, all he wanted to do was sleep. He *had* to sleep. He'd tell them everything…later.

"Son. Don't you think you could have called?"

Eric heard the anger, no matter how quiet his dad's voice might be. Dad was angry with him for the way he'd hurt Mom, which was something Eric could understand. Now. In fact, he understood a lot of things he never had before, now that he'd experienced those protective paternal feelings himself, firsthand.

He rubbed the back of his neck and felt the tiredness there creep right on down into his bones. Bracing himself, he turned to look his father straight in the eyes. "Sorry, Dad. I just didn't think I could afford to stop. I was afraid that storm was going to catch up with me before—"

"You didn't *stop?*" Lord help him, his mother had found her voice. And it was as sharp-edged and scratchy as he remembered it. He felt an unexpected surge of emotion as she rounded on him, all puffed up like an angry hen. "You mean, you drove all the way here from…what, L.A.? With that tiny baby in the car? Without *stopping?* Eric Sean Lanagan, I swear—"

"I stopped when she needed feeding or changing," he protested. And damned if he wasn't starting to feel like that kid again, defensive and resentful—until he caught a glimpse of something way back in his father's eyes, something he'd have sworn was laughter. He managed a smile then, though his face felt stiff with it; it had grown unaccustomed to that particular exercise. "She's a real good baby—took to traveling like she was born to it. *I'm* tired, though…" He made no attempt to cover his yawn, then felt his smile turn crooked. "What about it, Mom? Still got a bed here for me?"

She didn't say anything for a moment, just looked at him with her chin high and her arms folded across her chest, riled up and breathing hard. He had the feeling she might be holding her arms like that because she was using them to keep herself together. There was a shiny, fragile look around her eyes that made him want to pull his gaze away from her—only he couldn't. She looked so tiny…so much smaller than he remembered. He wondered if it was because she'd actually shrunk, or because he'd grown.

Then…"There always has been, Eric," she said in a furious, breaking voice. And there was a suspenseful little silence, like the moments between the lightning and the thunder.

It wasn't a thunderclap but something much smaller that broke the silence—a series of snuffling, snorting noises. Eric turned toward it—he was well-conditioned to that noise by now—but his mother was there before him, reaching into the nest of blankets in the infant carrier and making crooning sounds. Startled, he glanced at his father, but his dad wasn't looking at him. His dad was watching his mother as she lifted the little one from her carrier and held her up so they could both look at her…and look, and look, and look.

Eric stood and watched them all from what felt like a great distance, or—the more apt analogy came to him—as if he were seeing them through the lens of one of his cameras. There was Emily, blinking and squinting the way she did when she was getting herself waked up, working her way through her repertoire of expressions. His father's expression he couldn't read at all. But his mother's…oh, man. His mom's face was rapt, radiant, beautiful. The everpresent camera in his mind clicked madly away, and his photographer's heart grieved for the priceless moment…the once-in-a-lifetime shot lost.

His emotions were a mess, a hopelessly tangled, senseless knot, and because he didn't want to begin to try to pick those emotions apart, he said gruffly, "Her formula and stuff are in the diaper bag. It's in the car. I'll get it." And he fled from the warmth and love and security he'd come so far to find and plunged back into the darkness he'd grown accustomed to, the darkness and all-enveloping loneliness.

And the cold.

He'd forgotten about that cold. It shocked his body but cleared his mind, so that when he came back into the kitchen he was violently shivering but better prepared to deal with it all—his dad's questions and his mom's fussing, and Emily's much less complicated demands.

"It's snowing," he announced as he placed the diaper bag on the kitchen table.

But nobody was paying any attention to him.

"So, your flight got delayed, huh?" The young man at the car rental counter clicked his tongue in sympathy. "Too bad—happens a lot, these days. You're lucky you got in at all. I imagine they're gonna be shutting down here, pretty soon."

"Shutting down?" Devon glanced up from the rental agreement fine print she'd been speed-reading through and frowned. "Not the interstate, I hope."

"No, no—I meant the airport. Although, they'll probably close down the interstate, too. This one's supposed to be bad—a real Arctic Express."

"Wonderful..." She wasn't sure whether or not she'd be using the interstate, but it didn't sound like good news; the interstate was probably the last thing that would close, and if that happened it didn't bode well for the lesser roads.

Her perusal of the agreement completed, she nudged it toward the young man with an inaudible sigh of vexation. Devon didn't like monkey wrenches thrown into her well-laid plans.

The rental agent jerked his eyes away from their rapt appreciation of her hair. He gave a covering cough and murmured, "Okay, Ms. O'Rourke, if you'll initial here, here, and here, and then sign at the two *X*'s, we'll have you on your way. That's one Lincoln Town Car, non-smoker, with CD changer and GPS."

"Snow tires?" Devon asked hopefully.

"Uh, all our cars are equipped with all-weather tires, ma'am. But it can be hard to find your way around in a blizzard, especially at night. If you've got very far to go, you might want to think about getting a hotel someplace close by, and just riding it out.''

She shuddered inwardly. The size of the airport had come as enough of a shock to her; the idea of being stuck in one of the adjacent hotels was appalling. ''I'm sure I'll be fine,'' she said briskly as she picked up her keys. ''It's only about thirty miles or so from here, I believe, and I have the GPS. Now, if you'll just tell me which one's mine...'' She hitched the strap of her traveling combo handbag-laptop-attache case over her shoulder and reached for the handle of her rolling carry-on.

The rental agent gave a ''don't say I didn't warn you'' shrug. ''It's right outside that door there, ma'am—space number sixteen.'' He paused, then, unable to help himself, added, ''Must be important, to send you out on a night like this.''

''Oh, it is.'' Devon's smile wasn't pleasant. The court order stashed away in her attache case seemed to flare and glow in her mind's eye. Too bad, she thought with grim satisfaction. Mr. Eric Sean Lanagan was about to learn the hard way that one simply did not skip out on Devon O'Rourke, *or* her clients.

For the second time that night, the barking of the dogs awakened Lucy. This time she was actually in bed, cozy and warm and snuggled against Mike's back. It seemed like only minutes since she'd closed her eyes.

It had been after midnight by the time she'd gotten Eric and the baby settled in Eric's old room—he'd insisted on staying there instead of in the clean guest room, bedding down amongst all the boxes of dusty books and old clothes ready to go to the church rummage sale. He'd also insisted on keeping Emily with him, though Lucy had offered to take her—begged to take her—and let him get some decent rest.

Oh, but it had been hard to see him looking so exhausted. So drained and distant—like a stranger. This wasn't the Eric she remembered, the son she'd yearned for and dreamed of welcoming home again. In her husband's arms, in the privacy of their room she'd at last allowed herself to cry for that boy whom she knew in her heart she was never going to see again.

"Oh, Mike," she'd sobbed, "he's so different."

"He's grown up," her husband replied, stroking her back.

"Yes, but…I don't *know* him. He wouldn't even let me hug him. And…oh, Mike—a *baby!* I never thought—"

"Hey—you wished for grandkids, remember?" His voice was wry and amused…reassuring. "Goes to show you—be careful what you wish for. *Someone* might be listening."

They'd laughed together, then, and she'd fallen asleep with Mike's arms around her.

Now, she poked him and hoarsely whispered, "Mike—wake up. The dogs are barking. I think someone's here."

"Oh, Lord—not again…" He lifted himself on one elbow and squinted at the alarm clock on the nightstand, muttering thickly a moment later, "Tha'can't be right…"

Lucy was already out of bed and struggling into her favorite old bathrobe, the fuzzy yellow one that Mike said made her look like a newly hatched baby chick. A glance out the window told her the storm was continuing unabated, but aside from that, she couldn't see a thing—no car lights coming up the drive, nothing but darkness and swirling snow.

But there was definitely someone out there; she could hear a distant thumping noise, now. Someone was pounding on the door. The *front* door, which only a stranger would use.

"What in the world?" Muttering breathlessly, she hur-

ried—barefoot and as quietly as possible—out of the bedroom and down the stairs. Mike, grumbling under his
breath, was close behind her.

She ran down the dark hallway, flipping light switches
as she went. Through the frosted front door glass and heavy
storm door she could make out a faceless, huddled form
silhouetted by the outside lamp. It kept shifting from side
to side and appeared to be wracked every few seconds by
violent shivers.

It took Lucy only a moment to open both doors—being
country-raised, it would never have occurred to her not to—
and then for a second or two more she stared open-mouthed
at the apparition standing on her front porch. Surely, it
could *not* be an incredibly beautiful young woman with
wild and windswept hair—*crimson* hair that glowed like
fire in the porchlight, yet glittered with a crystalline frosting
of ice. Her bare hands clutched a coat together under her
chin—a cloth coat, some sort of raincoat, it appeared to be,
totally unsuited to an Iowa blizzard.

"I'm so s-s-sorry to b-b-bother you so late," said the
apparition. "My…f-flight was delayed, and I was
afraid…they were g-going to c-close the roads, and then it
t-took longer than I…th-thought it would to f-find…" All
at once the lovely frozen mask of her face seemed to crack,
and her eyes took on a look that bordered on panic.

That was more than enough for Lucy. "Oh, good grief,"
she exclaimed, and clutching a handful of snow-dusted coat
sleeve, hauled the alien visitor inside. It was on the tip of
her tongue to add a roundly scolding, *"What in the world
were you thinking of?"* when she felt Mike come up behind
her.

His polite "Can we help you?" struck Lucy as a silly
question; obviously, if anybody'd ever been in need of
help, it was this girl.

But for some reason, maybe the very conventionality of

it, the words did seem to revive the young woman's spirits. Her face once again arranged itself in its perfect mask, and she drew herself up and thrust out her hand in an abrupt way that to Lucy said "Big City" as plain as day.

"Hello—I'm Devon O'Rourke. I hope I've found the right place. I'm looking for Eric Lanagan."

Startled, Lucy blurted out before she thought, "Eric! But, he said—" then caught Mike's eye and the tiny but unmistakable shake of his head and stopped herself in time. She finished it only in her mind: *He said the baby's mother was dead.*

"I'm afraid Eric's asleep right now," Mike said smoothly, falling back once more on those polite conventions that sounded so ludicrous to Lucy, given the circumstances. "Would you like some coffee? Is there anyone with you? I don't see your car."

At that the woman seemed to hesitate, glancing uneasily back toward the door as if she feared she might have entered some sort of trap. It was what came of living in the city, Lucy thought. Nobody trusted anybody anymore. Probably, she reflected, with good reason.

"It's down there—" the woman gestured vaguely toward the dark windows "—somewhere. I couldn't get it up the driveway. I think it might be stuck in a ditch." She gave a shiver, then a resigned sigh. "And no, there isn't anybody with me." A look of surprise flitted briefly across her face as she said that, as if she couldn't quite believe she'd admitted such a dangerous thing.

Mike chuckled in his reassuring way. "We're Eric's parents. You're safe here. Tell you what—let's all go in the kitchen while we figure out what to do, shall we? Lucy?"

"Right," said Lucy.

But her mind was racing. Maybe it was because she was already emotionally battered, and on top of that, jittery from getting woken up out of a sound sleep twice in one night, but the woman's suspicious nature seemed to be rubbing off on her. She had an uneasy feeling about this girl, this Devon O'Rourke. Protective maternal instincts she'd all but forgotten and long presumed dormant were springing to life inside her. Maternal instincts that had somehow expanded to include not only Eric, but a baby girl named Emily.

Devon was an early riser and lifelong insomniac, so she was neither surprised nor particularly annoyed to find herself awake in total darkness. A myopic squint at the illuminated face of her digital watch told her it was nearly 5:00 a.m., which seemed to her a reasonable enough getting-up hour—though even if it hadn't, it would never have occurred to her to go on lying in bed, trying to force herself back to sleep. An utter futility, she knew from experience.

She sat up, groped for the lamp on the nightstand and turned it on. Throwing back the comforter, she swung her feet to the uncarpeted wood floor, shuddering at the unexpected coldness of it. She wasted no time finding and putting on the slippers she'd so generously been given last night, along with the flannel pajamas she was currently wearing and the bathrobe draped across the foot of the bed.

Strange people, these Iowans, she thought as she pulled the bathrobe around her shoulders, pausing to sniff the worn, slightly stiff and nubbly flannel. *Soap, fresh air and sunshine...* She could almost see the bathrobe flapping on a clothesline in a stiff spring breeze.

These Iowans, these Lanagans—Eric Lanagan's parents. She wasn't sure what to make of them. She'd never met anyone quite like them before. Most people, she was sure, even out in the country like this, would have been suspicious, even frightened at finding a stranger at their door in the middle of the night. But these people had not only invited her in, they'd insisted on making her fresh hot coffee, giving her dry clothes and a bed for the night. What kind of people would do such a thing, in this day and age?

Of course, she *had* mentioned Eric's name. No doubt they'd taken her for a friend of their son.

That thought made her squirm with an unfamiliar guilt, which she shrugged away. It was their fault if they'd jumped to the wrong conclusion; they'd no business being so trusting.

Hugging the bathrobe around her, she paced to the windows, and in doing so discovered two things. One, that the storm responsible for her demoralizing fiasco last night was showing no signs of abating; and two, that she was ravenously hungry. Those facts led her to two more obvious conclusions: One, she wasn't likely to be leaving here any time in the immediate future; and two, someone was bound to be getting up soon, this being a farm, after all. Didn't farmers always get up at the crack of dawn? She felt certain no one would object if she made coffee, and maybe some toast.

She left her room, tiptoeing, and made her way to the stairs. She could see well enough; someone had thoughtfully left a light burning in the downstairs hallway—and somehow she *knew* this wasn't usual, that it had been left on this particular night for *her,* the stranger in the house. She felt again that annoying twinge of guilt.

Her descent of the stairs wasn't as quiet as she'd have liked. A couple of the steps creaked—a sound that seemed appallingly loud in the sleeping house. She paused once to listen to see if she'd woken anyone but heard only the howling of the wind.

Downstairs, she found that the light in the hallway provided plenty of illumination to the kitchen as well, so she set about making coffee in that soft, forgiving twilight. She'd watched Eric's mother—*Lucy,* yes, that was her name—make coffee last night, so she knew where everything was; Devon was the sort of person who noticed and remembered details like that. She easily found bread and a toaster, popped in two slices and rummaged in the refrigerator for jam—Devon never ate butter—while the coffeemaker filled the room with heavenly smells and friendly sounds. She had located a jar of what looked as if it might be homemade apricot preserves when she heard, from close behind her, something that made her scalp prickle.

A snort of surprise.

And then, a most definitely unfriendly *"Who the hell are you?"*

Adrenaline surged through her, in part due to the shock of that unexpected voice, but certainly compounded by the fact that the jar of preserves she'd been in the process of reaching for had just gone shooting out of her hands like a bar of wet soap. For a few seconds she was too busy to give much attention to the owner of the voice as she grabbed at the jar, juggled it ungracefully and finally managed to clasp it to her chest, rightside up, thank God, against her wildly pounding heart.

Immediate disaster averted, she turned to face the man she'd come so far to find, and heard a hiss of indrawn breath and then a sound, not words, just a mutter of denial and rejection.

Oh, yes, and rejection was plain in his face, too. But that much she'd expected. For the rest, well, what *had* she expected?

Someone younger, for one thing. According to Emily's birth certificate Eric Lanagan was twenty-eight—barely two years younger than Devon. Based on the way he'd been behaving—ignoring the court's order, running away—she'd pictured him as some arrogant, irresponsible kid.

She hadn't expected him to have so much *presence*—and presence wasn't an easy thing to manage in tousled hair and bare feet, in pajama bottoms and a bathrobe hanging open—a flannel bathrobe, moreover, that was almost the twin of the one she herself was wearing.

She hadn't expected a face with so many hard edges and sharp angles. Bathed in the warm yellow light of the open refrigerator, it still appeared pale as chalk, shadowed and gaunt.

She hadn't expected him to look as if he'd just confronted a ghost.

Her next thought was that he looked instead like a man who wanted very much to strike her down where she stood—and might well have done so, but for the baby in his arms.

She gulped involuntarily and, eyeing the baby sideways as if it were a possibly dangerous wild animal, plunged into breathless explanations. "I didn't mean to startle you. I came in late last night. In the storm. Your parents—" She was talking too quickly; her voice kept bumping up against her galloping heart.

My God, what was that all about? Devon O'Rourke didn't scare easily, and besides, this was the man who'd befriended her sister, the man Susan had named as the father of her child. In spite of the harshness of his features, except for that brief flash of anger in his eyes, he didn't look at all like someone capable of violence. In fact, there was something about him that was almost…oh, good heavens, the word *sweet* was the one that came most insistently to mind, with that endearing distraction, the juxtaposition of a fuzzy pink head and tiny waving fist against a naked, hard-muscled masculine chest. Her heart gave another horrifying lurch.

She could be in no danger here—not from this man—not right this minute, anyway.

Was she? He was coming toward her. Her mouth went dry. She couldn't help it—she backed into the open refrigerator.

"I didn't ask you how you got here. I asked who the hell you are." His hand shot out, narrowly bypassing her head, and to her utter dismay, she flinched. He noticed it, too, and lifted one disdainful eyebrow, lending the half smile he gave her a devilish slant.

"You trying to warm things up in there?" he asked dryly as he plucked a bottle of formula from the refrigerator.

Feeling incredibly foolish, Devon ducked sideways to get out of the way while he closed the refrigerator door—and felt even more foolish when the toaster popped up just then and made her jump again. At the same moment, the coffeemaker launched burping and gurgling into its incongruously merry finale.

Never more glad to have something to do, she turned to the task of assembling a plate for her toast, a spoon for the preserves and a mug for the coffee. And all the while her unwelcome companion worked right alongside her, so close she had to be careful not to bump elbows with him as he ran tap water into a bottle warmer, plugged it in next to the toaster and plunked the bottle of formula into it.

Neither of them spoke a word, at least not to each other. The baby made impatient snorting, snuffling noises, which Devon was sure were a prelude to something much more disruptive. Eric responded with something that was probably meant to be a croon but in Devon's opinion more resembled the ratchety sound a tiger makes when it purrs. If she'd hoped to use the interlude of activity to gain back a measure of her normal confidence and self-control, that sound alone would have made it an uphill battle. She felt the strain of it in her spine, her temples, the back of her jaw.

After she'd poured herself a cupful of strong black coffee and taken a testing sip, she leaned back against the counter and watched sideways through the steam as the man lifted the bottle from the warmer and, expertly juggling the baby, squirted a few drops of formula on his wrist to test its temperature. She couldn't help but notice that his hands, though large, were sensitive looking, with long-boned agile fingers, and that not even the boyish lock of nut-brown hair that had fallen across his forehead did much to soften his hawkish profile.

"You must be Eric," she said after a long silence, and was pleased with her cool, friendly tone. "And this is Emily?"

"Okay, so you know who *we* are." Still intent on what he was doing, it was a moment or two before he cocked that sardonic half smile once more in her direction. "You still haven't answered my question."

Eric was fairly proud of the way he'd handled the situation so far. Especially considering the shock it had given him to walk into the kitchen expecting to find his mom up early and making breakfast, the way he remembered her doing most all the mornings of his growing up. And instead seeing…*her*. Like coming face-to-face with a damn ghost.

It was all he could do to make himself look at the woman. He kept his eyes on the little one instead, and found himself smiling way down inside the way he always did when he watched her eat and listened to her make those hardworking squeaky drinking sounds. He felt himself go calm and quiet, and didn't look up when the woman told him, in her brisk lawyer's voice, what he'd already guessed.

"I'm an attorney. I represent Gerald and Barbara O'Rourke, Emily's grandparents. I have a court—"

"I know *what* you are." He was able to keep it low, but couldn't quite manage soft. The words grated between his teeth like he was chewing on glass. "Now you tell me *who* you are, or I swear you're gonna be out that door, blizzard or no blizzard."

"I'm afraid I won't be leaving right away, Eric." Now her voice was just as hard-edged as his. "Not unless that baby goes with me. I have a court order—'' A gasp interrupted her, and both of them jerked like guilty children toward the sound.

Eric's heart gave an exultant leap. For there was Lucy, coming through the kitchen doorway, wearing a look he remembered well—the look of a mama bear charging to the aid of her cub.

Chapter 3

Before his mother could say a word, Eric sang out with false cheer, "Hey, Mom!" He motioned her into the room with a savage little jerk of his head. "Say hello to the viper you let into your house last night."

Then he got out of her way while his mother swept past them both, her house shoes making sandy noises on the linoleum floor. When she reached the table she halted and rounded on them, fired up and vibrating like some kind of self-contained energy source. And, darned if Eric even remembered that old yellow bathrobe she was wearing, the one that had made her seem to the little boy he'd been like a tiny broken-off piece of sunshine.

"What's this?" she rasped in that rusty-file voice of hers, glaring at her houseguest. "Devon? Something about you taking Emily? What's this about a *court order?*"

The lawyer's mouth popped open, but Eric, who was beginning to enjoy himself, got there first. "That's right, Ma." He lifted the bottle and squinted at what was left in

it before placing it on the counter, then shifted the little
one to his shoulder. "This lady has chased me—" he said
that in a crooning tone as he patted "—all the way from
L.A. She means—ah, *there* you go, darlin'—to take Emily,
here, away from me."

Beside him, Devon carefully put down the piece of toast
she'd been holding and dusted crumbs from her hands, like
someone preparing to do battle. Folding her arms across
her chest, she turned her head toward him and said in a
low, even tone, "I wouldn't have had to *chase* you if you
hadn't skipped town. You do know I could have sent mar-
shals to arrest you and bring you back by force?"

His mother heard that, and exclaimed, *"Arrest you?"*
She glared, outraged, at Devon, then glanced wildly toward
the back porch door. For one lovely moment Eric thought
she might be about to do what he'd threatened to do—
throw her houseguest out on her rear, blizzard or no.

Apparently that thought occurred to Devon, too, because
she pushed away from the counter and appealed to Lucy in
a hurried and breathless voice. "Mrs. Lanagan—Lucy—
please believe me, that's the last thing—"

"You said you were a friend of Eric's!"

She shook her head emphatically. "No. I said I was *looking* for Eric. I'm sorry if you misunderstood."

From his spectator's spot at the counter, Eric sourly muttered, "Lawyers."

Devon shifted her attention back to him; he could feel
her eyes even though he still couldn't bring himself to look
directly at her. That once had been more than enough.

"Look," she said, "it doesn't have to be like this." He
had to admit that quiet but vibrant voice would be a real
killer in the courtroom. "I wanted to come myself, to meet
you in person and, perhaps, appeal to your sense of compassion."

"Compassion!" With one word, she obliterated the emo-

tional shell he'd built around himself, like popping a balloon.

"—and fairness—"

"Good God—*fairness?*" Eric was so incensed he could hardly believe what he was hearing, much less articulate a reply. All he could do was stare down at the upturned face of the baby, now asleep and snoring gently on his chest, keep swallowing hard over and over again, trying without success to ease the knots of emotion inside him. Knots of fear, and anger and fierce protective devotion.

"Yes, fairness." Having put him out of action for the moment, Devon was appealing once more to Lucy. "I'm an attorney, Mrs. Lanagan. I represent the O'Rourkes—"

"O'Rourke?" Lucy sounded like a startled frog.

"Emily's grandparents. Parents of Susan O'Rourke, Emily's mother. They've filed a petition for custody—"

"Wait a minute," Lucy interrupted, "didn't you say *your* name was O'Rourke?"

Eric swore softly but savagely.

"Mrs. Lanagan...please—"

"Hey," Mike said from the doorway, not even trying to smother a yawn. "What's going on?"

Eric let out his breath in an audible hiss. He had mixed feelings about his dad walking in just then. On the one hand, the interruption was at least something of a safety valve; he could feel tensions easing, not only in himself but in the room as well, as though everyone in it had taken the moment to retreat and regroup. On the other hand, his confidence in his own adulthood was having a hard enough time finding its compass in this house where he seemed to be constantly and confusingly tilting back and forth between being someone's father and someone's son.

"Mike." Lucy pressed a hand to her forehead. "She's a *lawyer.* She says she has a court order. She means to take Emily away."

"Now wait a minute." Devon had a hand up as if to ward them all off. "That's for a judge to decide. All my clients want is a fair hearing. They have a right—"

"Your *clients?*" Three faces turned toward Eric, wearing almost identical expressions of surprise, as if, he thought, they'd all forgotten he was there. The little one chose that moment to stir on his shoulder and draw a long shuddering breath. He shifted her into the cradle of his left arm and began automatically to rock her, soothing her, soothing his anger. "Who're you kidding? Just who are you, really? Come on, quit lying to us."

"I'm not—"

"Evading, then. Come on—your name's *O'Rourke.*" His lips curved stiffly, though he felt no amusement at all. Bracing himself, he forced his eyes to meet the ones he'd been so steadfastly avoiding. "Did you think I wouldn't notice? Or did you think I'd consider it a coincidence that you happen to look just like her?"

Well…not *just* like her, he realized now that he *was* looking at her, really looking, for the first time. Hardship and drugs had robbed Susan O'Rourke of the beauty and vitality she'd been born with, long before Eric had ever laid eyes on her, dulling the fiery hair to a coarse and tarnished bronze, turning luminous alabaster skin to the color and texture of dirty chalk. But it was the eyes that made him understand, maybe for the first time, just how cruelly Susan O'Rourke had been cheated of everything she could have—*should* have—been. The eyes that glared back at him now held sparks of green fire. They glowed with life and energy and intelligence. Staring into them made him burn with sadness and anger, remembering Susan's eyes, especially the way he'd seen them last—sunken pools, shadowed with hopelessness and despair, fading to flat, final emptiness.

"Susan was my sister."

The words broke the tension that had been building in that dimly lit kitchen, like a baseball hurled through a window. Totally engaged with each other in some sort of tug-of-war of wills, Devon and Eric both ignored Lucy's gasp, Mike's small gesture warning her to be still.

"I wasn't trying to evade anything," Devon went on, in a voice utterly devoid of emotion, speaking only to Eric, now. "And I certainly didn't intend to lie to anyone about my identity. I simply didn't think it was relevant. As I said, I'm here acting as attorney for the O'Rourkes—period. The fact that they also happen to be my parents, and that the baby you're holding is my niece, has no bearing on anything. You know that a judge has ordered you to submit to tests to prove your claim of paternity. *If* you are, in fact, this child's father, then you will have an opportunity to explain to a judge why you think you, a single man with a globe-trotting lifestyle, should be granted custody of an infant over a mature and loving couple able to provide a secure and stable home."

Loving couple. Stable home.

To Eric the words were knives, stabbing at his heart. He caught his breath and held it, afraid that if he let it loose all the rage and grief inside him would come with it. And he didn't want to take that risk, not while he was holding the little one. He'd promised—he'd sworn on his life—to protect her. He'd vowed to make sure none of it touched her, *ever*—neither the violence nor the ugliness of the images in his mind.

"Mr. and Mrs. Lanagan—please, hear me out. Let me explain…" He could hear Devon appealing to his parents in that cold, intelligent voice, so different from Susan's. Susan's voice had been higher pitched, sweeter, but cracked and ruined, so that she sounded like a little girl with a sore throat.

"Eric, you have to keep my baby safe. Don't let them

get her. Please…promise me you won't let them have her. Please…''

"I will…I will. I promise.''

Those were the last words Susan had ever heard. In the next moment the monitor's alarm had gone off and nurses had come running, shoving him roughly aside. He'd stood then almost exactly as he was standing now, holding the little one just like this, gazing down at her perfect, innocent face while his insides filled up with the ache of an angry sadness, and elsewhere in the room people went on speaking to each other in words that had no meaning to him.

"It's true, Lucy…Mike.'' Devon had her back to him now, addressing his parents as if they were a jury—which was, he understood, just what they were: a jury of two. Her voice was vibrant, but the emotion in it seemed calculated to him; she sounded like an actress—a good one—doing a scene from a play.

"Susan—Emily's mother—was my younger sister. She ran away from home five years ago, when she was fourteen. My parents tried everything they knew of to find her, without success. We hadn't heard a word from her in all that time—we didn't know whether she was alive. We probably still wouldn't know, except that when your son brought her to the hospital, she was unconscious and *he*—'' she tossed a little nod toward Eric ''—claimed he didn't know her last name. They listed her as Susan Doe. Eventually, the police identified her from fingerprint records my parents had given when they'd filed the missing person report. They'd had us both fingerprinted when we were kids, apparently.'' She paused for just a moment, and Eric saw her touch her forehead as if that troubled her, somehow.

Then she drew a regrouping breath and went on. "Of course, my parents rushed to the hospital. They were too late. Susan had died.'' With flawless timing, she let the words hang there.

Lucy, his mom—tough as nails on the outside but, as Eric well knew, with a marshmallow interior—made a distressed sound. He saw her reach for his dad's hand. To hide her triumph, Devon turned from them and took two slow steps toward Eric. Her eyes burned into his as she continued her relentless summation...burned with that cold green fire.

And in spite of himself, in spite of *everything,* he found himself admiring her. He thought, my God, she's incredible. *Incredible.* How, he wondered, could a woman look so damn beautiful so early in the morning, with smudged makeup, uncombed hair and wearing his dad's old flannel bathrobe?

How could someone so damn beautiful be so damn *wrong?* And how could looking at someone that beautiful make him feel so full of...what *was* it he felt? Not hate—hate was cold, bitter, a decay in the soul. This was something white-hot in his gullet, like a slug of straight whiskey; a fire underneath his skin, an electrical charge delivered straight to his brain. Watching her, listening to her, made him burn with anger, seethe with frustration, vibrate with excitement.

Damn her. She made him feel—there was only one word for it—aroused.

"She'd regained consciousness," Devon said softly, still speaking to his parents but holding *his* eyes, "long enough to provide the information for her baby's birth certificate. Since she had named Eric Lanagan as the father, Emily had been released to his custody." Displaying a nice flair for the dramatic, she whirled back to face her real audience. "Since then, he has refused to allow my parents—Emily's grandparents!—to visit her. You can imagine how much grief this has caused these people—to find their lost child after so many years only to lose her forever—" at which point, predictably, Lucy sniffed, coughed ferociously and dabbed at her nose "—and then on top of it, to be denied the chance to see and hold their grandchild. I'm *sure* you can understand why Susan's parents are hoping to have the chance to raise their daughter's little girl."

"Like a second chance," Mike said, and there was a suspicious gruffness even in *his* voice.

"Exactly…" It was a sigh of satisfaction. Eric half-expected her to add, "I have nothing further, Your Honor."

He looked defiantly straight at them, then, because he could feel them all watching him. Three pairs of eyes arrayed against him, full of questions and accusations. His mom and dad sitting close together at the table, Lucy with one hand clutching Mike's and the other clamped across her mouth and her eyes suspiciously bright. And Devon standing, half facing them, with one hand on the back of a chair and her head turned toward Eric, as if she'd just finished addressing a jury. As, of course, she had. And it was obvious to him that he'd already been found guilty.

He had to get out of there, blizzard or no blizzard. He had to find a way to calm his mind, prepare himself for the battle ahead. He could put the little one down in his room—she'd sleep awhile, yet—and go someplace peaceful and quiet.

And he knew, suddenly, just where he could go. The place he'd escaped to so often during the turbulent years of adolescence.

But first, he couldn't hold back the question. One question. He hurled it at Devon and it shattered the silence like a shovelful of gravel slung against a wall.

"Why'd she run away?"

"What?"

Ah—was it only his imagination, or had Devon suddenly gone still…still as a marble statue? Except, he thought, no statue had ever had hair that vivid.

"You heard me," he said harshly, staring at her so hard

his eyes burned. "If your parents' house was such a great place to raise a kid, why did Susan run away from it?"

Her eyes shifted downward to the hand that rested on the chair back, for that moment the only thing alive in her frozen face. Then she pulled in a breath, drew herself up, and said stiffly, with none of the previous vibrancy, "My sister was always…a difficult child. She was headstrong, spoiled. Rebellious. I imagine she ran away because she didn't like my parents' rules. I'm sure she thought she was being mistreated—"

He couldn't stop a laugh; it made a sound like blowing sand. "No kidding." Tucking the little one more securely into the cradle of his arm, he pushed away from the counter. No one said a word when he moved toward the door.

Halfway there, though, he turned. Again, he felt as if he had no choice as he softly said, "Tell me something, Devon. How can you do this? To Emily. After—"

"What?" She'd gone wary and still again, just like before. "After what? I don't know what you're talking about."

He took a breath, then shook his head. No. He couldn't do it, couldn't say it, not with his parents—his mom—sitting right there. Instead, he smiled a hard little smile. "Susan used to say she had nobody—you know that? Nobody who cared a damn about her. *Nobody in this world,* that's how she put it. That includes you, doesn't it? You said, you *imagine* she *probably* thought she was being mistreated. Don't you *know* what was going on in that house? Where were you when your sister needed you?"

It was cruel, and he knew it. It wasn't like him; he knew that, too. He felt the weight of his mother's reproachful glare and fortified himself against it, bracing himself to meet instead that other pair of eyes…green-fire eyes.

There was no flinching this time; she lifted her chin and those eyes stared back into his. "I was away—in law school—when Susan left. I'd have been there for her, if I'd known—''

"Yeah, keep telling yourself that," Eric said softly. He turned and left them there.

His going left a void that wasn't quite silence. To Devon it felt like a sort of hum, a current of tension and distress that was almost audible.

She heard Lucy exclaim, "I don't know what's happened to him, I swear," and probably would have gone after her son then and there if her husband hadn't tightened his hand on hers and held her where she was—a tiny, private gesture. She also saw the tight, shiny look of worry on Lucy's face, the tense and skittery way she sat, like a little brown bird perched on a fence, half a heartbeat away from flight.

"How 'bout some of that coffee you made? Sure smells good." Mike's gaze, thoughtfully appraising, rested for a long moment on Devon, and she felt a curious tickle of unease. She couldn't have explained why; his eyes held only kindness and compassion.

They've seen a lot, those eyes. They understand too much.

"I'll get it," said Devon, and was surprised when her voice came out sounding as rusty as Lucy's. "How do you take it?"

"Black is fine."

"Lucy?"

"What? Oh—yes...black for me, too."

Devon busied herself with the cups, and it didn't seem strange to her that she, the guest, was serving coffee to her host and hostess. She was bemused and dismayed, though, to find that she felt shaky and nervous doing it.

I'm probably just hungry, she told herself as she bit savagely into cold leathery toast.

Chewing stolidly, she thought about the scene that had just played itself out in the predawn quiet of a farmhouse kitchen…her first meeting with the Opposition. Her thoughts weren't happy ones. She hadn't handled it well. She'd allowed herself to be blindsided, and that *never* happened. When she thought about *why* it had happened, all she could come up with was an appalling list of mistakes. *Her* mistakes. Devon hadn't gotten to be where she was—that is, one of the most respected and feared young attorneys in Los Angeles—by making mistakes.

Mistake number one, she'd failed to prepare herself. So far, the information she'd been able to assemble on Eric Lanagan was proving to be woefully inadequate. Most of what she knew was in the form of statistics gleaned from Emily's birth certificate: age, race, state of birth. From that, with the help of her firm's private investigators and a judge's court order, she'd been able to put a trace on his credit cards. Finding him, tracking him down—that had been the easy part. Finding out *who* he was—that was where she'd slipped up.

Mistake number two, she'd fallen victim to her own preconceived notion of what kind of person Eric Lanagan was.

Which had led directly to Mistake number three, seriously underestimating her opponent.

And why not? she furiously asked herself. Twenty-eight-year-old man with no employer of record befriends nineteen-year-old homeless woman and gets her pregnant—that sure said Punk-Sleazebag-Loser loud and clear to her! Didn't it?

She'd come prepared to despise Eric Lanagan and to fight him tooth and nail on behalf of *her* parents for custody of her sister's child. But she hadn't expected *this*. Hadn't expected him to have parents who would unhesitatingly take her in in the middle of a blizzard and give her a bed and pajamas and an old flannel bathrobe that smelled of sunshine. She hadn't expected Eric Lanagan to have such an interesting and compassionate face, and eyes—like his father's, she was startled to realize—that gave the impression they'd seen way too much of the world's failures and cruelties.

And, she thought with a curious little flutter high up under her ribs, it was damn hard to despise a man while he was holding a tiny baby in his arms, tenderly, expertly feeding, burping and then rocking her to sleep.

"So—you live in Los Angeles, then?"

Devon jerked her gaze and her attention back to the two people who were sitting at the table, sipping coffee and watching her—one warily, the other with that quiet curiosity she found so unnerving. She chewed toast, drank coffee, swallowed.

"That's right—downtown L.A., actually." It was Mike who'd asked, but she addressed her reply to Lucy as well. And all the while she was telling the Lanagans about her high-rise corner condo—from one side of which, on a clear day, she could see the Pacific Ocean, and from the other, snow-capped mountain peaks—making bright, tension-easing conversation, with another part of her mind she was gnawing and nibbling at the problem—the enigma—of their son, like a dog with a thorn in its paw.

I need to find out more. I have to get to know him.

Footsteps thumped on the stairs, making no effort to be stealthy. Devon's heart lurched, and so did her hand; she swore under her breath as hot coffee slopped onto the front of the flannel bathrobe. Again Lucy started to get up, and again Mike held her where she was. The footsteps clumped down the hallway; a bulky shape flashed past the service room, past the open kitchen doorway. The door to the back porch opened, then banged shut. A moment later the outer door did, too. Three pairs of eyes jerked toward the windows, as if pulled by the same string.

"Chore time," Lucy announced. And this time when she pushed back her chair, her husband didn't try to stop her.

The windows were filled now with a swirling, milky light. Dawn had come, and no one had noticed.

Devon retreated to her room while around her the farmhouse awoke to the routines of a snowy winter morning. Footsteps clumped up and down stairs, doors banged, buckets rattled—activity as incomprehensible to Devon as some mysterious ritual performed by aliens. She wished she could be interested in, or at least curious about what was going on. When, after all, was she ever again likely to find herself on a *farm?* But all she felt was frustrated. Thwarted. Boxed in. She had things to do, important things. But right now none of those objectives seemed achievable. Without the means to accomplish her purpose, without the ability to change her circumstances, she felt powerless—and Devon O'Rourke did not like feeling powerless.

She'd have to call her office, at least—let them know what had happened. Still too early for that, though; the offices in L.A. wouldn't be open for hours. Even if she'd had her cell phone with her, which she didn't. What had she been thinking of, to leave it in the car? And where, exactly, *was* the car?

Pacing to the windows did nothing to soothe her restlessness. In fact, it made her feel even more as if she'd been shut into a box—all she could see out there was a wall of swirling white. Now and then the snow thinned enough to unveil shadowy shapes—nearby, the gnarled skeletons of great oak trees, and farther away, the hulking mass of a huge old barn, the kind she'd heretofore seen only on the pages of calendars and in children's picture books. She couldn't see any sign of the rented Lincoln Town Car complete with GPS—though she knew it had to be out there, somewhere, under all that snow. She hoped it wasn't in the road, at least. She hoped it wasn't—though she suspected it might be—in a ditch.

Someone, a bulky and indistinguishable shape in a parka, was crossing the snowy swath between the house and the barn, accompanied by two smaller shapes which romped and frisked in excited circles around the bulky one. Mike, apparently, because a moment later there was a soft tapping at Devon's door, and Lucy put her head in.

"Hi—" her voice was scratchy-soft, her smile strained. "I just wanted to check and make sure...Mike and I have to go out and do chores. Since Eric's not...uh... Can you keep an ear out for the baby in case she wakes up?"

Suppressing panic, Devon gulped and said, "Oh—sure, yeah, that's fine. No problem."

"Eric's gone out." Lucy gave an embarrassed little shrug and left it hanging.

"So I gathered. But, if you don't mind my asking—" Hell, she'd ask it anyway, in utter exasperation. "Where could he possibly go, in *this?*"

Lucy's smile slipped, became gentler, less strained. "Oh—the barn, I imagine." She stepped into the room, still holding the doorknob, and leaned against the partly open door. She was wearing quilted snow overalls, Devon saw, over a thermal turtleneck pullover. "It's where he always used to go when he was upset about something...or mad at us." Devon hadn't said a word or changed her expression, but Lucy suddenly shrugged and looked uneasy. "Well, you know how kids get."

"Not really," said Devon in a companionable sort of way. "Never having had any myself."

Lucy made a sound like swallowed laughter. "Well, you were one—and not so very long ago, either. You must remember what it was like."

"Not really," Devon said dryly.

Lucy looked at her for a moment as though she didn't believe her, then smiled again, that same soft little smile, and for some reason this time it seemed almost unbearably poignant. "You said your sister was headstrong and rebellious? That pretty much describes Eric, when he was growing up. Maybe that's part of what drew them to one another, do you suppose? Kindred spirits...."

Her eyes flew to the windows and she drew herself up, looking fierce and faintly embarrassed. "I've got to see to my animals. Sorry to bother you—just wanted to make sure—"

"Go ahead. I'll look in on the baby, no problem."

"Okay...well...shouldn't be long..." Halfway out the door, Lucy turned back to sweep Devon with a quick, appraising look. "If you need any warmer clothes, help yourself to whatever's in the closet. It's mostly just things I haven't gotten around to giving away, anyway."

"Okay, thanks." Devon stepped quickly forward when Lucy would have closed the door. Wedging herself into the open space she said in a low voice, terrified that she might wake the sleeping baby, "Uh, you said Eric's in the barn? I really do need to talk to him. Do you think it would be okay if I..."

"I'd wait a little while," Lucy said, and her smile was more wry, now, than sad. "Give him time to work it off."

Thwarted once more, Devon gave a little huff of frustration. "Work *what* off?"

"Whatever it is," Lucy said softly, "that's eating him up inside."

Chapter 4

After Lucy had gone, Devon went back into her room and for a few minutes stood with her toes curled up inside her oversized slippers, frowning at nothing and dithering over her choices. Her choices seemed annoyingly limited.

She needed to talk to Eric—that was absolutely number one on her priority list. But Lucy had asked her to wait awhile, so she couldn't do that. At least, not right this minute, which was when Devon preferred to do things.

In the meantime, though, she could get dressed. Should get dressed. But the clothes she'd taken off last night were still unpleasantly damp, and neither they nor anything else she'd brought with her for what she'd expected would be an overnight stay in a nice hotel seemed remotely appropriate for an Iowa farm in a blizzard. Lucy had invited her to help herself to whatever she might find in the closet, and as unappealing as that prospect was, she supposed she'd have to take her hostess up on her offer unless she wanted to spend the entire day in borrowed pajamas and an old flannel bathrobe.

Perhaps she could take a shower. Oh, she longed to take a shower; not only could she have used the morale boost, her hair was also sorely in need of the taming only a good shampooing could give it. And no time like the present, when she had the house all to herself.

But then she realized—if she took a shower, she wouldn't be able to hear the baby if she cried.

That was when it hit her—she was alone in the house…with a baby! An extremely *tiny* baby, moreover. A helpless infant no more than a few weeks old.

Panic seized her. Her heart pounded; she began to sweat. Oh, God—what did *she* know about babies? She couldn't remember ever having touched one, let alone picked up one, fed one, changed a diaper. Oh, God, she thought, what am I going to do if it wakes up?

A series of images flashed through her mind, vivid as a slide show: a tiny fist waving against the backdrop of a masculine pec that was enticingly adorned with a smooth brown nipple. A big hand with long, sensitive fingers rhythmically patting a blanket covered with pink bunny rabbits and yellow ducklings. A tiny head covered with red-gold down bobbing just below an angular beard-stubbled jaw.

She gave a snort, laughing at herself—though mysteriously, her heart still pounded.

Get a grip, Devon. Think about it—if he can do it, how hard can it be?

She could handle one little tiny baby. She was a grown woman, more intelligent and capable than most. Of course she could do something millions of people, all kinds of people, even some not-all-that-bright people, managed to do quite capably every day. And just to prove she could, she took a deep breath, squared her shoulders, opened the door and stepped out into the hallway.

The door directly opposite hers was open. Devon could see a tumbled bed, and on it what was unmistakably a fuzzy yellow…her heart gave a leap before she recognized it as a bathrobe, the one Lucy had been wearing this morning. The master bedroom, then. The door next to it was open, too—obviously a sewing room or workroom of some sort, eclectic and joyously cluttered. The door at the far end opposite the stairs was the bathroom. That left only one door—the one next to Devon's.

That door was closed. Never one to waste time once she'd made a decision, before she could even *think* about chickening out she marched up to it, seized the doorknob and turned it. Quickly and silently she pushed open the door and stepped inside. Then she just stood there, absolutely still, while her heart banged itself silly against her ribs.

Eric's room. She knew instantly that it was his, and that almost nothing in it had changed since he'd left it, probably as an eighteen-year-old heading off to college. The bedspread and curtains were faded blue denim, the furniture old, scarred and brown. There was a desk topped with a hutch, the shelves of which were filled with books, mostly paperbacks. A stereo and a revolving carousel that held an assortment of both tapes and CDs took up most of the space on a long, low dresser, along with a lamp with a parchment shade and a base shaped like a horse's head.

One surprising thing: on the walls, where she would have expected to see posters of rock concerts or sports stars, maybe some shelves lined with athletic trophies, instead there were photographs—dozens of photographs, of people and animals, buildings and landscapes, both in color and black-and-white, all expertly matted and framed. Devon recognized several shots of the barn she'd seen from her window this morning, one bathed in glorious sunset light, another—this one dramatic in black-and-white—against a backdrop of a stormy sky, still another in happy primary colors, red, green and blue, like a child's crayon drawing.

There were portraits—lots of portraits, mostly casual—of people Devon didn't know. There was a very pretty, whole-some-looking girl with freckles and a perky smile, and an incredibly old but still beautiful woman with tragic eyes and a face that looked as if it might, at any second, break into laughter. She did recognize Mike and Lucy, photo-graphed both together and separately. And, good Lord, was that—no, it couldn't possibly be—but it *was*—Rhett Brown, the former president of the United States, standing beside an old rope swing hanging from a huge tree limb. And sitting in the swing was none other than Dixie, the First Lady!

All this Devon observed in a few seconds while she was trying hard *not* to look at the one thing in the room that was trying to demand her attention. Which was a nest sur-rounded by pillows in the middle of the blue denim bed, and in the nest, what appeared to be a small snowdrift of pink bunnies and yellow ducklings.

No sense in trying to avoid it. She walked toward it slowly, tiptoeing, dry-mouthed, her heart still bumping along, gathering speed like a runaway wagon. Her knees touched the edge of the bed. She caught her breath, then leaned over to get a better look, and felt a giddy urge to laugh—not with amusement or anything like it, but simply a release of tension. And a profound sense of wonderment and awe. Tears sprang to her eyes; she found that she was hugging herself, trying to stop herself from shaking.

The cause of all this unheralded emotional turmoil was lying on her back, but propped with pillows so that she was rolled almost on her side. One tiny fist lay like a half-open blossom against a plump pink cheek. Her mouth was open, and from it issued a soft but unmistakable snore.

Susan's baby. My niece.

Devon drew a shuddering breath. "Hello, Emily," she whispered.

She put out a finger but pulled it back before she touched the fat, velvety cheek. She stood for a long time—looking, and looking, and looking.

The barn had always been Eric's special place of refuge, since the day he'd bravely and defiantly climbed the forbidden ladder to the loft, off-limits to a five-year-old, and discovered the newborn kittens his sister Ellie's cat had hidden there in the hay.

Back then it had seemed to him a safe and friendly place, warmed even on days like this by the body heat of the animals winter-quartered there, the busy and contented sounds they made filling all the spaces inside the barn so that the storms howling outside its walls seemed far, far away. In the summertime, its dim and dusty emptiness made a different kind of refuge, a cool, quiet escape from sun and responsibilities and the hot, sweaty work he'd hated so.

The camera in his mind had loved the play of light and shadow inside the old barn, a montage of patterns and colors, constantly changing: shafts of sunlight slanting through open doors, shimmering with dust motes; moonlight glimpsed through windows fogged with drifts of spiderwebs; shadows leaping across a rough-plank wall, brought to life by a swinging lantern; heat lamps bathing newborn calves in pools of molten gold....

But that was pure enjoyment. Other times he'd come to the barn, like now, with his emotions in turmoil, his heart full of rebellion and his mind full of questions. At those times it wasn't enjoyment he'd been looking for, but peace. Acceptance. And if not answers, at least the patience to wait for the answers to come.

More often then not, back then, he'd been able to find those things here—and why that was, he wasn't sure. Though later in his life he'd wondered if it was because inside the barn's walls, everything—from the spiders in the rafters to the cows with their new calves—seemed so simple, all of life reduced to its basic elements: food and shelter, birth and death. And everything beyond those walls, like the noise of the storm, had seemed, for that moment, at least, far away and therefore inconsequential.

He'd been a kid, then. Naive, to put it mildly. He found that out later in his life, too, about the same time he'd discovered that some of those things outside the barn were closer to him than he'd thought, and there was no escaping their consequences after all.

So, what was he doing now, running off to his childhood refuge when he had damn little hope of finding peace, there or anywhere else? Certainly not acceptance, not of any kind of scenario that would involve giving up Emily to this woman—this *lawyer*—and her parents. Not answers, either. Or ideas. He'd used up his last one, bringing the baby here, to the place he'd been surprised to realize he still thought of as home. For all the good it had done him, or her.

No—as far as answers and ideas went, he was fresh out. And he hadn't much hope of finding any new ones waiting for him in his mom's old barn, either. Stupid idea.

Still…amazingly, there *was* something calming about working alone in the early morning quiet, cleaning out stalls by the gentle light of a hanging lamp. It had been a long time since he'd wielded a pitchfork or shoveled manure—not activities he'd ever relished in his youth—and he was mildly surprised to discover it felt good to work up a sweat. He'd actually taken off his jacket and, finally, even his shirt.

His mom and dad had been in and out, starting the morning chores. He'd stopped shoveling long enough to ask his mom who was looking after the baby. She'd given him a searching look before answering, "She's still asleep. I asked Devon to keep an ear out for her."

He'd had nothing to say to that, and had just nodded and gone back to shoveling, using the physical activity and his own sweat to dampen down the fiery sizzle of anger in his belly.

After that, his parents, no doubt remembering his old habits, had pretty much ignored him. Still, he'd been glad when they'd finished the chores and gone back to the house, and the quiet he remembered, if not the peace, had settled once more around him.

When he again felt a cold blast of arctic air and heard the storm's howl rise abruptly from a muted roar to a banshee's scream, he thought it must be his mom or dad come back, probably to tell him the little one was awake. When he saw instead the bundled shape of someone that couldn't possibly be either of his parents, his heart gave a leap, then settled down to a quick, angry thumping.

He watched in impassive silence while the figure, clumsy in snow-dusted parka and rubber chore boots several sizes too big for her, struggled to push the door closed against the buffeting wind. She gave a wordless cry of victory when she succeeded in dropping the latch into its cradle, then whipped around and leaned against the door, breathing hard.

She looks scared to death, Eric thought, amused. *As though she'd just managed to escape a pack of ravenous wolves.*

Oh, he wanted to feel contempt for her, this thin-blooded California girl, threatened by a little snowstorm. He tried. But…dammit, there was something fierce, even triumphant about the way she threw back the hood of her parka and shook out that fiery hair of hers, and try as he would, he couldn't manage to convince himself it was contempt he really felt.

She came toward him, absently brushing snow from her coat and looking around her like someone who'd been magically transported to an alien world. Rather the opposite, he thought, of Dorothy finding herself in Oz.

"What do you want?" he asked before she'd gotten far; he couldn't explain why he didn't want her coming close to him. "She awake?"

"What? Oh—no, Emily's still sleeping, or was when I left. Anyway, your mom…" Apparently fascinated by the barn, she'd finally got around to looking at him, only to do a double take and interrupt herself with a blunt, "Aren't you *cold?*"

Eric glanced down at his naked chest. "Only when I stand around," he said meaningfully, and twirling the scoop, rammed it, with more energy than was necessary, under layers of dirty, wet, trampled-down straw. He heaved the shovelful toward the pile he'd been building in the center aisle without checking to see if his visitor was out of the way or not, and got an infantile satisfaction when he heard her exclamation of dismay.

Didn't slow her down a bit. Out of the corner of his eye he saw her skirt the manure pile, brushing straw off of her parka sleeve now, instead of snow, and come to lean her elbows on the gate of the stall next to the one he was working in.

He went on shoveling, thinking if he ignored her she'd take the hint and go away. No such luck. Apparently lawyers didn't understand subtlety. Looked like, if he wanted to get rid of the woman, he was going to have to use more direct measures.

He stopped shoveling, and scoop held at the ready, said, "What do you want?" just as *she* opened her mouth to say something. A lifelong habit of good manners—for which he could thank his mom and dad's stubbornness—made him halt and give her a sardonic go-ahead shrug.

"I was going to say I didn't know you were a photographer."

It wasn't what he'd expected. He lowered the shovel blade to the floor and leaned on the handle. "My mom been blabbing?"

"No. I went to check on the baby and saw the photos in your room. I asked about them, and she told me they were yours. And that you're a professional photographer."

He gave a soft grunt and corrected it. "Photojournalist."

She said, "Ah," and went on looking at him in a searching, appraising kind of way he found intensely annoying.

"Don't look so surprised," he said after a moment, smiling without amusement. "What did you think? Yeah, I have a profession, even earn a living at it, pay taxes and everything. You just assumed I was some homeless street person?"

"Why *shouldn't* I think that?" she shot back, riled and defensive. "How else would you have met my sister, much less—"

"Got her pregnant?"

Devon closed her eyes and held up a hand to stop him in case he meant to say more, which he sure as hell didn't. As far as Eric was concerned, any conversation with this woman was a waste of time.

"Look," she said, taking in a long draught of air through her nose—the smell of which seemed to surprise her a bit, since her eyes got watery and she blinked and gave her head a little shake to clear it before she went on. "I just thought, since we apparently got off on the wrong foot this morning—" She broke off. Eric was shaking his head.

"Oh, I don't think so, lady," he said softly. "I think that's pretty much the only foot I ever want to be on with you."

She looked at him in silence, then said just as softly, "Aren't you forgetting something? Emily is my niece. If you *are* her father, we're now family, you and I—distasteful as that may be for both of us. Like it or not, Eric, we have that little baby in common. And I'm sure we both want the same thing, which is what's best for Emily.''

Eric made a rejecting sound and turned away. Looking at her had again become impossible; his eyes felt seared by her image.

As before, she didn't take the hint and back off but instead pressed her advantage, coming right into the opening of his stall, invading his space. He wanted to shut her out, command her to leave, but again, an ingrained courtesy forced him to stand and listen to her voice, that poised, confident voice, so different from Susan's, and insidiously gentle, now.

"Look, Eric, I think I understand how you feel. You must have loved Susan. As I did. I think…my sister was very lucky to have found someone like you, after such a difficult and unhappy adolescence. At least, maybe she finally found some happiness, at the end. I know losing her was hard. My God, it was hard for *me,* don't you realize that? Hard for my parents—for all of us. And I know you must love your daughter very much. But Eric—'' she put out a hand and touched his arm, and he felt a shiver go through him, sharp and cold as a knife. "Even you must admit that your job… Your mother says you have to travel most of the time. Don't you think a stable home, with two loving parents, would be a far better environment for a child than what you, a single—''

He made a violent movement, shaking her hand off of his arm as if it were some particularly loathsome variety of bug, and glared at her with burning eyes. "You think you understand *me?* Lady, let me tell you something. You don't understand anything. You got that? *Nothing.*'' Breathing hard, he turned away from her again.

Lady, don't make me do it, he silently prayed. *Just go. Get the hell out of here. Don't make me say it.*

It was rejection as emphatic as anything Devon had ever

experienced, a door slammed rudely in her face. But it wasn't her way to flee in ignominious defeat. She stood in frozen silence, staring at the naked back he'd turned to her, at muscles bunched and rigid as stone.

Her eyes felt as if they'd been scorched; she kept blinking, trying to soothe their burning. His sudden withdrawal had shocked her; she'd thought—she'd been certain—she was saying the right things. Getting through to him. She'd sensed his pain and grief—surely she'd been right about that much.

Part of her shock was anger at herself, because once again she'd let Eric Lanagan take her by surprise. Once again she'd misjudged him. I can't read him, she thought, fighting an unfamiliar sense of failure. *He's right—I don't understand him.*

"Look—" he flung out an arm and she stiffened, composing herself to face him. But he kept his back to her as he went on, in a voice that had gone low and guttural, "I might as well tell you—you're going to find out anyway, soon enough. I'm not the baby's—Emily's—father."

Again, it wasn't what she'd expected—the admission, not the fact. Inwardly in turmoil, outwardly calm, she nodded, though he couldn't see it, but didn't say a word. After a moment he rounded on her, fierce and defiant.

"I was working on a piece—a photo essay—for the *L.A. Times.* About teenaged runaways. That's where I met her— Susan. I didn't know her last name—didn't know any of their names. It took me months, living with them on the streets of L.A., but I finally won their trust—some of 'em, anyway. Susan was one. She seemed…special to me, right from the first. There was something about her, you know?" He stopped and looked away, and Devon felt an ache, the beginnings of a lump in her throat.

A tiny movement from Eric tugged at her attention; she let her eyes follow the ripple of his throat when he swallowed. But then, without permission, somehow her eyes just continued on down, slaloming over the planes of a chest still shiny with sweat. Irrelevantly, she thought, *He lied. He is cold.* She could see his nipples had gone boldly erect, hard and sharp as buttons.

There was something in the silence. She jerked her gaze upward and found his eyes on her. And the darkness in them seemed more anguished, now, than angry.

In mounting suspense she waited, and after a moment he went on, in a voice so raw and sharp she thought it must hurt his throat to talk. "We got to be friends. *Friends*—" he interrupted himself with a sharp angry gesture "—*not* lovers—we were never that. She trusted me. Told me her story. She told me—" he clenched his teeth hard; she could see the muscles work in his jaws "—she'd been abused— sexually. By her father. *Your* father. For years. Until she finally got strong enough, desperate enough, and decided to take her chances on the streets." He stopped, breathing hard, waiting for her reaction.

She didn't give him one. Couldn't have if she'd wanted to. She'd gone cold, hollow. The truth was, she felt nothing, nothing at all.

"Go on," she finally said, without expression.

He did, wearing a tight, off-center smile, and if her lack of response surprised him, he didn't let it show. "She survived, the way so many of them do—working as a prostitute, panhandling, a little shoplifting. Got into, then out of drugs."

He let out a breath, picked up the shovel, then stood it on end again, flexing his grip on the handle. Releasing tension. "When I met her she was clean—and pregnant. Didn't know who the father was, though. I took care of her, or tried to. Saw to it she had food, vitamins, things like that. I just about had her talked into moving into a shelter. I'd made all the arrangements. I went to pick her up and that's when I found her—she was in labor, bleeding. Barely conscious. I drove her to the hospital, got her there in time to save the baby.''

Silent now, he watched himself twirl the shovel, around and around in the straw. Then he looked up at Devon from under the lock of hair that had fallen across one eye, his face suddenly younger, more vulnerable than she'd ever seen it.

She didn't want to see that. She hated him. *Hated him.*

He went on, inexorably. ''That's all she could think about, you know? Her baby. Was her baby okay, and please save her baby. She held on to my hand and asked me— begged me—to keep her little one safe. Don't let them get her—that's what she said to me. *Please—don't let them get her.* She told them I was the father, and they let me hold her, just for a minute. I stood there and held that little girl and watched them try to save her mother's life. They kept pouring blood into her, everybody yelling back and forth and shocking her with those paddles. But it didn't...it wasn't enough. It wasn't enough.'' His clenched jaws relaxed, and his voice trailed away on an exhausted breath.

Through the shimmering haze of her anger, Devon saw him draw a hand across his face, then straighten up and turn toward her, silently waiting. Waiting, she realized, expecting her to say something. She became aware that she was shaking—a tight inner tremor that wouldn't even show on the outside. To him she knew she appeared cool and unruffled, calm and unmoved. Oh, but the trembling, deep, deep inside.

She couldn't remember ever being so angry. She wanted nothing more than to flee, to simply walk—no, *run*—away and leave him there. Leave him with his vicious and unconscionable lies.

''She lied.'' She heard herself say it in a calm, cold voice. ''Susan always was a little liar.''

It was her exit line, and she did walk then, *not* run—that would have been undignified—away from him, with her spine rigid and her chin high. She got as far as the door, pulled back the latch and felt the wind battering against the boards and it seemed to her like some fearsome beast trying to gain entry. Hurriedly she shoved the latch back in place and sagged against the door, leaning her head against it as a shudder shook her through and through. She felt defeated, trapped, cornered—caught between the storms within and without.

Chapter 5

*U*nbelievable. That was all Eric could think of as he watched her walk away from him. The woman was simply unbelievable. Made of solid ice. Not a compassionate bone in her body. He'd wasted his breath on her. Furious with himself for trying, he twirled the shovel around and jammed it viciously into the layer of matted straw at his feet.

Something—maybe the silence—finally got to him. He realized that she hadn't opened the door, letting in the expected blast of cold and noise. He stopped his shoveling. Hating himself, contemptuous of himself for wondering about her, he couldn't stop himself from turning to look.

What's she waiting for? he silently raged when he saw that Devon was still standing by the door. *Why doesn't she go on and get the hell out of here?* He desperately wanted her out of his space, his place of sanctuary, his peace. Because if there'd ever been a moment in his life when he'd needed those things, it was now.

He wondered again how she could turn her back on her sister like she'd done. Even if those people were her parents, how could she protect them, let alone even *think* about giving them custody of a baby girl? She must have known what was going on in that house. She must have. At the very least, *suspected*. Maybe she even... *Maybe...*

That was when his body grew still, giving his mind a chance to listen to the tentative rustlings of a new idea.

Devon had been standing with her back to him and her head bowed, her forehead against the door. And maybe it was because she was some distance from him and the light was dim, and that he couldn't see that beautiful, arrogant face, but it struck him all at once that what she looked most of all was...vulnerable.

No way! He wanted to argue with himself, totally reject the thought. But he couldn't. That was when it came to him—the notion, the possibility that would change everything. Change his perspective. Make it a whole new picture.

What if... Oh, he'd read it somewhere—about people suppressing memories that were too painful to bear. He began, now, to wonder if this cold-hearted attitude of Devon's might be nothing more than armor she wore to protect herself from truths she couldn't bring herself to face. *If...*

What if—it seemed not only possible, but made all kinds of sense—*Devon* had been a victim of abuse as well? Everybody had different ways of coping with the bad stuff in life—he'd learned that lesson well enough. What if the only way *she'd* been able to deal with that, grow up and live a normal life in spite of it, had been to block it out of her mind?

What did he know, after all, about her life, Susan's—any of it—growing up the way he had in a home as normal and wholesome as apple pie? He'd been judging the woman. And he'd been taught better. How many times had his mom and dad both told him he had no right to judge someone until he'd walked a mile in their shoes?

He wanted in the worst way to hate Devon O'Rourke. It would make things a lot simpler for him if he could. Hating what she stood for and what she meant to try and do to him and the little one, and at the same time having his feelings for the woman herself turn soft and sympathetic on him—that was something else entirely. He could see how that kind of conflict was going to make for some serious emotional turmoil.

Slowly, slowly, Devon's mind grew quiet again. *It's not his fault,* she reminded herself. *He only knows what Susan told him.* And, she told herself, *it wasn't really Susan's fault, either. She was disturbed, sick. More so than I realized.*

She took a deep breath and squared her shoulders. She had to try and talk to Eric. Make him understand that.

If only he weren't so damned difficult.

It struck her suddenly how quiet it was in the middle of such a storm. *Storms—both inside and out.*

Too quiet...

An awareness, a presentiment—not of danger, just of *something*—gripped at her spine, making her turn abruptly with her heart inexplicably pounding. She saw that Eric was leaning on the handle of his shovel, intently watching her, as if she were some unfamiliar new animal whose behavior and responses he couldn't be sure about. Her breath caught, and that same awareness, a tiny frisson, shivered down her spine.

Defying her own uneasiness, she forced herself to walk toward him, managing a casual stroll, hands jammed deep in the pockets of her borrowed parka. He watched her for a few moments, saying nothing, then hefted his shovel and went deliberately back to pitching straw.

This time Devon was prepared, and sidestepped the shovelful of smelly hay he carelessly heaved her way. Safely past the danger zone, she leaned her folded arms once more on the stall gate and quietly watched him work while she waited for her pulse rate to return to normal.

For some reason, it didn't. It wouldn't.

There was something fascinating, almost hypnotic about the way his body moved. The bunch and ripple of muscles in his torso as he bent and straightened, the way the light played over his back and shoulders, shiny wet with sweat, the lock of hair that dangled across one eye every time he leaned forward....

She tore her gaze away.

Impossible.

This couldn't be happening. She wasn't supposed to be attracted to a man who'd just hurled the most vile and unspeakable accusations at her and her family. The man, moreover, whom she was about to annihilate in a court of law. The enemy.

Know thine enemy....

Girding herself with reminders of her reasons for being where she was, Devon took a deep breath. She looked up, down, all around, everywhere but at that perfectly ordinary body—she insisted it *was* ordinary—before she cleared her throat and dove in. "Um. It's quiet in here."

As a conversation starter, it proved a miserable failure. Eric grunted and went on shoveling. "Peaceful," Devon added hopefully.

That won her a snort. "Yeah. That's why I like it."

"Ah." *An actual sentence.* Encouraged by a tone that was at least not *un*friendly, she drew another breath and shifted gears. "Eric—" she began, and was interrupted by a flurry of flapping noises from somewhere in the gloom overhead. She gave a shriek, to her own disgust, then asked in a hushed and shaken whisper, "What was that?" She was thinking of bats.

"Bird, probably." Eric paused long enough to point the handle of his shovel toward the hayloft.

"Really?" And it was only relief that made her sound so breathless and eager. "What kind?"

He shrugged and reluctantly set aside his shovel, then looked at her the same way—reluctantly, as if he didn't quite know what to do with her. "Doves, sparrows, maybe an owl. Probably lots of birds up there in the rafters. Looking for shelter." He gave her a crooked, reluctant smile. "Didn't you ever wonder where birds go when it storms?"

She shook her head as she watched him stroll toward her. Fascinated by the sudden change in him, she felt uneasy too, like a bird herself, watching the cat prowl closer.

He held her eyes while his voice lowered and grew growly. "'The north wind doth blow and we shall have snow....'"

She knew it was a quote of some kind. And that he expected her to recognize it. Unable to think of a word to say, Devon just looked at him; her heart had quickened again.

Separated from her by the width of the stall gate and not much more, Eric halted. His eyes flicked upward to touch her hair before coming back to snare hers.

"'And what will the robin do then, poor thing?'"

It occurred to her suddenly, irrelevantly, that he had beautiful eyes. Warm and golden-brown, like brandy.

"'Sit in the barn,'" he prompted, answering his own riddle. "'Keep herself warm...'" He stopped there, watching her, his head slightly canted, eyes quizzical and searching.

She shook her head, still at a loss for the answer he seemed to expect. Heat and the scent of his body enveloped her. "I don't—I'm sorry—"

"It's a nursery rhyme." His voice was curiously gentle. "Don't tell me you've never heard it."

"Oh, well." She felt the vestiges of her panic drain away, and defensive disdain take its place. "I'm afraid I'm not very familiar with nursery rhymes." She looked away, holding herself rigid and aloof. She hated him for making her feel at such a disadvantage, especially when she didn't know why she should. She didn't have children, why *would* she know nursery rhymes? Chin lifted, she prepared to defend what seemed to her a perfectly understandable ignorance.

When she found his eyes on her, curious, and curiously intent, the words faded to a whisper and died on her tongue.

Softly, he said, "Didn't your parents read you nursery rhymes when you were a little kid? You know—'Mary Had a Little Lamb,' 'Jack and Jill went up the hill'...stuff like that?"

Devon shifted, once more fighting down anger. She was trying her best to establish some kind of rapport with this man, and he wasn't making it easy. Dammit, she wasn't used to being the one under fire. *She* was the one who was supposed to do the cross-examining, not the other way around.

"I'm sure they did," she said in her coldest voice. "That was a long time ago."

She pushed off from the gate and turned away from him. She didn't want to be angry with the man any more than she wanted to be attracted to him; both were equally unprofessional—and unproductive. For the first time he'd been talking to her—actually *talking*. She wanted it to continue. She couldn't let her personal feelings get in the way of finding out all she could about him. The enemy.

Know thine enemy.

She moved a few steps away from him and paused to take deep breaths, gulping in air that was cool and smelled only of damp hay and animal waste, with no unsettling traces of a hardworking and unnervingly attractive man.

She said brightly, "I can see why you—and the birds—like it in here. It's cozy. It's not even that cold."

Unaccountably, inside the borrowed parka she was sweating herself, now, and she could feel a heat flush in her fair, redhead's skin. She unzipped her coat and was fanning the two halves to cool herself when Eric pushed open the stall gate. She felt vulnerable without the fence between them, like a lion tamer without the chair.

"I see you helped yourself to my closet," he said in what she thought seemed a conversational, even mildly friendly tone.

She looked down at herself, at a faded gray sweatshirt imprinted with a dark blue bucking horse and the word *BRONCOS* in block letters arranged in an arch above it. "Your mom's closet," she defended herself. "She told me to help myself—I didn't exactly come prepared for this." She waved a hand in the general direction of the howling storm beyond the barn walls, then looked up at him curiously. "Why, is this yours?"

"Was. When I was in high school." He gave a grunt of surprise. "Can't believe Mom kept it all these years."

"Well, I personally am rather glad she did," Devon said dryly. "I hope you don't mind if I borrowed it?"

He looked slightly affronted. "Good Lord, why would I? Probably wouldn't fit me now, even if I wanted it."

Devon plucked the sweatshirt away from her chest so she could look at it again, and a wash of cold air swept under it and peppered her sweat-damp stomach with goose bumps. She felt her breasts grow hard and tight. "Broncos…" she said, fighting down shivers. "I suppose that's your team mascot?"

"Yeah." He smiled that reluctant, lopsided smile. "Used to be the Indians, back when Mom was in school, but a few years before I got there somebody evidently decided that was politically incorrect, so they changed it to Broncos.''

Devon smiled back. It came easier, this time. "I can understand that, I guess. 'Native American' doesn't have quite the same punch to it."

"Hard to make a good cheer out of it." As if he'd realized he was openly smiling at her and feeling guilty about it, Eric's brows suddenly knitted in a frown. "So, what was yours?"

"What?" She'd been gazing at his chest again, thinking how incredibly smooth it was, except for those hard-pebbled nipples, noticing that his skin was dusky but thinking it was more with the flush of exercise than suntanned. Caught, she felt her heart thud against her ribs and her breath grew sticky. "What was my...I'm sorry?"

"Your high school mascot." His eyes watched her, intent and amused, with that particular masculine awareness that said he knew very well what she'd been looking at and what she was thinking. "Where'd you go to school— L.A.?"

"Canoga Park, actually." She frowned and touched her forehead. "Our school mascot? Oh, God, I don't know— some sort of animal, I think. I really don't remember." Desperately, she blurted out, "Aren't you freezing?" Grasping at anything, just to change the subject. "Without a shirt? Aren't you afraid you'll catch cold?"

"You just said it wasn't cold." Oh, definitely amused.

"I said it wasn't *that* cold," she said tartly. "That's a relative observation."

"Ah," said Eric, his smile tilting.

Suddenly, irrationally, she wanted to hit him. "Don't put words in my mouth," she snapped. "I'm a lawyer, remember?"

"Oh, I'm not apt to forget that." When had he moved closer to her, with his arms folded across his chest and his hands tucked in his armpits? And he was no longer smiling at all. Just that quickly, it seemed, the cease-fire was over. His voice rumbled in his chest like distant artillery fire. "Look—let's cut the crap, okay?"

"What?" She held her ground. She was proud of that, when what she really wanted to do was turn tail and run. *This isn't supposed to happen,* she thought again.

"You must have had a reason for coming all the way out here in a blizzard to find me." His voice was soft, but there was a dangerous light in his eyes. He came closer still, leaned toward her. "What the hell is it you want?"

It took all her willpower not to step back, leaving her no reserves with which to control the tremor in her voice. "I told you. I wanted a chance to talk to you. I thought we should at least *try* to understand each other. As I said, we're going to—" She stopped, belatedly remembering that he wasn't the father of Susan's baby, and that they wouldn't be family after all. Lamely, she finished, "I thought we might get to know one another, that's all."

There was a long pause while he studied her, and she tried—utterly without success—to decipher the emotions that flickered behind his whiskey-brown eyes. The only thing she could be certain of was that there was no longer any anger in them. And why she found that more unnerving she had no idea.

He'd rejected her overtures before, bluntly and even cruelly. She expected him to do so again. And once again he surprised her.

"We could do that," he said softly. She stifled a tiny, gasp as his hand came from nowhere to touch her jaw, lightly brushing the place where it curved into her neck.

She couldn't stop a shiver. And instantly, as if he'd felt it, he lifted his head and looked intently into her eyes. "You had some straw," he said, and then… "Are you afraid of me or something?"

"Afraid?" It came out sharp and angry, not at all convincing. "Of what? Why would I be? I'm a—"

"A lawyer...I know." His voice was dry, his eyes amused; she could see at their corners the beginnings of the laugh lines he'd have when he grew older.

"I was going to say, a *grown-up*," Devon coldly replied. "Childish games don't impress me."

Something flared again in his eyes, so close to hers. And again, she knew with utter certainty it wasn't anger. "Then why," he said in a silken whisper, "is your pulse so fast?"

She realized then that his fingers were still curved around the side of her neck, and that his thumb was stroking up and down, up and down over her throat, measuring the ripple of her swallows. His hand was warm, and far from objecting to his touch, she felt an insane desire to melt into it, like a friendly cat.

This isn't supposed to happen. This can't be happening...not to me. Not to me!

She said nothing—how could she? For a time measured only in heartbeats she held herself absolutely still while Eric measured her pulse with his thumb, and, she thought, her soul with his eyes.

Then, just when she thought she wouldn't be able to stand the suspense one second longer, he gave his head an almost imperceptible shake, murmured something she couldn't quite hear, released her and turned away. Her neck felt cold where his hand had been. She had to resist an urge to cover the spot with her own hand.

"Not because of you, that's for sure," she said as she hooked the two halves of her parka together, masking the panicky unevenness of her voice with motion as she jerked at the zipper and yanked the hood over her head.

She might have saved her breath. Eric was yards away from her now, and totally occupied with pulling a black turtleneck shirt over his head. His back was turned to her and his movements as unself-conscious as if he were alone. Frustrated, Devon stared laser beams at his back, but it was her eyes that burned. Burned and stung until tears came. Alarmed, she hurled herself around like an out-of-balance top, so full of confused and contradictory wants and urges she knew her only salvation was to flee.

Look at me, damn you! Answer me....

No—don't look at him. She never wanted to have to see him again. Speak to him again

Touch me again...

Damn this storm! If only she could get away from this place, these people. Jump in her rented Lincoln with the GPS, drive to the city and take the first flight back to L.A. and let the authorities deal with Eric Sean Lanagan. The man was a loose cannon—she'd been crazy to think she could reason with him!

Reason? How could she possibly reason with a man who wouldn't even talk to her like an adult?

The northwind doth blow and we shall have snow,
And what will the robin do then, poor thing?
She'll sit in the barn and keep herself warm....

It came to her then—a tiny flash of memory, clear and bright and sweet as a single raindrop splashing onto her upturned face.

And hide her head under her wing.

She uttered a stricken sound, somewhere between a laugh and a whimper, and turned and ran—literally—to the barn door. Throwing her weight against it, she shoved at the old-fashioned wooden latch until it gave and the wind opened the door for her. Mindless and uncaring, she plunged into icy howling whiteness.

Inside the barn, Eric swore furiously as he sprinted to close and latch the door Devon had left open to the blizzard. His anger was for himself, not her.

He was an idiot. *An idiot.*

What in the world had gotten into him? He could neither explain nor excuse his behavior, except…he was thinking that maybe he'd been too long in the dark and slimy underbelly of L.A., living among people who'd so long ago lost the ability to speak to the sun-dwellers that they no longer tried to make themselves understood.

Cold, now, he stood in the vast open center of the barn with his head thrown back, staring up into the gloom that shrouded the loft and rafters like fog. Like my brain, he thought bitterly. Nothing seemed clear to him anymore. He was lost—not so much in the sense of *what* or *where,* but *who.* I don't know who I am, he thought. I used to, but now I don't.

Somewhere in those mean Los Angeles streets, he'd lost himself.

He thought of Emily, wondering whether the way he felt about her had anything to do with his having lost himself, but if it did, his fogged mind couldn't piece it together.

He thought of his mother, and the fact that he hadn't let her hug him hello, and shame weighed so heavily on him it sagged his shoulders. What kind of son am I? he wondered. *What kind of man?*

He thought of Devon O'Rourke. *The enemy.*

Before this morning that was all she'd been to him. One of *them,* the O'Rourkes. His enemies. In the jumble of phone messages left on his answering machine, in the pile of legal documents shoved into his mailbox, it had never occurred to him to associate the name Devon O'Rourke with lawyers. He'd seen the name, but in the turmoil of his life, hadn't registered in exactly what context. Probably he'd assumed it was one of the parents; Susan hadn't mentioned a sister.

Then, this morning he'd walked into the kitchen and come face-to-face with Susan's ghost. A lawyer, she'd said, and then her name: Devon O'Rourke. And the pieces had fallen into place.

Except that *place,* it seemed, was a cement mixer. Everything was going around and around inside his brain. He'd come out here to the barn, to the peace and quiet he remembered, hoping the churning would stop and let him sort things out. Instead, he'd had a few more shovelfuls thrown into the mix, and now things were murkier than ever.

It didn't help that she was so damn beautiful.

He found himself thinking about that—Devon's looks. As a photographer Eric had had experience with more than his share of gorgeous women, a good many of them real stinkers as human beings. As a result, he liked to think he wasn't all that impressed with pure physical beauty. He couldn't have explained why he was so knocked out by this particular woman, especially since this morning he'd have definitely put her in the stinker category, no question about it.

What was it about her that fascinated him so? So she had sea-green eyes and hair an incredible shade of deep, vivid red he couldn't even think of a comparison for—so what? So did thousands of women, probably. So she had skin so fine and clear—*and soft!* The sensory memory jolted him viscerally, a twisting in his belly so powerful it made him groan out loud.

What was I thinking of, to touch her?

What *had* he been thinking? He'd been thinking about that hair, and not how beautiful but how vulnerable the back of her head had looked, bowed against the barn door. He'd been thinking, not about the shape of her breasts but

the way she'd shivered in his borrowed sweatshirt. He'd
been thinking, not about the unusual shade of green her
eyes were, but the panicky look in them when he'd told
her a nursery rhyme, and asked her questions about her
childhood she couldn't answer.

He'd been thinking about what it might have been like,
her childhood, and how, being a stronger person than Susan, she might have figured out her own better ways of
surviving.

He'd been thinking about all those things and a whole
lot more—Susan, and Emily and all the throwaway kids
he'd met during the months of living on the streets of Los
Angeles—and suddenly he'd wanted, not just to touch her,
but to *hold* her. As he'd held Susan. Put his arms around
her and fold her close and whisper into her hair that she
was okay, she was safe, now.

That was the way he'd meant to touch her. But then he'd
felt how smooth her skin was, and her pulse racing against
his fingertips. And he'd wanted to hold her, not just because
she was vulnerable, but because she was a woman. Not just
because she was cold, but because she ignited a fire inside
him. Not because she'd looked so lost, but because he felt
lost, too.

The enemy. Oh, she was that, and he couldn't let himself
forget it, even for a moment. No matter how beautiful or
damaged or vulnerable she was, Devon O'Rourke was still
the dragon he had to vanquish in order to keep his promise
to a dying mother. He meant to keep that promise, no matter what it cost him. This was a fight he had to win, because
the alternative was unthinkable.

Devon O'Rourke was his enemy. But hadn't he heard it
somewhere—or read it, more likely? An old saying: *Keep
your friends close…and your enemies closer.*

The cement mixer inside Eric's brain ground slowly to

a halt. Still with his head back, gazing into the rafters, he drew a quick, catching breath and closed his eyes. *Yes.*

His instincts, it seemed, hadn't been so far off after all. It was clear to him, now, what he had to do. In order to win this battle he was going to have to get very close to his enemy, very close indeed. The O'Rourkes had the law and blood on their side; all Eric had was the secondhand testimony of a woman who wasn't available now to tell her own story. His one witness—his *only* witness—was the vulnerable and possibly damaged child locked inside the memory of Devon O'Rourke.

Somehow, he *had* to find a way to set her free.

Chapter 6

As if the gods understood that Devon, a Californian born and bred, was in no way equipped to deal with such things as blizzards, the storm seemed to let up a little as she fought her way back to the house. The wind dropped; instead of the feral wail and shriek she'd almost grown accustomed to, a lovely whispering silence fell. Snow still swirled, but not in an impenetrable curtain. It lent an almost Christmas-card quality to the farmhouse huddled on the crown of the hill beneath the stark bare branches of trees.

Oh, God—Christmas. She remembered, then, with a small sense of shock, that Christmas was only a few days away—she'd lost track of exactly how many. Back in Los Angeles, in a world a universe away, Christmas decorations would be wilting in eighty-degree sunshine, and shoppers coming to blows—sometimes worse—over the last available spaces in the mall parking lots. An unheralded wave of homesickness swept over her, filling her with an intense longing for a freeway traffic jam, a nice hot Santa Ana wind.

Christmas was no big deal to Devon. She personally didn't go in for a lot of the sentimental trappings, but she wasn't one of those people who got mopey and depressed during the holidays, either. Her shopping had been done weeks ago with a minimum of fuss, all her purchases gift-wrapped at the store where she'd bought them and now stacked neatly on the bed in her seldom-used guest room. She never bothered with a tree, since she was so rarely home to appreciate it. On Christmas Eve, as always, she would have dinner with her parents at their home in Canoga Park. As for the day itself, she was currently "between relationships" so there would be no leisurely Christmas morning cuddle with mugs of eggnog in front of a gas log fire. Devon planned to catch up on some paperwork, and later perhaps drop in on one or more of the holiday parties to which she'd been invited. Or, maybe she'd skip them all and go to a movie. The advantage of being single, she thought, was that she could do pretty much anything she pleased. Which was the way she liked it.

As she approached the house, two medium-sized dogs—they'd sounded much larger in the dark last night—came romping out to meet her. Not being accustomed to dogs—or animals of any kind—and remembering the ferocious-sounding welcome they'd given her upon her arrival, Devon froze in her tracks. Holding her hands and arms close to her chest and trying to look as stumplike as possible, she ventured in a quavering voice, "Hello, doggy. Nice doggy...?" However, no doubt smelling familiar clothing, they greeted her like a returning prodigal, with wriggling and giddy joy.

"*Nice* doggy," Devon confirmed as she pushed past wet, questing noses and clomped on up the snow-dusted steps to the back porch.

Shedding her muddy boots and snow-crusted parka in the service room, as instructed, she went into the kitchen.

Her cheeks and fingers were tingling, her nose running; she felt exhilarated for having survived all Mother Nature could throw at her. And something else—a curious sense of…almost of expectation…of the warmth and light and welcome that awaited her there. Odd—when she'd never felt like that coming into her own home, or even her parents' home when she was a child. Had she?

Such a simple, basic thing. A feeling of home, of welcome and security. Why couldn't she remember even that?

As it turned out, the kitchen was empty. But it smelled of coffee and bacon and maple syrup, and there were two places set at the oval oak table. More dishes, washed and stacked in a drainer in the sink, suggested Mike and Lucy had already eaten.

Never a big breakfast eater at the best of times, and with a stomach full of knots left over from that confrontation with Eric in the barn, Devon poured herself a cup of coffee which she sipped standing at the counter, frowning at nothing while she digested unaccustomed feelings of disappointment and loneliness.

"Crazy," she muttered to herself, not even sure what she meant by it. Only silence answered her.

No, not quite silence. She became aware all at once of a sound, one that had been there all along, but one so familiar, so much a part of her customary habitat, it hadn't registered. The faint and distant clickety-clack of computer keys.

Carrying her coffee, she wandered down a dim hallway toward the front of the house, head cocked and ears pricked like a hunter alert to the snap of a twig or the rustle of leaves. On one side of the house a formal living room stood dark and, Devon suspected, seldom used. Across from it an open doorway spilled warmth and light and busy noises into the hallway murk.

Devon announced herself with a polite "Knock knock"

as she stepped into what was obviously these people's real "living room," and a welcoming clutter of books and family photographs, afghans and worn but comfortable furniture.

"Come on in." Mike was peering intently at a computer monitor that was sitting on an old wooden desk placed endwise to a window through which Devon could see snowflakes swirling amongst bare black branches. A moment later the keyboard clatter ceased and he turned from the screen, peeling off a pair of dark-rimmed glasses as he rose with a welcoming smile.

"Oh, please," she said, holding up a hand, palm outward, "don't stop. I'm sorry—I'm interrupting you." But she couldn't keep curiosity out of her voice, and, she was sure, her face. The desk was piled high with papers and books, and a low table under the window held a sophisticated combination printer-scanner-fax machine. Granted, Devon hadn't much firsthand knowledge, but it seemed to her a little much for a farmhouse in the middle of Iowa.

"No problem," Mike cheerfully assured her. "I was just killing time. Deadline's still a ways off. Did you find breakfast? I think Lucy left it in the oven to keep warm."

"What? Oh—yes, thanks…" She waved her coffee cup and offered an apologetic smile. "Actually, though, coffee's all I want right now. I had some toast earlier, so I wasn't really hungry. Maybe later?"

"That's fine." There was a pause, and then, with a cautious smile, he asked, "Eric still shoveling manure in the barn?"

Devon murmured an affirmative and managed to avoid his eyes by taking a sip of coffee, but not before she'd caught the compassionate twinkle in his eyes.

"Where's Lucy?" she asked as she turned away to begin a casual exploration of the room.

"Take a guess." He pointed at the ceiling as he joined

Devon in front of an old upright piano topped with a collection of framed photographs she was looking at without really seeing. "First thing Lucy did this morning after chores was unearth the bassinet and her rocking chair. She's taking to this grandmother business in a big way."

Devon would never be mistaken for a sentimentalist. She gave him a quick glance, and her mouth opened to tell him the truth in her customary blunt and forthright manner. But something—an unexpected constriction—suddenly made it impossible, and instead she swallowed the words with an audible sound she tried to hide in a gulp of coffee.

Mike wasn't fooled. "What?" he prompted gently.

Devon shrugged, keeping a shoulder turned to him, avoiding his eyes. "Nothing—I was just..."

"I take it she isn't." It was matter-of-fact. And not a question.

She gave him another quick, hard look; then, letting go of a breath, nodded. "He admitted it to me just now—down in the barn." Oddly, right now she felt no sense of victory.

After several long seconds of silence, Mike murmured on an exhalation of regret, "Well, Lucy will be disappointed."

Devon felt an alien bump of empathy. Startled, even a little frightened by it, she moved on to the fireplace, where still more photographs crowded the mantelpiece and a fire sputtered and crackled with a merry eccentricity that could only be real wood.

"You don't seem surprised," she remarked, holding her hands toward the fire even though they weren't cold, watching them so she wouldn't have to look at the gallery of photographs arrayed before her. She couldn't have said why; normally she liked photographs. Moreover, these were Eric's family. She wanted to know more about him, didn't she? And here they all were, his entire family spread out in front of her, all those friendly eyes and wholesome smiles. Nice people…good people.

Mike had come beside her again. "Oh, I was pretty sure Eric wasn't Emily's biological father."

Devon tilted her head and fixed him with a look of honest curiosity. She was a lawyer; she hadn't missed the precise and, she was sure, deliberate terminology. "May I ask why?"

He smiled, though not with his eyes. "Oh, I don't know, the way he told us, I guess. Eric's always been careful with words—what comes of having a writer for a father. What he said was, 'she's *mine.*' You understand? Not, 'she's my daughter,' or 'I'm her father.'" The smile made it to his eyes then, just as his mouth tilted into irony. "I know my son."

Once again she was caught unawares, this time by the poignancy in that particular combination of words and smile. "I'm sorry," she said abruptly, frowning at her coffee cup. "I know this is awkward—my being here. Like this."

"Wasn't much anybody could have done about it." Mike gave a little shrug. "Couldn't very well let you freeze to death on our doorstep."

Devon laughed. "Well, yes, actually, you could have." Somber again, she looked him straight in the eye—one of her best weapons in the courtroom—and said earnestly, "You have to believe I never meant it to be like this. The storm—"

"What did you mean it to be like?" His interruption surprised her. Suddenly alert, she realized the eyes that gazed back into hers, eyes that before had held only gentleness and compassion, now held a keen and probing light. "Just curious," he said quietly, studying her, arms folded on his chest. "Seems a little unusual for an attorney to personally take on something like this. Why didn't you let the authorities handle things?''

Devon made a sound, a soft, unamused laugh, and turned her back on the homey crackle of the fire. ''You're right, it is unusual for the attorney to get personally involved. I chose to, for several reasons. I definitely would have handled it differently if Emily hadn't been my niece—that's one. However, since in the normal course of things, Emily winds up in foster care and your son possibly in jail on contempt charges—'' Aware that her voice had developed a hard and brittle edge, she abruptly changed both her tone and tactics, schooling her gestures and body language as she would in handling a delicate courtroom situation.

''You have to understand,'' she said, one hand upraised, quietly earnest again. ''I had no idea what kind of person your son was, what his background was, nothing. Except that my sister Susan evidently trusted him and thought enough of him to leave her baby in his care, even though she knew he wasn't the biological father.'' Her poise slipped and she gave another mirthless laugh. ''Of course, my sister was a homeless, screwed-up kid, probably a drug addict, so what does that tell you?''

She told me she'd been abused by her father. Your father.

She gulped cold coffee and just did manage to keep from choking on it. The struggle for control hardened her voice again as she continued, ''So, the upshot of it is, I had our firm's P.I. track him down. Once we had this as his home address, and credit card gasoline receipts started popping up showing him heading east on a direct course to Iowa, it wasn't hard to figure out where he was going. I thought I'd beat him here, actually. I thought the unexpectedness of my being here, waiting for him, would demonstrate the futility of running, and that I could convince him the best course of action for everybody concerned would be for him to bring Emily back to Los Angeles voluntarily. For Susan's sake, I didn't want to see him arrested. And I definitely didn't want Emily in the hands of social services.''

"Especially," Mike said dryly, "at Christmastime."

Devon looked at him and made a faint "Humph" sound. "Believe it or not, I never even thought about that. I keep forgetting it's Christmas." She looked around, only then realizing that, comfortable and warm as the room—the whole house—was, she hadn't seen any sign of holiday decorations. No Christmas tree or wrapped presents, no creche, no wreaths or garlands, not so much as a twinkling light or red velvet bow.

Mike had followed her gaze, and apparently her thoughts. "I know what you mean. We've been having the same problem around here. Been meaning to do it—the boxes of decorations are sitting upstairs in Lucy's work room. Tree's in a bucket on the back porch. Just haven't gotten around to it. Lucy's been in a mood this year...." He paused, then added softly, "She's been missing the kids more than usual. Eric's coming home was…like the answer to a prayer."

Eric. Devon didn't want to think about Eric, didn't want to hear his name or remember those unsettling moments she'd just spent with him down in the barn. And yet, she knew she must if she was to regain—and maintain—the upper hand here, where she was so clearly out of her element.

"This is all so different than I imagined," she said on an exhalation, strolling to the window and on the way trailing her fingers idly across an antique wind-up Victrola and a worn recliner draped with a brightly colored afghan.

Behind her, Mike's voice sounded amused. "Considering how little you knew of my son, I'm sure it is."

The desk, the computer monitor, were right in front of her. She touched the monitor, remembering things he'd said before. She said brightly, conversationally, "You said you're a writer?"

"Journalist, actually. I write a nationally syndicated column—just twice a week, now. And once a month on a rotation for *Newsweek*."

Devon turned to stare at him. "Wow. I'm sorry—I feel I should know who you are." She smiled her regret, meaning it. "The truth is, I don't have much time for reading newspapers and magazines—mostly what I read are legal briefs and court documents."

"Ouch," Mike said with a good-natured wince. "I hate to say it, but it sounds boring as hell."

She smiled. "It can be. But not always."

"Sounds as though you like what you do." Again his eyes had turned probing.

"Yes, I do." But she was never comfortable talking about herself, and steered the conversation firmly back to the subject she was most interested in. "So you're a writer—sorry, journalist—and Lucy's a farmer. That's an unlikely combination, isn't it? How did you two meet?"

"A long story. Part of the family folklore."

Devon waited, but he said no more. She gave a dismissive shrug and said lightly, "I hope you'll tell it to me some time." But she was conscious of the same vague disappointment she'd felt, coming in from the cold and finding the kitchen empty. Plagued by unfamiliar and perplexing emotions, she fought down irritation and tried again. "Eric's not an only child?"

"We have a daughter, four—no, almost five years older." He picked up a framed photograph from the mantel and handed it to her. "Rose Ellen. She's a biologist—works for the government. She and her husband are out of the country at the moment—in fact, most of the time these days."

Devon recognized the pretty, wholesome-looking girl

she'd seen in so many of the photos on the walls of Eric's room. After a moment she nodded and handed it back. "A biologist—wow. And Eric's a photographer." She was on the verge of asking how such a thing had come about when Mike interrupted her.

"Photojournalist," he corrected firmly.

Devon laughed. "He said exactly the same thing to me, you know—down in the barn."

"It's an important distinction." Mike's eyes were smiling. "As is writer versus journalist."

"I'll remember that." For the first time, she felt some of her own awkwardness and tension ease. "I saw the photographs upstairs in his room," she said, touching one or two of the frames on the mantelpiece before turning to a collection hanging on the wall next to the fireplace. "Did he take these as well?"

"No, not those."

Alerted by something in his voice, Devon leaned over to peer at one photograph in particular, a dramatic picture of helicopters flying in formation over a jungle river at sunset. As beautiful as it was, there was something subtly menacing about it. "This looks familiar. Is it Vietnam?"

"It is." Devon turned to look at him; for once he hadn't moved up beside her, but stood a little way off, hands in his pockets. "Those are my dad's. He was a photojournalist, too. A pretty famous one—Sean Lanagan. He was killed in a helicopter crash during the Tet Offensive. Which I realize you've probably never heard of." He tilted his head toward the wall of photographs. "Those came from magazines, actually—some of them. Others I got from my mother. My personal collection, the ones he'd sent me from all over the world when I was a kid, were lost in a fire years ago."

He paused, then went on in a musing tone, still gazing at the photos. "Eric idolized his grandfather. Always wanted to be just like him." Again his smile tilted crookedly. "Until recently, I think his biggest disappointment had been not having a war to go to."

He said it lightly, but thanks to the nature of her profession, Devon's emotional intensity radar was acute. *Issues,* she thought.

Moving abruptly away from the photo wall, she caught sight of a snapshot on the mantelpiece, similar to one she'd seen upstairs, of a laughing young man standing under a huge tree, one knee on an old-fashioned wood plank and rope swing, holding on to the ropes. "Oh, my God," she cried, snatching it up, "*please* don't tell me—this can't be President Brown!"

Mike chuckled; it was the first time Devon could remember hearing anyone actually make such a sound. "Oh, that's Rhett, all right. I suppose we should have something more dignified—an official presidential portrait, at least, but Lucy likes that one. She's always thought Rhett is inclined to be a little too full of himself, and she wants to make sure he doesn't forget where he came from." Devon was staring at him, speechless. He laughed. "You didn't know? Rhett Brown is Lucy's brother."

Realizing her mouth was open, she hurriedly closed it—and then her eyes as well. "I had no idea," she said faintly, "Until I saw the picture upstairs." And then, in a burst of candor brought on by chagrin, snapped, "I can't believe this. Yesterday I thought your son was just some homeless unemployed bum my drug addict sister picked up on the street. Today I find out he's the nephew of the former president of the United States."

A husky voice, dry and amused, responded from the doorway, "The two aren't necessarily mutually exclusive, are they?"

Devon jerked toward the voice.

"Hello, son," Mike said mildly, "did you find your breakfast?"

"Not yet, but I will." Eric let his eyes slide past Devon as he moved into the room. Okay, so he was deliberately—perhaps childishly—ignoring her. And yet, so acutely attuned to her he could hear her breathing, quick and shallow like his own. "Baby still asleep?"

"Your mother's up there with her," his dad said. "Haven't heard a peep out of either one of 'em." He ran a hand over his chin, looked from Eric to Devon and back again. "Uhh, guess I'll go see what they're up to...."

"I'll go. She's my kid." Eric wanted to kick himself for the surliness in his voice.

He felt like even more of a jerk when his dad merely said, touching his arm as he moved past him, "You'd better get your breakfast first—you know your mother, she's not going to want to see your face upstairs until you do. And," he added with a chuckle on his way out the door, "you'd better change out of those pants before she sees 'em, too."

"Some things never change," Eric growled into the silence his father's going left behind.

Devon laughed, a light but artificial sound. "Sounds like you might have a few issues with your father."

He let himself look at her then, having had time to prepare himself for the shock that always came from seeing her, time to school his features so as not to let it show. Though...he felt the jolt a lot less this time. Maybe he was getting used to her. Beginning to see her as Devon, instead of Susan's Ghost.

"What is this...*issues?*" he drawled as he studied her. "We don't communicate. We're father and son. So what else is new?" His voice was edgy because he was thinking that if the woman could look as beautiful as she did wearing his dad's castoff bathrobe, somebody's old chore coat and his high school sweatshirt, he sure would like to see what she looked like in her own clothes. What would they be, he wondered—gray flannel suits for the courtroom, maybe? Something softer, more feminine for the evenings. Royal-blue, or a deep forest-green, he thought, dressing her with his photographer's eye.

"I don't know," Devon drawled back, mimicking his own tone as she touched the computer monitor that was sitting on his dad's old desk, "your father seems like a pretty good communicator to me. I didn't find him hard to talk to at all."

Eric snorted. "Yeah, well, maybe that's because you're not his son." He added under his breath as he turned away from her, "And you haven't let him down as many times as I have."

"What?"

He watched his fingers trail lightly over dusty piano keys, making no sound. "Nothing. Forget it."

"I'm sorry," she persisted, moving closer to him, "what do you mean, you 'let him down'?"

He lifted an eyebrow at her and smiled without humor. "Take a guess."

But he saw that she was frowning, and genuinely perplexed. He let out a long slow breath while he thought about whether to answer her or not. It wasn't his problems—*issues*—with his family he wanted to talk about, and certainly not with *her*. What he needed to do was get her talking about *her* family, *her* issues. On the other hand, maybe one way to get her talking and remembering was to start the ball rolling himself.

For a few more seconds, though, he didn't say anything; not being used to personal confidences, it was hard to know how to begin. Finally, he reached up and took down a photograph—the biggest one—from the top of the piano. Smiling because that particular one always made him smile, he handed it to Devon.

She gave him a curious glance. "Who is it? Looks old—the picture, I mean, not—"

"It's my great-great—Lord knows how many greats—grandmother. Lucinda Rosewood."

"She looks a lot like your mom." Devon was holding the portrait like an open book in her two hands, her normally flawless forehead marred by a tiny frown.

Eric nodded. "She's named for her."

Her eyes flew wide, colliding with his, and he felt himself start as if he'd been splashed with cool green water. "Oh—she's much prettier, of course. Your mom is, I mean. This lady—God, she looks so *severe*."

Eric laughed and shifted so he could look at the portrait of his ancestor with her. He caught the faintest whiff of something from her clothing...could it be mothballs? "Those pioneer women always do, don't they? Like they could lick their weight in wildcats." His throat was husky. He cleared it, and as if it were a signal of some kind, Devon looked up at him and handed the picture back.

Instead of returning it to its place, he held on to it, and said hoarsely, "There's a legend in our family about Grandma Rosewood—I must have heard it a thousand times at least, growing up."

"Legend?" Her voice was hushed, and...was it his imagination, or did there seem to be a catch in *her* breathing?

He didn't look to see why. He was too close to her...the heat from her body was seeping through the weave of his shirt, soaking into his skin. Her scent was in every breath he took—a warm, woman's scent, without even a lingering hint of mothballs.

He cleared his throat again. "Yeah...according to this legend, Grandma Rosewood saved herself and her baby from a Sioux raiding party by setting fire to her own house and barn. Then she tied her baby up in her apron and climbed down the well and hid there while the fire burned all the way to the river.''

"Looking at that picture of her," Devon said in a light, laughing voice, "I can easily believe it."

He reached up to set the portrait in its place. "That's how long this farm has been in our family. Handed down from generation to generation, for more than a hundred and fifty years."

"Wow...some legacy."

"Yeah, well, it's a legacy that's going to end with my mom," Eric said, and his voice was neither light nor laughing, but hard and heavy, like the weight that had come to be in the middle of his chest.

Chapter 7

"Why?" She was frowning, her eyes sharp and intelligent, clear and green as glass.

He felt a wild little ripple run through him, a reprise of what he'd experienced in the kitchen this morning during his first run-in with her. There was something about the woman that got to him. Excited him. Turned him on. It wasn't the way he wanted it, but what could he do? The only thing he knew for sure was that he couldn't deny it.

"Why?" he croaked, angry with himself for many reasons. "Because *I* sure as hell am not cut out to be a farmer. I never wanted to be a farmer." He jerked away from her and paced to the fireplace, ramming the fingers of one hand into his hair as he waved the other at the array of faces looking back at him from the mantelpiece. "Who does that leave? My sister? Okay, Ellie's nuts about animals—she always planned to be a vet—but then she got involved with Save the Whales and Orangutan Rescue, and became a government biologist instead. She and her husband work together now. They go all over the world saving endangered wildlife—important stuff. You think she's going to come back here to Iowa and run a *farm?*

"Who else? My mom's brothers?" He snorted derisively as he touched their portraits in turn. "You've already 'met' my uncle Rhett, here, the former president of the United States. His kids…my cousin Lauren, she's a lawyer, married to a Native American sheriff. They live on a reservation out in Arizona. My cousin Ethan's a doctor. He's married to Joanna Dunn—you know, the rock star, Phoenix? Can't see either of them coming back here to take up the family business, can you?" Devon shook her head, but he wasn't looking for an answer.

"Then there's my cousin Caitlyn…" He paused. Small seismic tremors were rippling through him, the beginnings of something of too great a magnitude to be called an idea. More like an inspiration.

Caitlyn. Of course.

He cleared his throat and glibly continued. "She's a social worker—works for a non-profit human rights organization of some kind. Nobody really knows exactly *what* Caty does…" Which was a lie. *He* did, actually, and was probably the only member of the family other than Caitlyn herself who did. "Except that she travels a lot. Definitely not the type to sit home on the farm.

"Her dad, my uncle Earl—better known as Wood— teaches school in Sioux City. He's a great guy, but he abdicated years ago. After my grandparents died, both of my uncles left my mom to sink or swim here on her own—and she might have sunk, too, if my dad hadn't come along when he did. Gwen always said it was Providence…" He stopped, because a lump had come unexpectedly to his throat.

He was trying to swallow it when a voice close behind him softly prompted, "Gwen?"

She'd startled him; he'd almost forgotten he had an audience, he'd had this discussion with himself so many times. He turned with Gwen's portrait in his hands. Frowning at it, he said thickly, "My mom's great-aunt, I think. She lived with us when I was growing up." He took a deep breath and looked around the room. "This was her sitting room—Gwen's parlor, we called it. Come to think of it, this is the first time I've been here since she died."

"I'm sorry."

It was the standard, automatic response. Eric shrugged it off. "She was over a hundred years old—I'm not sure exactly how much over, but quite a bit. Hey—it had to happen."

"Is that her picture?" She held out a hand, and Eric, nodding, handed it over. "One of yours?" He nodded again, wondering how she knew. "She looks like a neat lady," Devon said, making what might have been an inane comment sound as though it came straight from the heart.

Eric said nothing for a moment, gazing down at the face he'd photographed so many times…this one a favorite of his, the lovely aged face turned slightly away from him and lifted joyfully to the sun. "She had the most incredible voice," he said, trying again to laugh. "Like music…always just a grace note away from laughter."

"But," said Devon thoughtfully, "her eyes seem sad."

The observation both surprised and touched him. Looking over at her, standing almost shoulder to shoulder with him, shorter than he was though not by much, his eyes on a level with the top of her head, he felt a sudden and intense wave of longing, and had no idea what it was he was longing for.

"I always thought so," he said gruffly. "Mom said it was because her husband was killed in the Second World War. Anyway, she never remarried." He paused, looking around him at the room he'd never before seen without Gwen's presence in it, hearing in his mind's ear the music of her laughter. Regret made his voice even harsher when he added, "I didn't make it to her funeral."

She looked up at him, and he forced himself not to waver under the impact of that intent green gaze. Reminding himself that it had been his own idea, this sharing of the secrets of his soul. "Why not?"

He shrugged and looked away again. "I was in Africa at the time. There was a famine…."

"There's always a famine in Africa, isn't there?"

"Yeah," Eric said dryly, "and that's apparently what the whole world's attitude was at the time, because this particular famine didn't even make the evening news here. Just stuck away somewhere on the back pages of the international section of the newspapers. Old news." Except to the children who were dying, he thought bitterly. "It was a story I thought needed telling."

He feels things more deeply than most people…and not only that, unlike most people, he also gets involved. Devon was experiencing disquieting stirrings, the awakening of new impressions and perspectives. She was surprised to identify one of those as respect.

"Were your parents upset with you for not coming home for the funeral?" she asked in a careful, gentle tone, as she would if she were interviewing a particularly fragile witness.

Eric considered a moment, then let out a breath. "No," he admitted almost reluctantly, "they pretty much understood."

Devon let the words lie there in the fertile silence. She watched his face as he gazed down at the portrait of the old woman in his hands, then let his eyes travel slowly across the mantelpiece, touching each photo there in turn.

Finally, bringing his gaze back to her, he muttered it again, as though in awe, "They understood."

There was silence again, and it became too hard to maintain contact with those eyes. She jerked hers back to the family photo gallery. "Well. You do have quite a family." It sounded lame. It wasn't what she wanted to say. She felt a new burning in her belly and identified its source with a small sense of surprise.

Envy. I envy him. You have a *wonderful* family, she wanted to say. Even scattered all over the world, you can feel their warmth, their love. *I envy you.*

"Not what you expected?" His voice had a cool and bitter edge. Jerking her eyes back to him, she saw that his smile had slipped off center, and knew what he was thinking even before he said it. "That's what you get for pre-judging people."

She opened her mouth to protest, wanted to deny it, to explain. A soft snort forestalled her.

"You know what's funny?" Eric said, and there was no rancor in his voice. Only wry amusement. "You're probably still doing it. Right this minute. Right now you're probably thinking, Wow, what a great family, right? From one extreme to the other. But you know what? The truth is generally somewhere in the middle. Hey, I love my family, but they're not perfect." He snatched up a photograph, a black-and-white wedding picture she thought might be his grandparents'. "It's like this photograph. We'd call it black-and-white, but if you look closely, it's actually a whole bunch of different shades of gray." He thrust it at her, a little self-consciously; she thought he wasn't comfortable on the soapbox.

Cautiously smiling, she said, "Does that mean you no longer believe I'm a complete one hundred percent ogre?"

He paused, obviously caught off guard. Then a smile

flickered behind his eyes as he said somberly, ''Not a hundred percent. Maybe…fifty.''

''Okay,'' Devon triumphantly breathed, ''we're making progress.''

There was another pause before he answered without the smile, a wary and thoughtful, ''Are we?''

And she couldn't answer him, not the glib and confident affirmative she'd planned. *Where is this going?* she wondered with a stab of panic. Last night she'd set off in a blizzard, full of self-assurance, certain of her path. Today, in a warm house, safe from the storm, she felt lost, afraid to put a foot forward or say a word lest it lead her into hidden peril.

What had changed? This man, Eric Lanagan, with his gentle eyes and hollow cheeks and fierce hawk's nose…he was still her adversary. That much hadn't changed. What was different, she realized, was the battlefield. She was accustomed to seeing every contest in terms of…yes, black and white: me—my client—against them. But like the photograph in Eric's hands, this landscape seemed to be all in shades of gray. She was like a lander on a new planet, picking her way over unfamiliar terrain, never knowing when or from where the dangers might come.

He was waiting for her answer, she realized, watching her with unreadable eyes and lopsided smile. She murmured something ambiguous, but even before she finished she could tell he'd stopped listening. His head tilted, and his eyes lifted toward the ceiling.

''The baby's awake,'' he announced, returning the wedding picture to the mantel and heading for the door. Halfway there he paused and gave a jerk of his head, inviting—no, ordering—her to come along.

Devon's heart thudded; she opened her mouth, words of panicked protest already tumbling from her tongue. But he shook his head and made an imperious gesture with his hand, reminding her suddenly, remarkably, of his mother. "Come on," he said gruffly, a masculine version of Lucy's rusty voice, "it's about time you met your niece."

Mike had found Lucy sitting on Eric's bed, holding the baby up in front of her, rather the way she'd hold a hymnal, even though she couldn't sing a note.

"It's the 'Looking Over,'" she explained in response to his amused question, watching the baby's murky blue eyes flick across her own face. "You know, like in *The Jungle Book?* We humans do it, too, you know. Sort of our way of saying welcome to the world…" She caught her breath in wonder as the baby's tiny mouth suddenly popped open in a smile—a real one, she was sure of it. "I've been looking for Eric," she said when her awed and tremulous breathing had gotten back to normal. She paused, and then… "Do you think she's really our grandchild?"

Mike coughed and shifted around the way he did when he was trying to avoid answering her. Which was generally when he knew she wasn't going to like the answer he had to give her.

She caught a quick breath and went on before he had to. "Doesn't matter, really. If Eric says she is, that's good enough for me."

She turned the baby this way and that, studying the way her eyes changed in the light. "I think her eyes are going to stay blue."

Mike cleared his throat in a relieved sort of way. "Could be green, like her mother's."

Lucy gave him a look. "How do you know her mother's eyes were green?"

"Devon's are."

"Oh, you noticed that, did you?" She slyly teased him just so she could enjoy the fluster in his mutter of response. After a moment, though, because it had been on her mind, she said slowly, "Mike, tell me really. What do you think of her?"

"Devon?" His eyes flicked toward Lucy, then away. "She's pretty," he said cautiously, making her smile. "Seems smart."

"But, what?" Lucy knew the nuances in her husband's voice.

He came to sit beside her, tickling the baby's cheek with one long forefinger to stall for time while he thought.

"Just…something about her," he said, "reminds me of Chris."

"*Chris! Our* Chris?"

"The first time Wood brought her here for a visit—remember? We were all sitting around the table having lunch, and Gwen remembered she'd known Chris as a child. Turned out she'd grown up around here, gone to school with Wood. She hadn't told him."

"Hmm…and she had good reasons not to, as it turned out." Lucy frowned at the baby, whose eyelids were growing heavy.

"Yeah, well, the point is, you know how she always seemed so cool and calm, her face was like a beautiful porcelain mask. And all the time there was so much going on inside her…so many secrets she was hiding behind that mask."

"And you think *Devon*…"

He shrugged. "I don't know. Like I said, there's just something about her that makes me think of Chris, that's all."

"Well," Lucy said darkly, "she's sure not hiding the fact that she means to take Emily away from us—from Eric, I mean."

"Yeah, and right at Christmastime, too." Mike's tone was somber, but when he looked at her Lucy could see the teasing twinkle in his eyes. "Sure doesn't seem right, after you wished, and then it looked like you had your wish granted.''

"Sometimes Providence works in mysterious ways," she reminded him. "You, of all people, should know that, *Cage.*" Lucy nudged against him and shared with him their secret smile. "Just think—all those years ago—if those hoodlums hadn't tried to kill you, firebombing your town house—"

"And if my girlfriend hadn't picked that night to break up with me, and I hadn't been out walking off my grief, they'd have succeeded."

"Right. And if you hadn't run from them and gotten off the interstate in that thunderstorm and wound up lost and run your car into a ditch and holed up in my barn on the very same day my hired hand quit—oh, Mike…"

"I'd never have met you," he huskily finished for her when her voice choked and he saw that her eyes were filling up.

She was glad when he slipped an arm around her, and the storm-ripples of awe and fear that always came with that terrible thought died peacefully in the sunshine of long-established love. "Anyway," she said on a quick, restorative breath, smiling down at the now-sleeping baby, "it's not over yet. I have a plan…."

"Shush!" And Mike silenced her with a squeeze a half second before Eric and Devon walked into the room.

They look guilty as hell, Eric thought. Like a couple of kids caught necking in the hayloft. And he almost smiled.

"How's she doing?" Eric gave the baby a nod as he eased into the room, keeping all the awkwardness he felt inside. "I thought I heard her fussing."

"Nope," said his mother serenely, "not a peep. I think she wore herself out making faces at me—she dropped off a minute ago. We were just going to put her down." She stood up with Emily in her arms, putting action to the words.

"Here—I'll take her." He plucked the baby from his mother's arms more abruptly than he meant to, a fact of which he was acutely aware and instantly regretted. He was aware, too, of his father's eyes…calm, quiet, more appraising than accusing.

Uncomfortable, he picked up the formula bottle from the nightstand and frowned at it. "She didn't take all her bottle? She'll probably just catnap, then wake up in a few minutes and want the rest. I can take it from here, if you, uh, if you want to…" *Get lost?* He stopped, frustrated. How *did* one tactfully dismiss one's parents?

Which was one thing his plans for drawing Devon out of her shell hadn't taken into account. Those plans were going to require a considerable amount of privacy, and that was a commodity it had just occurred to him might be in short supply to him, living under his parents' roof.

"Well, all right, if you're sure…" His mother's eyes wavered, then slid past him to pounce on Devon, who was trying hard to look at ease and succeeding about as well as he was. "Have you had breakfast? There's French toast and bacon in the oven—did you find everything okay?"

Devon had been concentrating with all her might on becoming invisible. Now, brought so abruptly into the conversation, she did something she almost never did. She floundered. "I'm not—that is, I don't normally—uh, I had some toast earlier. I'm sorry—you shouldn't have gone to so much…" And appealing for salvation to the only person available, she threw Eric a look of desperate entreaty.

He gave his mother a pained look. "We'll grab a bite later, Ma, okay? Quit worrying about feeding us—we're not kids."

It was impatient, though not at all rude, which Devon thought might be about normal for grown-up offspring when speaking to their parents. And it struck her how different it was from the way she customarily spoke to her own parents—always with polite reserve, more as she might a client or a stranger.

"Well," said Lucy briskly, unperturbed by her son's bluntness, "I guess you know where to find the food when you get hungry. I know I've got plenty of things I should be doing." She paused to give Devon a smile. "Just let me know if you need anything, okay? Mike?"

Devon caught the look she exchanged with her husband as she bustled him out of the room. They left the door wide-open as they went, she noted with amusement. She glanced at Eric to see if he'd noticed, and saw that his expression had gone from pained to sardonic. He tilted his head toward the open door and muttered under his breath, "Jeez, you'd think I was twelve."

Discovering that she was smiling, Devon ducked her head in an unsuccessful attempt to hide it.

"What," Eric demanded, "you think it's funny that they still treat me like a kid?"

"No," she said, "but I think it's probably normal."

He paused in his slow, rocking pacing to look at her. "Oh, yeah? Did your parents do that when you were a teenager? Make you leave your door open when you had a boy in your room?" And there was something about the way he watched her, all of a sudden, something almost…crafty. Something that set off her lawyer's radar.

"Oh, I'm sure they must have," she said lightly, walking away from him to avoid his eyes.

"What do you mean, 'they *must* have'? Don't you remember?"

"No, actually, I don't." She said it absently as she paused, pretending to study the revolving rack of tapes and CDs on the battered wooden desktop. But she was too aware of her own heartbeat. She felt a curious sense of uneasiness, and wondered if this was what animals felt when they caught the distant odor of fire.

"You have an interesting assortment of musical tastes," she remarked as a means of changing the subject. Though not only for that reason. It *was* interesting to her, what kind of music he liked. At the very least, she reasoned, it was a way to learn more about the man who was to be her adversary. A way of finding out what made him tick. CDs—rock bands and country music stars from roughly ten years ago—took up most of the space in the carousel, but there were also some older tapes, folk and gospel music, mainly. And one cluster of CDs from the Vietnam era that particularly intrigued her.

"*Had,* you mean." Eric was leaning sideways to look over her shoulder. "Those are at least ten years old. And some of 'em aren't even mine."

She hadn't realized how close to her he'd come with his relaxed, baby-rocking stroll. Now she inhaled his scent with every breath, and it flooded her system like high-test fuel, kicking her pulse into a new and faster rhythm. It struck her first how clean he smelled—not just freshly showered, but *wholesome,* without any hint of either nervous sweat or cologne, cigarette smoke or booze or artery-clogging fast foods—compared to the people who inhabited the courtrooms and law offices and jail meeting rooms she was accustomed to.

And that wasn't all. There was something else, too, something unfamiliar to her, something warm and sweet and faintly earthy that could only be coming from the sleeping baby.

"Those are Mom's—the gospel stuff," Eric was saying. "And the Parish Family tapes, too—that's Dixie's family, you know? The folk singers?" He made a disgusted sound when Devon only looked blankly at him. "Jeez, I thought everybody knew them. Their stuff is in the Smithsonian."

Devon muttered something vague. Her head was swimming; she couldn't think. It had to be his nearness—something to do with his animal heat, his masculine scent, maybe even something to do with the baby in his arms. She snatched a CD from the carousel and thrust it at him. "What about these? You must not even have been born when they were popular."

He leaned closer, brushing her arm with his. "Creedence Clearwater Revival? Those are my dad's."

Something in his voice made her risk a glance at him. And she wished she hadn't. His brown eyes seemed to flare with a golden light, giving the gaunt features so close to her own a hawklike fierceness so unnerving she wished with all her heart she could tear her gaze away. But she couldn't.

"I bought him a bunch of those Vietnam-era CDs for Christmas one year. I was really into the period—because of my grandfather, you know?—and I knew Dad had lost all his stuff in a fire, way back before he met my mom."

"That was thoughtful." Devon could barely hear herself. Her voice had gotten lost somewhere in the thundering pulses inside her own head. "I'll bet he really liked it."

"Yeah, he did." His eyes, gentle again, dropped to the baby in his arms. Released from that strange golden spell, Devon realized then that Emily had begun to squirm and scrunch her face into alarming expressions and make angry, snorting noises.

"Ah...ready for the second course, are you?" Eric was speaking again in the crooning voice that reminded Devon of a tiger's purr. It resonated under her breastbone, and she surprised herself with a nervous sound that was horrendously close to a giggle. He shot her a look. "You want to hold her?"

"Oh—God," she gasped, cringing away from him. "No—that's okay, you go right ahead—"

"Come on, she's not going to bite you."

"Oh, but I—"

"Here—hold out your arms."

"What? How—"

"Just hold 'em out—you know, like somebody's trying to hand you a load of laundry. A pile of legal briefs—I don't know. *Something.* Hell, anything but a baby, I guess."

"Oh, God," said Devon faintly. "I think I'd better sit down." She backed up until she felt the bed come against her knees.

"Don't tell me you've never held a baby before," Eric teased as he followed her. His smile was sardonic, though his eyes held a softer gleam.

"As a matter of fact, I haven't," Devon bristled in her own defense, glaring at him. "I'm a *lawyer,* for God's sake! I don't think I've ever even *touched* a baby. When *would* I have?"

He chuckled, in a way that made her think instantly and vividly of his father. "Don't feel bad. Neither had I, until they put Emily, here, in my arms, right after she was born. You'd be surprised how easy it is. I know I was. Pure instinct. Here—let me show you." He bent toward her with the pink and yellow bundle in his arms.

Trembling, Devon tried to think of all the other times she'd been scared nearly out of her wits and somehow found the courage to hang on to them in spite of it—taking the bar exam, facing a judge and jury in open courtroom for the first time, interviewing a serial killer... She took a deep breath and forced herself to lift her arms.

"No, no—the other way—the left one. They like to hear your heartbeat. That's right. Now, you kind of make a cradle...yeah, that's it. Hold her against you...not too tight." He looked up at her from his half crouch and smiled. "See? What'd I tell you? Like rollin' off a log." He straightened up and folded his arms on his chest, looking as if he'd just won a case. "Instinct," he said smugly.

What instincts? I don't think I have any—not the mothering kind, thought Devon wildly. She was too overwhelmed to speak. Emotions of so many different kinds and colors were careening around inside her, out of control and bumping into one another and creating unimaginable chaos and confusion.

In all that confusion she was sure of one thing: the baby in her arms wasn't any happier about the situation than she was.

"I think you'd better take her," she said in a choked voice, gazing in utter horror at the baby's red, contorted face. "Here—quick! *She's going to cry.*" She said that the same way she might have said, *She's going to explode.*

"She just wants her bottle," Eric said easily, reaching with one long arm to snag it from the nightstand. "Yeah…there you go." He spoke in his ratchety croon as he popped the nipple into the baby's already-open mouth. Instantly, the angry, alarming noises were replaced with greedy gulps, snorts and snuffles. Eyelids tipped with barely visible red-gold lashes drifted half-closed in blissful satisfaction. "What'd I tell you?" Eric said, smug again. And then added, "Here—take over."

And somehow or other *she* was holding the bottle and he was beaming down at her as if he'd just created a miracle, something on the scale of the discovery of fire. All she could do was glare up at him, first in panic, then confusion. Because, in some indefinable way the smile had blurred the sharpness and softened the shadows that made his face sometimes seem so forbidding…and in that same indefinable way she felt something soften and blur inside herself. In panic she tore her gaze from that disturbing, utterly mesmerizing face and fastened it instead on the tiny pink one nestled in the crook of her arm.

''Hold her snug against you—they need the body contact while they're nursing,'' she heard Eric murmur.

I can't do this, she thought. *I can't.* Oh, how she hated feeling soft and blurred. *Vulnerable.* She hated the quivery awe in her chest, the peppery sting of tenderness in her nose and eyes, the ache in her breasts. And most of all she hated the sudden and terrible longing…the inexplicable wish…that Eric would come to sit beside her on the bed, that he would put his arms around her and enfold her and the baby both in the warmth and safety of his masculine protection.

Ridiculous! What was this? Hadn't she spent her entire adult life making herself strong enough, powerful enough, and feared as any man, just so she wouldn't ever have to feel like *this*—helpless, vulnerable, longing for a man's protection? *This isn't supposed to happen!*

She rose abruptly, just as Eric was saying, ''Probably ought to stop and burp her—she's a real little pig—''

''*You* take her,'' she said in a tight, airless voice. With more deftness than she'd thought herself capable of, she thrust baby and bottle into Eric's arms, turned and fled from the room.

Chapter 8

"It was like…she couldn't even stand to touch her," Eric said. He was sitting at the kitchen table, watching his hands turn a coffee mug around and around on the red-and-green plaid tablecloth that had magically appeared there since breakfast. "Mom…you think it's possible for a woman to have no maternal feelings whatsoever?" *Or…feelings of any kind?*

"Devon? Oh, I can't believe that." Lucy threw him a smile over one shoulder. "She was probably just nervous. A lot of people are, around new babies."

"Yeah, well, I wish you could have seen her." He pushed the mug away on an exasperated exhalation, then sat and bleakly gazed at his mother as she went back to rolling cookie dough into balls on the countertop.

Which was when it occurred to him that the back of her green sweatshirt was adorned with the rear view of a very fat black-and-white cat wearing a Santa hat; he assumed the front view of the cat would be on the corresponding side of the sweatshirt. Since breakfast, it seemed, his mother had metamorphosed into a Christmas elf.

Now that he thought about it, since this morning the whole house had broken out in Christmas. The sweatshirt, the tablecloth, Christmas songs drifting in from the CD player in the parlor, cookies baking in the oven, filling the air with the rich dark smell of cinnamon and cloves. Molasses Crinkles, he realized as he watched his mother's hands deftly spoon gobs of thick brown dough, roll them into balls, dip them in sugar and then, the final touch, with a fingertip touch a single drop of water to the sugared top of each cookie, so they'd crack when they baked. What memories it all brought back. Those cookies had been his favorite, and he bet he hadn't tasted them in almost ten years. She'd probably made them especially for him.

At some point in the future he'd probably have to think about that, maybe even decide whether it touched or annoyed him—or both. But at the moment he had something else on his mind. *Someone* else. Devon. Naturally.

What am I going to do, he thought gloomily, if she *doesn't* have any feelings? About the little one, at least—he'd seen pretty convincing evidence of other kinds of feelings, down there in the barn this morning.

The little one. He thought then about his own feelings, and the need he still had, after all these weeks, to hold a part of himself safely aloof from feeling too much for a child he knew he had no real claim to. Saying her name, even in his mind filled him with fear. Even the word "baby" made him feel vulnerable. "Little one"—that was better. Nothing to do with his heart, only a small person for whom he was responsible. A helpless being he'd sworn to protect.

On that score, on a purely legal level, once the DNA tests proved he wasn't the baby's father, his custody claim wasn't going to have much of a leg to stand on. So, he'd figured his only hope for keeping the little—Emily—out of her grandparents' clutches was to get to Devon's emotions—break her down, get her to remember what it had been like, growing up in that house. At the very least, get her to remember and acknowledge what it was that had made her little sister run away from home—and stay away, at the cost of her own life. But what if, he thought now, the memories are too painful for her to face? *What if she's buried the memories—and the feelings—too deep? What if I can't get through?*

Then…it will have to be Caitlyn.

"Son? You want to give me a hand out here for a minute?" His dad had opened the back door just wide enough to put his head through, letting in eddies of damp snow-scented air to swirl through the warm, spice-saturated kitchen.

"Yeah—sure." As he pushed back his chair, Eric saw his mother throw another smile over her shoulder, this one aimed over his head, toward the back porch door.

Watching his parents' silent communion, he felt a pang of something that wasn't *quite* envy, but rather an acknowledgement sense of being on the outside of an exclusive club—one with a membership of two.

Once upon a time, he'd wondered if the kind of love his parents had was really as rare as it seemed. Now that he'd been out in the world for the past ten years, he knew beyond any doubt that it was. And that was a bleak and lonely thought.

Even with the storm windows up, the porch was cold as a meat locker. It smelled of mud, evergreens and freshly cut wood.

"I took off another four inches—that should be enough." Mike gestured vaguely at the wet sawdust and pine boughs scattered on the floor, the tree leaning against the wall. "Your mother likes to use the extra branches to put around."

Yeah, Dad, Eric thought but didn't say aloud, I know. *I used to live here, too.*

He didn't blame his father for treating him like a stranger; not really. He'd been just a kid the last time they'd spent any time together. The few brief and very awkward visits in the years since, some even more awkward phone calls hardly counted at all. Now, here he was a grown man, and it seemed neither of them had figured out how to work it yet.

"I thought we could—oh—okay…" His father hastened to grab the other side of the eight-foot tree Eric was already lifting and together they eased the freshly cut stump into the stand. "That looks pretty straight," Mike said, standing back to get a better perspective.

"I'll hold it, if you want to tighten the screws," Eric said, and then silently cussed himself as he watched his father lower himself to his knees with a stiffness that hadn't been there before. His dad getting old? Eric wasn't prepared for that. Not by a long shot.

"You know, son," Mike said, squinting up at him through the evergreen boughs, "I couldn't help but hear what you were telling your mother just now—about Devon. The baby…."

Eric glanced at his father, then quickly away. His feelings just then were ambiguous, as they had been since long before he'd pulled his car up to his parents' back door. While the child—the son—in him was bristling at the merest hint of parental interference, the adult—a brand-new parent himself—cautiously hoped for some much-needed advice. So as not to betray that fact, he eyeballed the tree, straightened it minutely and unnecessarily, and said, "Yeah? What about it?"

"You said…you didn't think she had…any feelings…for the baby.'' Mike's head and shoulders had disappeared into the foliage, and his words came in muffled grunts. ''But…I think…you're wrong about that.''

What else is new? Eric-the-son wanted to say. Eric-the-new-father drew a careful breath and gruffly said, ''Yeah? Why?''

''Think about it.'' Mike sat back on his heels, gave the tree a measuring glance, then transferred the glance to Eric. ''If she didn't have any feelings toward that baby, why would it bother her just to hold her? Shouldn't be any different than holding…say, a doll. Or a sack of groceries. Right?''

Eric didn't say anything. He stared at the tree, then gave it a quarter-turn. His father studied it with tilted head, muttered, ''A little bit to your right—that's it, hold it right there,'' and dove into the branches again.

''Now, Devon, it seems to me—'' slightly out-of-breath, it came from the depths of the tree ''—is a young woman who likes to be in control.'' There was a pause before Mike emerged to gaze up at him again, this time balanced on the ball of one foot and the opposite knee. ''That sounds like a cliché, I know, but in her case I think it's important. There's a good reason she's a lawyer. Lawyers get to call the shots, see? Tell people what to do. Anyway, to a lawyer, emotions are commodities, something to be polished up, spin-doctored and sold to a jury.'' He smiled crookedly and stuck out a hand. After the briefest of hesitations, Eric gripped it firmly and braced himself against the pull of his father's weight. ''*Real* emotions—particularly her own,'' Mike said with a grin when he was on his feet again, ''probably scare that woman to death.''

Eric made a disbelieving sound and shook his head, but it was only for show. To his surprise, his father seemed to know that. Instead of arguing with him, he touched his arm and moved closer in a companionable, man-to-man sort of way.

"Son, let me tell you how it is with women and babies. I don't know what, but there's something that happens. Put a woman close to a baby, and she goes all soft and runny inside. Even the most sensible no-nonsense woman'll suddenly start cooing in babytalk. Take your mother—when she was younger, she'd fight a bare-knuckle brawl to prove how tough she was. She felt she had to, I guess, trying to run this place alone, all that responsibility, being the boss. I had a devil of a time just getting her to admit she needed me.

"Then your sister Rose Ellen was born…" He paused, laughing softly, and for some reason Eric found himself laughing the same way. "Ah, man." Mike shook his head. "I remember once, Ellie was only a couple of weeks old. I walked into the bedroom, and there was your mother, leaning over the crib, crying. Nearly scared me to death— I thought for sure something was wrong with the baby. But your mom shook her head and kept looking at Ellie, who it turned out was sound asleep and perfectly fine, and all she could say was, 'She's so beautiful—'" He broke off with a cough, and Eric, all too familiar with how it was with guys and emotions, turned away with an embarrassed laugh of his own.

"The thing is," his father said after a moment, stopping him just before he could escape back into the kitchen, "there aren't many emotions in this world more powerful than those of a mother. You've heard of maternal instincts? If Devon was feeling even a little bit of that, it is no wonder she ran."

After her demoralizing morning, Devon hid out in the bathroom for as long as she could find excuses to do so. She showered and shampooed, conditioned and deep-cleansed, tweezed and clipped, brushed and flossed, blow-dried and styled anything and everything she could think of to which those activities could possibly be applied. Worse than the boredom was the full awareness that that was what she was doing—hiding out. And the worst of it was, she couldn't really understand *why* she was doing it. Devon O'Rourke wasn't a coward. She was not in the habit of avoiding issues and ducking confrontations—especially when such confrontations might be her only means of obtaining needed information.

But then, Devon O'Rourke did not ordinarily make a complete mess of things from the get-go, either.

She'd been over it a dozen times, and demoralizing as it was, it was still the only conclusion she could come to. She'd screwed up. Made one mistake after another. To begin with, she now realized, she should have just let the marshalls serve the court order and never gotten involved with these people at all. That was mistake number one.

Mistake number two: *What was I thinking of, born and raised in Southern California, to have tried to drive in a Midwestern blizzard?*

Number three—and after that so many more she'd lost count—all had to do with Eric. Damn him. She'd started out underestimating him. She'd told herself she wouldn't make that mistake again, but somehow he kept catching her off guard anyway. She didn't understand him. And all her efforts to do so seemed to result in more confusion, more misunderstanding.

All right, so what in the hell was she supposed to do now? Devon was accustomed to taking action, making things happen, not *waiting* for events to happen to her. But stuck here in an Iowa farmhouse, in a blizzard, she was both figuratively and literally—and she thought of the rented Town Car, out there in the snow somewhere—spinning her wheels.

The north wind doth blow and we shall have snow,
And what will the robin do then, poor thing?
She'll sit in the barn and keep herself warm,
And hide her head under her wing.

A shiver coursed through her, though the bathroom was warm and steamy as a tropical greenhouse. All right, so big deal, she'd forgotten that nursery rhyme—so what? *And so many others… Why? Why can't I remember my childhood?*
Where were you when your sister needed you?
Help me, Devon please don't leave me.
Damn you, Eric, she thought bitterly. Damn you.
It was hunger—and the delicious smells drifting up from the kitchen—that finally drove her downstairs. As before, she was vaguely disappointed to find the kitchen empty, though she did locate the source of at least one of the mouthwatering smells there. Cookies—dozens of them, spicy brown rounds with crackled tops—were spread out on trays on the kitchen table and covered with clean dishtowels. Though the smell made her almost dizzy, after a quick peek she let the dishtowel drop back over the cookies without tasting so much as a crumb; Devon rarely allowed herself to eat sweets.
While she'd been barricaded in the bathroom, it seemed, Christmas had arrived. The already cozy farmhouse kitchen had been transformed, as if by magic wand—or a battalion of elves, Devon thought wryly—into a department store window. A bright red-and-green tablecloth covered the oak table, and there were red cushions on all the chairs. A basket in the center of the table held pinecones decorated with cranberries and sprigs of evergreen. There was a wreath dangling against the glass part of the back door, and above each window, boughs of evergreen had been tied to the valance rods with red velvet bows. There were Christmasy towels and potholders on the counter, and Christmasy

covers on the toaster and blender, and Christmasy knick-knacks on the shelves above the microwave oven. Devon tried to tell herself it was ridiculously overdone; she wanted to believe it was tacky and gaudy and silly.

She tried, but she couldn't.

What she really thought it was, was pretty.

And being there in the middle of it all made her feel much the same way the cookies did—dizzy with longing and at the same time doggedly proud of the willpower with which she had always denied herself such things.

There was Christmas music, too, she realized, drifting in from a stereo playing somewhere in the house. Bing Crosby had just started "I'm Dreaming Of A White Christmas," when real voices joined in, picking it up on the next line. Men's voices, singing in harmony. *Men's voices?* Good God, Devon thought, one of them had to be *Eric*. Would he never stop surprising her?

Following the voices and the music, she crept down the hallway to the parlor. Yes, they were all there—Mike and Lucy, Eric and even the baby, asleep in her carrier seat—but instead of joining them right away, Devon paused in the shadows just outside the doorway to watch. Standing in the dark hallway and looking into that room, all aglow with Christmas cheer and family togetherness, she felt as if she were alone in a cold street, watching strangers through a lighted window. Watching something warm and real, but which she could neither feel nor touch. Something wonderful that she could never be a part of.

Across the room, Eric and Mike stood flanking a Christmas tree that towered almost to the high parlor ceiling. They were facing each other, each holding one end of a tangle of Christmas tree lights, though at the moment that was all they were doing—holding them—as they devoted their attention to the song they were singing with droll abandon. Though Eric's was the stronger voice, he was doing the harmony, while Mike backed up Bing on the melody. Lucy, their appreciative audience, perched sideways on the recliner chair with her chin in her hands and the baby's carrier at her feet, watching and smiling, but not singing. No one noticed Devon.

She didn't mind. She was glad of the chance to study Eric's family, she told herself, ruthlessly disregarding a persistent, mouthwatery hunger feeling that was centered much nearer her heart than her stomach. She told herself it was his whole family she needed to know more about, although after the first sweeping glance around the room, her eyes came back to Eric—just Eric.

She was struck by how alike they were, father and son—though she couldn't have broken the resemblance down to specifics. Eric was a little taller than his father, and a lot thinner, and he did have his mother's hawklike nose. And, she realized, her intensity, too—though it was possible that Mike's quiet way was something that just came with age. Like wisdom.

Barely thirty herself, it was hard for Devon to imagine herself or anyone her age old, but she knew with complete certainty that, like his father, Eric would still be trim and attractive when he was in his sixties—and well beyond. She could see it in his bones, the strong features unsoftened by excess flesh, in the shape of his head, the breadth of his shoulders. *And his hands...*

Oh yes, those big, long-fingered hands, so unexpectedly gentle when he'd touched her, this morning in the barn. Oddly, she could feel them still, on her face, her throat, the side of her neck. Feel her pulse throbbing against his thumb, and her body quivering inside, humming like a dynamo—some high-voltage power source. *So gentle...*

And they'd scared her to death. They still did.

She shifted restlessly, that strange vibration inside her a tickle she couldn't reach. And that movement was enough to give her away. Mike sang out, "Hey—Devon! Come on, join us."

"White Christmas" had ended. Someone else was singing now; Devon had no idea who, or what. She moved into the room, pretending an ease she didn't feel, avoiding Eric's eyes though her senses hummed with awareness of him and her skin still shivered with that memory of his touch.

"My," said Lucy from her perch on the recliner, "don't you look nice."

Devon's smile, as she murmured her thanks for the compliment, was wry. Her clothes—black silk pants and an ivory cashmere sweater—and hairstyle—a sleek and elegant twist—would have been entirely suitable for dinner in a hotel dining room, maybe a solitary nightcap in the lounge afterward. Here, in a farmhouse parlor in the middle of a snowy winter afternoon, she was well aware that she was ridiculously overdressed. Mike and Eric were both wearing nondescript jeans and sweatshirts, and Lucy looked decades younger than her age in matching green sweats with a Kliban Cat Santa on the front.

Well, so what? Devon thought. Too bad. After her marathon primp-session, she'd debated whether to put on something borrowed again. Considering the debacle she'd made of the day so far, she'd opted instead for the boost of confidence her own clothes might give her. So what if she looked like a city girl, and completely out of her element? That's what she was, dammit.

"You must be starving. Help yourself to some cookies and cocoa." Lucy casually pointed with her head to a tray on the coffee table. "We sort of missed lunch—got so busy decorating, I guess we all lost track of time—so we're filling up on snacks to tide us over till dinnertime." Her grin wasn't even remotely repentant. "There's some popcorn around here, too, someplace. Mike, where did you—oh, there it is.'' Mike had reached behind him to retrieve a giant Tupperware bowl from the desktop. He handed it over to Lucy, who stretched to add it to the hospitable jumble on the coffee table. "Don't be shy, dig in."

What else could Devon do? Her own fault she'd missed out on breakfast, of course, but she *was* starving, and it had been a very long time since that piece of toast and cup of coffee in the dark early morning. One cookie wasn't going to ruin her!

Seating herself on the edge of the couch, Devon picked up a napkin and selected a single cookie from the half-empty plate. The rich, spicy aroma made her lightheaded. She bit into the cookie and it was so delicious she actually closed her eyes. It was all she could do not to croon.

"Molasses Crinkles were always Eric's favorite," said Lucy with a pleased and reminiscent smile.

Mike chuckled. "Don't even *think* about stopping at one."

Devon had already taken another cookie. She envisioned her thighs blowing up like off-road tires.

"Have some cocoa," Lucy urged. "It's the old-fashioned, made-from-scratch kind, not instant." She gave a contented sigh and wrapped her arms around her knees. "I think hot cocoa just goes with a snow day and a roaring fire."

Devon felt the same way about white wine, preferably a nice Napa Valley chardonnay, but she didn't say so. Probably not so much as a bottle of wine in this entire house, she thought, as, in complete surrender to the inevitable, she poured herself a cup of steaming cocoa from the thermal carafe on the tray.

She was taking a cautious sip when her eyes collided with Eric's across the rim of the cup. She gulped instead, and felt a delicious warmth spreading all through her insides—similar in effect to a slug of good brandy.

Brandy…yes. That's what his eyes are like. Brandy.

Had he been watching her all that time, she wondered, with his mocking smile and whiskey eyes? Her heart skipped and jumped beneath her ribs, but she defiantly refused to let herself look away. She blew gently on her cocoa and stared back at him through the fog of rising steam.

"Speaking of snow days," Lucy announced to the room at large, "the noontime weather report says the storm is supposed to be over by tomorrow. Should be ending late tonight."

"Thank God," Devon muttered, tearing her gaze away from Eric's with a determined shake of her head. He and his father went back to untangling the strings of lights and bickering about whether to begin installing them at the top of the tree or the bottom.

Mike contemplated the end of the string he was holding. "Doesn't this white one have to go at the top? For the star?"

"Okay," Eric countered in a disgusted tone, "if you do that, what're you gonna do with the plug? It's got to hang all the way down the back of the tree. Shoot, you're gonna need an extension cord just to reach the socket."

"You're going to have an extension cord, no matter what."

"Of course," said Lucy, looking thoughtful, "there's no telling how long it'll take them to get all the roads plowed…"

"What about you, Devon?" Eric was watching her again, with that curious and unnerving intensity she'd seen in his eyes before. "How do *you* do it—bottom up, or top down?"

"I wouldn't know," she said dismissively, veiling her eyes with her lashes as she sipped cocoa. "I don't usually have a tree, since I'm generally at my parents' house for Christmas."

"No *tree?*" Lucy sounded horrified.

"Okay," said Eric, "so how do *they* do it?"

"How should I know?" Devon snapped. Why did she feel as though she were in the witness box, being cross-examined by a hostile prosecutor?

"You were there, weren't you? When you were a kid? Don't you remember—"

"No," said Devon, seething with inexplicable anger, "I *don't.*" It was too warm in that room, stifling, rather than cozy. Under her cashmere sweater, her skin felt damp and itchy.

"What I think is," said Mike, "we should get an artificial tree." That was met with a loud duet of protests that effectively broke the tension. He put up both hands, laden with lights, as though to shield himself from a shower of thrown objects. "No—wait—hear me out. That way we'd only have to put the lights on once, see? Then we just leave them on when we take the tree down."

But nobody was taking him seriously, not even Devon. It was as impossible for her to imagine a fake tree in that farmhouse parlor as it would have been to envision herself serving cookies and hot cocoa to guests in her Los Angeles apartment.

And just like that she felt a wave of homesickness for her own apartment, for the serenity of its uncluttered furniture and neutral colors...its cool, quiet elegance, and sweeping city-view.

"*I* remember," Lucy said with an air of amazement, "when we still used real candles on the tree."

"Come on, Ma."

"No—it's true. It was when I was a little girl—I'll bet Rhett would remember. Earl might have been too small. We had these little metal candleholders that you clipped onto the ends of the branches. Then there were special little candles that fit into the holders."

"Wasn't that dangerous?" Devon asked, conscious of the century-old wood-frame house around her.

"They were only lit once," Lucy explained. Her face was wistful, and her features blurred and softened with it so that she seemed almost to become that little girl she remembered. "That was Christmas Eve. They turned the lights out, Mama'd get her guitar, and everybody'd sing 'Silent Night.'"

"Except *you,* I hope." Leaving the light-stringing to his dad, Eric had moved close enough to his mother to give her an affectionate bump with his elbow. He threw Devon a grin and explained, "Mom can't carry a tune to save her life."

"Pop couldn't, either," Lucy ruefully confirmed. "Who do you think I got it from? And passed it on to Rose Ellen, poor thing. Thank goodness you got Mama's voice, Eric—like Rhett and Earl. My brothers," she explained for Devon's benefit. "They used to sing with our mother—for church and weddings…community get-togethers, mostly." She looked up at her son and gave him a light swat with the back of her hand. "And I did *too* sing. Nobody cares that you can't carry a tune when you're a child."

"That's true." Eric sat on the arm of the couch and hitched himself half-around so he could reach for a handful of popcorn. "What about you, Devon?" He lifted an eyebrow, regarding her over one shoulder as his arm came within an eyelash of brushing hers. "You sing?"

Vaguely embarrassed by the question, she opened her mouth to answer it. And inexplicably couldn't. She wanted to look away from him and found that she couldn't do that either.

"That's the kind of reaction you get from most adults when you ask that question," Mike said kindly when Devon, at last, gave a helpless shrug. He paused to consider the arrangement of light strings on the tree. "I did a column about that once, years ago—it was after I'd gone to visit Ellie's kindergarten classroom. Ask a bunch of five-year-olds if they can sing, and every hand goes up. Ask an adult and ninety percent will shrug and look embarrassed. It's kind of too bad, really.''

Devon cleared her throat. "I never said I couldn't sing."

"Well, can you?" Eric's eyes glinted teasingly. So close to her, she found their effect more than ever like swallowing straight whiskey.

She lifted her chin and glared back at him. "I do well enough."

"Oh, yeah?" He tossed a kernel of popcorn into the air and caught it adroitly in his mouth. "So, let's hear you. Sing something."

"Eric!"

Devon gave an incredulous laugh. "Oh, sure, like I'm going to sing a solo right here!"

"A duet, then. I'll sing with you." He leaned back on one elbow, completely relaxed. His eyes caught hers and crinkled with smile lines. "I'll bet we'd be good together," he murmured under his breath, as though for her only.

Her breath made a surprised sibilance as she stared at him. *What's in that cocoa?* she wanted to exclaim. Unless she was badly mistaken, she was almost certain he was *flirting* with her. In front of both his parents, for God's sake.

In the next moment she was sure she *was* mistaken, that she was being overly sensitive, that she'd misjudged him. Again. Because Lucy was beaming at them both, hands clasped under her chin, and once again her eyes had a wistful shine.

"Oh, you know, I'll bet you *would* be. It would be so nice to hear you two young people sing Christmas songs together. That's always been one of my favorite things about Christmas—hearing the old carols. It makes me think of Mama and Papa, Christmases when the boys were both home—and when you and Ellie were kids, Eric—remember?''

The look she gave her son was suddenly fierce and accusing, and her voice had grown husky. ''We've missed you so much, Eric. These last ten years—''

''I'm here now, Mom.'' He spoke softly, but even from where she sat, Devon could feel the tension radiating from his body.

''It's getting late,'' Mike interjected quietly from across the room. He was peering out the windows. ''Time for chores.''

But Lucy wasn't going to be forestalled. ''For how long?'' she said in a choked voice, transferring her fierce and accusing glare from Eric to Devon. ''Until the roads are cleared?''

''Lucy—''

''Mom—''

''I'm sorry,'' Devon began. She put down her cup and was appalled to hear it clatter on the tabletop. ''It's not my—''

''Please let them stay.'' With the spriteliness of a little brown bird, Lucy hopped off the recliner and came to take Devon's hands in both of hers. ''Devon, why not? At least until Christmas. It's only a few days….''

She's so small, and yet there's so much energy, so much power in her, Devon thought. Eric's mother was a tiny human dynamo incongruously wrapped in a comic-strip cat. She shook her head, feeling dazed. ''I can't—''

''You stay, too.'' She threw her husband a brief, silent plea. ''We'd love to have you—wouldn't we, Mike? So, why don't you stay for Christmas—*all* of you?''

Chapter 9

The silence in the room seemed absolute. When, Devon wondered, as three pairs of eyes focused on her with varying degrees of intensity, had that cozy parlor begun to seem to her more like a hostile courtroom?

She freed her hands from Lucy's grasp and hitched herself uneasily on the couch's cushions. Beside her, she could feel Eric's body tense and come upright on the arm. In preparation for his mother's defense? she wondered.

Wait a minute, she wanted to shout, I'm not the villain, here, dammit! I'm not the one who took a baby girl and fled the jurisdiction in defiance of a judge's order.

"What day is it?" she demanded, her eyes darting around the room as if the answer must be somewhere in plain sight.

"December twenty-first," Mike supplied.

"There, you see?" Lucy straightened and tucked one wing of her chin-length hair behind her ear with an unmistakable air of triumph. "Nothing's going to happen until after Christmas anyway.'' She said that as if it were a done deal, as if the decision had been hers and hers alone to make. ''You might as well stay here—spend Christmas with us. Your parents will understand, won't they, if you miss *one* Christmas with them?''

''I don't know, I'm not...'' She let her voice trail off. She wasn't used to being steamrolled and didn't know how to respond.

At some point, Eric had quietly gotten up from the arm of the couch and was now bending over the baby carrier on the floor beside the recliner. Devon watched him hunker down, balanced on the balls of his feet, the fabric of his jeans stretching taut over the flexed muscles of his thighs.

He seems so much younger like this, she thought. With that gaunt face and those aged eyes of his turned away from her, nut-brown hair curling long on the back of his neck, broad shoulders angular and rawboned even beneath the drape of his sweatshirt.

Something twisted inside her chest, and she uttered a faint, unconscious sound of protest.

''Hey, you know what? It's Winter Solstice,'' she heard Mike announce.

Lucy gave a gasp. ''That's right, December twenty-first!'' She turned to her husband, eyes alight, and she was smiling again as if that moment of emotional intensity with Eric and Devon had never happened. ''Oh, that calls for a celebration.''

''Break out the champagne,'' Mike said, grinning back at her.

''Sorry,'' said Lucy, ''no champagne. Guess cocoa will have to do.'' She found their mugs, poured a dollop of cocoa into each from the carafe and handed one to her husband. Grinning at each other, with the air of observing an old ritual, they clinked the mugs together, and then Lucy turned to Devon and Eric with a sweeping gesture that included them both. "Come on, you two—join us in a toast to the shortest day of the year!"

Devon threw Eric a mystified look. His eyes met hers above the pinkish gold head bobbing on his shoulder, but without their warm, brandy glow they seemed remote and faintly mocking. Awkwardly, she lifted her mug toward her hosts, and as they did, drank down her last swallow of lukewarm cocoa.

"Well—chore time," said Lucy briskly when that was done. She was already halfway to the door. "Coming, Mike?"

"Right behind you." He paused in the doorway to lift his mug in a farewell wave. "Carry on, kids," he said with a wink, and then they were gone. Devon could already hear the clank of buckets coming from the utility room down the hall.

In the now-silent parlor, Eric watched Devon turn to him with a look of bemusement, and braced himself for her soft, disparaging laugh. Funny, he thought, a moment ago he'd been embarrassed by his parents' behavior; why now did he find himself preparing to defend it?

"What was *that* all about?" she asked in a hushed undertone.

"What was *what* about?" Without thinking, he had pressed his lips to the top of the little one's—no, Emily's—velvety-soft head and was breathing in the sweet, baby smell of her. He felt himself already growing calmer, quieter inside.

"I don't think I've ever toasted the shortest day of the year before," Devon said, regarding the mug in her hands with an expression on her face that barely avoided mockery. "I don't know, I guess it never seemed like cause for celebration to me. Is there some significance there that I've missed?"

"The cause for celebration," Eric gently explained, jog-

gling the baby in his arms and slowly pacing, "is that, from
now on, the days get longer. If you're a farmer, in a place
where you actually have winter, that means something,
yeah."

"Oh," said Devon. She set the mug on the coffee table,
not looking at him. He heard her take a breath, and it
seemed to him her shoulders had a slump to them now, as
if she felt defeated, a condition he imagined she wasn't
much accustomed to. "Living in L.A., I guess I never really
noticed."

Living in L.A., I guess you wouldn't, he thought. Whis-
perings of sympathy stirred through him, but he couldn't
think what to say to her to let her know how he felt—or
even whether he should. Better, maybe, that they should
stay enemies.

Holding his breath, he flipped the second lightswitch on
the plate beside the door, then murmured, "Hallelujah…"
as the tree erupted in tiny multicolored lights.

After gazing at them for a moment, he said without turning, "You don't have a clue what we're all about, here, do
you?"

"No," said Devon humbly, "but I'm trying."

He gave a surprised laugh. He didn't know what sort of
response he'd expected from her, but he knew for sure it
wasn't humility. He paced back toward her, gently joggling
the baby, inhaling again her uniquely soothing smells.
"Any chance of you taking my mother up on her invitation?

She gave a light, ironic laugh. "It sounded as though she
doesn't mean to give me a choice."

He acknowledged that with a smile. "She doesn't look
it, but Mom can be a real steamroller." He paused to settle
himself on the arm of the couch within arm's reach of her,
and instantly felt the tension in her mount, as if he'd
crossed some invisible line. "She does have a point,

though," he said after a moment, looking at her along one shoulder. "Nothing's going to be done about anything until after the holidays."

She shifted her gaze to the tree. "That's not the only consideration. There are my parents. They are expecting me, you know."

"So, go—be with them."

"Without you and Emily?" Her eyes lashed back at him with stinging green fire. "Not a chance, Lanagan."

He shrugged. After a moment she made an exasperated sound and abruptly rose and walked away from him, rubbing at her arms. "Is it true? Has it really been ten years since you last saw *your* mother?" She paused for a sharp, mirthless laugh. "It seems to me you and my sister had something in common."

Anger surged through him, and he forced himself to answer calmly. "Ten years since I was here for *Christmas*. I've seen my parents a few times in the meantime—other occasions, other events. Family crises… Not the least of which," he added wryly, "was having my uncle elected president of the United States." He paused. "But yeah…for Christmas, it's been a while."

"I'm sorry, but that's not my fault." She'd halted in front of the tree and was staring at it, and the lights splashed her face with a wash of luminous color, like stained glass. The photographer in Eric caught his breath in awe; his fingers itched to be holding a camera. "Look—your issues with your parents have nothing to do with me *or* Emily. It's not fair of you—or your mother—to use that to coerce me."

"Nobody's coercing you." He managed to keep his voice quiet, but his body refused to obey the same command. He left his perch on the arm of the couch and paced a few restless steps, while his fingers gently rubbed the baby's back in calming circles. Calming himself, not her.

"Hey, can you blame her for wanting to have me—and her first and only grandchild—with her for Christmas?"

She whirled on him, primed with the contradiction, "Emily's not—" then froze when she saw how close to her he was.

"Mom doesn't know that," Eric shot back before she could continue. "And even if she did, do you think it would make any difference? If *I* say the kid's mine, that's all that matters."

Her mouth opened, and he knew she meant to lash back at him. For some reason, though, the harsh words didn't come. Instead, she glared at him, breathing hard, and he glared back while his heart banged around in his chest like one of those crazy balls that keep gaining energy with every bounce.

It occurred to him that Emily had begun to squirm and fuss, picking up on the tension around her, he thought, and by the looks of things, was about to launch into a full-blown temper fit. And because he childishly wanted to blame someone else for that, he threw Devon a look of dark accusation as he went to collect a disposable diaper, the plastic jar of baby wipes and a fresh bottle of formula and retreated to the couch. Accusation, spoken and unspoken, hung in the room like fog.

By that time the baby was in full voice, which could be spectacular when a person wasn't used to it; he was surprised Devon hadn't gone running for cover at the first squall. Instead, she stood with her back to the tree and watched him with a tense, stoic look on her face while he got the diaper changed—something the kid didn't enjoy at the best of times. Then he had to get her calmed down enough to accept the bottle, and all the while his insides were swirling with emotions he didn't know what to do with and wasn't even sure he could name.

He thought about what his dad had said about maternal

feelings being so powerful. Obviously there were some powerful emotions involved in being a father, too. He'd known, for example, the first time they'd placed the little baby girl in his arms, that from then on there wasn't anything he wouldn't do to protect her. He wished he knew how to explain that to Devon.

The thing was, the feelings that kept coming over him whenever he was around Devon, the emotions churning around in him right now, for instance, sure as hell weren't maternal. He was pretty sure they didn't have much to do with being protective, either.

"Eric?" The voice was harsh in the peace that came abruptly, as the baby's mouth closed at last around the nipple and the room filled up with the hungry sounds she made when she ate.

He glared at Devon, primed and battle-ready, but something about the look on her face made him wary, and kept him silent. There was something wistful, almost bleak about the way she watched him, he thought. For the first time in a long time she reminded him of Susan.

What is she thinking? Is she…could she possibly be remembering?

His heart gave a *bump* of excitement and hope, and he softened his glare and waited.

"What did Susan intend to do with Emily?"

It was a long way from what he'd hoped for. *"Do?"* Frowning, he shifted on the couch, getting himself and Emily more comfortably settled. "What do you mean?"

"What was Susan going to do, after her baby was born? I'm sure—" a smile flickered weakly, then vanished. "I doubt very much that she intended to *die.*"

Eric didn't answer. Instead he stared down at the baby's face, watched it waver and blur.

"She was living on the streets, you said. So, did she have any kind of a plan?" Her voice was brusque—almost pug-

nacious. But when he looked at her, all he saw was the
same wistfulness that had touched him so often in Susan—
a stretched, fragile look around her eyes...a certain childlike softness to her mouth. She looked...lost, he thought.
And—yes, there it was again—*vulnerable*. "Was she going
to put the baby up for adoption? Keep her? What?"

He drew a careful breath. "I don't think she'd made up
her mind. Sometimes she'd talk about keeping her baby—
going into the shelter, getting a job... But then, I think—I
don't know, maybe the fear of failure would get to her, and
she'd be just overwhelmed by it all. You know—'What if
I don't make it? What kind of life will my baby have then?'
And by that time, she figured she'd be that much more
attached, and giving her up would be that much—"

"What was she like—my sister?" The interruption was
no more than a whisper.

Eric narrowed his eyes, but it did nothing to help the
pain that had come over him. Giving her up. It was a fear
that he understood in his gut, in the depths of his soul.
Looking at Devon became too hard, and because he didn't
want to look at Emily either, just then, he turned his head
away. "Tired," he said gruffly. "Defeated. Like most street
kids, old before her time—like...nineteen-going-on-a-
hundred."

He felt rather than saw Devon nod. After a moment she
asked in that same fragile whisper, "Was there a funeral?"

"She was cremated," he said bluntly. "I took care of
it—sorry, it was all I could afford. There's a marker,
though, where her ashes are buried. If you want—"

"Thank you. I—my parents would appreciate that." She
hesitated, staring at nothing, rubbing at her upper arms.
Then she walked quickly past him and out of the room.

But not before he saw that she was crying.

A Southern California girl born and raised, Devon had
never experienced the profound stillness of snow. Because

of it, and because she was still operating on Pacific Coast time, she slept late and awoke to a disorienting brightness that alarmed her before she was at least partly reassured by the numerals on the nightstand clock.

She threw back the covers and, accustomed now to the shock of the cold floor on her bare feet, rushed to the window. And caught back a cry with a quick intake of breath. After that, she could only look and look...and hug herself and shiver with a strange effervescent excitement. She was unaware, then, that what she was experiencing for the first time ever was only the exquisite delight countless children have known, awakening to discover a world made magic by a simple blanket of white.

Surprised somewhat by her eagerness to be out in it, she dressed quickly in borrowed clothes and hurried downstairs. She found the kitchen warm and cozy as she'd come to expect, humid with the smells of coffee and something she feared must be boiled oats, with the friendly sounds of a local radio station playing in the background, turned down low. Her heart did a peculiar little *bump* when she saw that Eric was there before her. She couldn't for the life of her think why; slouched in a chair with several days growth of beard on his face and an errant lock of hair giving him a vagabond air, he was hardly heartthrob material.

She couldn't help but think what a difference a day made. Yesterday morning, bare-chested and holding a baby in his arms, he'd confronted her in this kitchen with all the hospitality of a peasant encountering Frankenstein's monster. Today, he was sitting at the table placidly reading a book, a coffee mug and an empty cereal bowl on the table in front of him, and he only looked up long enough to mutter a neutral, "'Mornin'—help yourself to coffee and oatmeal."

And why on earth did she find herself wishing for more?

"Where are your mom and dad?" she asked as she pulled out a chair and sat down, curling her hands around a mug of steaming coffee.

"Feeding cattle," Eric said without looking up, as he deliberately turned a page. Under the stubble that darkened his jaws she could see a muscle working, and she felt a distinctly childish—and unsettling—desire to kick him under the table.

"How come you're not out there helping?" She was secretly pleased when he closed the book and pushed it away from him. Pleased, and yet another part of her couldn't think what had possessed her, to demand attention like a spoiled child.

"Somebody has to stay with the kid," he reminded her. He laughed without humor when Devon straightened as if she'd been poked, then ducked her head to meet her raised coffee mug and bury her face guiltily in the steam. "Don't worry, I wouldn't dream of asking *you.*"

She didn't reply, but sipped coffee and nursed a little ember of…was it hurt, or annoyance? So, I'm not the mothering type, she thought. So, I don't know how to hold a baby—what am I supposed to do, apologize for that?

Refusing to give in to the disappointment she felt, she tilted her head to study the cover of the book he'd been reading. "Harry Potter—I've heard of him. Isn't that supposed to be a children's book?"

"Yeah, so what?" He picked up his coffee mug and lifted an eyebrow at her over the rim. "Does that mean adults can't read it?" He took a swallow, gesturing toward the book with the mug as he set it back down. "Dad told me I should read it, actually. He's a writer—I can see why he'd like it."

"Why's that?"

"It's full of words," he said, then smiled when she laughed at that ridiculous statement. "Well, you'd know what I mean if you read it.'' Then, while laughter still warmed his eyes, he slyly asked, ''What books did you read when you were a kid?''

''The usual ones.'' She flung it back at him, defiantly, to let him know that, even with the laughter and the smile, he hadn't caught her off guard *this* time.

''What?'' he persisted, looking innocent. ''Nancy Drew…horse books…Beverly Cleary…*The Hobbit*—''

The Hobbit. She pounced on that—she'd read *Lord of the Rings* in college. ''Yeah, I read that.'' She said it with an air of victory, and before he could ask more questions, rose briskly, taking her coffee cup with her. ''What I want to do,'' she announced, ''is go outside and see the snow.''

''Believe me,'' he said dryly, ''it looks prettier from here.''

She turned to lean against the sink. Acutely self-conscious under his quiet, appraising gaze, she folded her arms across her breasts. ''Hey—I'm from L.A. This is a new experience for me. I intend to make the most of it.''

''I hope you've got your long johns on.''

''My what?''

''Long johns—thermal underwear?'' His glance swept her from head to toe, a touch as light as snowflakes. Inside the meaningless shell of her clothes, she felt slim and cool and naked. He nodded at the jeans she was wearing. ''In those, without thermals you'll freeze in five minutes.'' He made an exasperated grimace. ''It's not a damn Christmas card. Don't you know it's *cold* out there?''

She couldn't seem to answer him. It's true, she thought. Your voice *can* stick in your throat.

Impatient, brusque, he shoved his chair back and stood up. ''Come on—I'll find you some.''

She moved clumsily to one side so he could put his cereal bowl and coffee cup in the sink. He reached past her to run water into them, then gestured for her to go ahead of him. She obeyed, meek but resentful. And he says his *mom's* a steamroller, she thought. Maybe it was in the genes.

Oh, how she did *not* want to walk ahead of him up the stairs. She'd never felt so conscious of her body before. She tried to hold herself rigid, wishing she could somehow stop the sway of her hips, the stretch of fabric over her buttocks. She was breathless by the time she reached the top, and her heart pounded as if she'd climbed a dozen flights of stairs.

In the upstairs hallway, Eric slipped past her and into her room. She followed, and found him opening and closing drawers.

"Ah—here we go." He held up a pair of light blue knit thermals, top and bottom. "These ought to fit you—I think they're probably my dad's, so ignore the, uh…guy stuff." He tossed them on the unmade bed and pulled open another drawer, this one full of socks. "If you're going to go outside in this, dress in layers—especially your feet—got it? At least three pairs of socks. The boots you were wearing yesterday morning should be okay… Oh—and eat some breakfast. You'll need the energy to keep warm. There's oatmeal—"

"I *hate* oatmeal," Devon blurted out. Belatedly recognizing the rudeness of that, she hugged herself contritely, shivering even in the mild coolness of the bedroom.

"Suit yourself," Eric said with a shrug. He went out of the room, and a moment later she heard the door next to hers quietly close.

Still shivering, still resentful, she jumped belatedly to close her own door after him. Then, muttering words like *"Bossy!"* and *"Where does he get off!"* under her breath, she began peeling off her clothes.

It took a while, and by the time she was finished the room was strewn with discarded clothing, but she was sat-

isfied she'd donned enough layers to see her through an
Arctic trek. She felt enormous—like a pregnant whale, co-
cooned in layers of fabric and stuffed into jeans that felt a
couple of sizes too small now. And stiff—she could hardly
bend her knees. She walked like a B-movie monster. But
she was ready. And she could hardly wait to get outside.

Ignoring Eric's advice about breakfast—she really did
dislike oatmeal—she bypassed the kitchen and made
straight for the service porch, where she struggled into the
rubber boots and parka she'd worn yesterday. The boots
were a snug fit, now, and much less clumsy than they'd
been during her brief excursion to the barn. She stomped
them experimentally a few times, then clumped across the
porch and pushed open the outer door.

The air made her gasp, and at the same time she wanted
to whoop with sheer glee. It was like the coldest *coldest*
champagne she could imagine—effervescent, exhilarating,
breathtaking. She paused for several moments, breathing
deeply, blinking in the incredible brilliance of the morning.
It's not a Christmas card, Eric had said. No, she thought,
it's a thousand times more beautiful…more wonderful.

She'd barely reached the bottom of the steps before the
dogs came bounding to welcome her; apparently they were
old friends, now. Once the amenities were out of the way,
the two Border collies went tumbling and romping off
through the blanket of snow that covered the yard, rolling
and leaping, yipping excitedly as if, she thought as she
watched them, laughing, they were trying to demonstrate
for her its marvelous possibilities.

Although, romping in snow was one thing, she discovered as she floundered her way down the hill on what she
hoped was the driveway, taking her bearings from the tops
of fence posts she could see sticking out of the drifts at the
bottom. Walking was another. She'd fallen down several
times by the time she reached what she assumed must be

the road. In addition to making a clumsy spectacle of herself, snow had managed to find its way inside her boots, and her hands were red and aching, though she tried her best to keep them warm by tucking them deep in the pockets of her parka.

She halted at the bottom of the lane, hip-deep in snow, and turned first one way, then the other, sighting along the line of fence posts, a curving row of stark black dots against all that blinding white. She shook her head, then looked again. Panic flashed briefly through her mind, followed by bewilderment, and finally, pure stubborn, muleheaded disbelief.

Where in the hell was her car?

Eric, who had been following Devon's erratic progress down the hill from a discreet distance, lifted his camera and snapped several quick pictures before moving on. He'd taken more than a few already—a fact he hadn't decided, yet, whether to share with their principle subject. Based on what he knew of Devon so far, he wasn't ready to trust her sense of humor—wouldn't have given odds, in fact, that she had one.

"Waiting for a bus?" he inquired as he approached the bereft-looking figure half buried in snowdrifts.

She jerked toward him, blowing on her hands—bare, of course. When it came to weather, the woman obviously had no sense. Her face brightened, but only briefly. She made an annoyed grimace, lifted her arms and let them fall back to her well-padded sides. "I can't find my car." She sounded so astounded, Eric couldn't help but smile. "It has to be here *somewhere*," she insisted, glaring at him as if she thought *he* must have hidden it, somehow. "I couldn't have walked *that* far in that damn blizzard."

"Then it must be here." Scratching his chin and making exaggerated "Hmm, let's see…" noises, he looked up the road in the direction from which he knew she'd have come, studying the patterns the wind-driven snow had made along the fence. Resisting the urge to lift his camera one more time, he plowed his way around Devon and halted beside a drift larger and slightly more rounded than the others. He gave the side of the drift a kick, and was rewarded with a solid-sounding *thunk*.

"Oh, my God. It's my car. It *is*. I don't believe it." Devon had wallowed her way to his side, and was already trying to brush away the blanket of snow that had completely buried what appeared to be a spanking new luxury car, navy-blue—ignoring the fact that her bare hands were cherry-red with cold.

"For God's sake, here—put these on before you get frostbite," he said as he roughly bumped her arm with the hand he'd pulled from the pocket of his parka.

She looked at him—first, in surprise, at his face; then uncomprehendingly at his hand. When she saw the pair of heavy, thermal-lined ski gloves, she jerked her eyes back to his, and he saw in them the beginnings of a glow that spread slowly over her whole face, a kind of *lightening*, not unlike a sunrise.

"Thanks…that was nice of you," she said as she took the gloves from him and awkwardly put them on. She sounded breathless, but it might have been the cold.

"Don't you know you lose most of your body heat through your hands and head?" he growled, holding up the blue-and-white knitted ski hat he'd pulled from his jacket's other pocket. "Here, hold still." He kept his expression pained as he turned her toward him and yanked her closer, so she wouldn't know what he was thinking.

As he lifted the ski cap and pulled it roughly over her cold, damp hair, he was thinking what a shame it was to cover it up and how heartstoppingly beautiful those wild, flame-red curls were, part of the reason he'd felt compelled to focus his camera lens on her again and again on her ungainly trek down the lane, the one spot of color and warmth in a frozen black-and-white landscape.

As he tucked away an errant curl with a gloved finger and tugged the cap ungently over her ears, he was thinking how young and fresh and sweet she looked, with her nose and cheeks all rosy and her mouth blurred and trembling with the cold…and how fiercely, how intensely he wanted to kiss her.

Chapter 10

"What am I going to do?"

The question, asked in such a small voice, with stark appeal and unheralded meekness, startled him. It so closely echoed his own thoughts just then. Swallowing to dampen down the desire that coiled in his belly and lingered like the taste and smell of something delicious and forbidden at the back of his throat, he let his gloved hand drop away from her.

"I knew it was in the ditch—I knew it, I *knew* it. How am I ever going to get it out of there?" More upset than she'd ever thought she could be, Devon pressed a gloved hand to her forehead. What am I going to do? she thought. *What was I just thinking?*

She'd been thinking how it might feel to kiss him, thinking about his mouth. His lips would be cold and firm, warm inside. Thinking about it with such intensity, her whole body now felt bereft...cold. She shivered with the shock of it. *Oh, God, what am I going to do?*

"Don't worry about it—I can pull it out with a tractor. No big deal." He was moving away from her; she wanted so badly to call him back. To have him put his arms around her and hold her until she stopped this infernal shivering.

"And then what?" She flung out an arm, taking in the buried road.

Eric paused to glance back at her. "They'll get it plowed—eventually."

"*When?* New Year's?" She was irrationally furious. Even the highway department, it seemed, was determined to keep her here against her will.

Against her will? But how could that be, when in her deepest buried heart what she really wanted to do was stay?

He paused, shrugged. "They usually do the interstate first, then the main roads, any emergency stuff—police, fire department, hospitals, things like that. Doubt if they'll get out here until tomorrow, the earliest."

"Tomorrow…that's the 23rd, right?" She stared across the frozen landscape, eyes narrowed against the incredible glare as she did the calculations. "By the time we'd get to the airport, get a flight—if we're lucky…" She shot Eric a look and her lips curved stiffly. "Your mom's right—we'd be getting back to L.A. just in time for Christmas Eve." It was hard to admit defeat. She took a deep breath and puffed it out in a cloud of vapor. "Looks like your family's got an uninvited guest for Christmas."

Eric's smile was as sardonic as hers. "Mom'll be happy."

"And you're not?" She asked it curiously as she came trudging up beside him, and felt him shrug.

"It's a reprieve, not a pardon."

"Look." Devon halted and touched his arm so that he had to stop too, though she could see it was grudgingly. "Do you think we could…I don't know, call a truce or something? Just until after the holiday? Even armies in the middle of fighting wars do that.'' She took a breath and closed her eyes, fighting for the self-control that usually came naturally to her, then said, all in a rush, "I didn't mean for this to happen. But I'm here, you're here, and I just think we should make the best of it. For your mom's sake, if nothing else."

Eric said softly, without looking at her, "You sound as if you care."

"Of course I do." And Devon was mildly surprised to realize she meant it. She wondered when it had happened. When, exactly, had these Lanagans begun to be people that mattered, instead of simply adversaries?

Eric's eyes swept over her with calm appraisal—and something else she couldn't identify. Daringly, she forced herself to meet and hold his gaze. "Okay—truce, then," he said, and held out a gloved hand.

"Until after Christmas," she reminded him, extending hers.

His smile slipped sideways as he took her hand in a well-padded grip. Her heart gave a *bump,* and she was sorry when he released her hand and continued on up the lane toward the house. Too soon, her renegade heart protested. *Stay with me…*

"Aren't you going to show me around?" Hands in her pockets, heart pounding harder, now, she watched him turn back to her.

He raised one eyebrow. "I thought you were cold."

"Well, of course I'm *cold.*" And to prove it, her voice was bumpy with shivers. "Dammit, after what I went through to get into these layers, I want to make the most of it. This is probably the only chance I'm ever going to have to see an actual farm, you know—especially in snow."

"An *'actual'* farm? As opposed to…what? A virtual farm? A fictitious farm?" But he was grinning as he trudged back to join her. He gave her a mocking glance as he turned and threw his arms wide. "Okay, there you have it. Over there is the actual barn—you saw that yesterday. Next to it are the actual corrals, and down there are the hog shelters—where the lights are burning, see? That's for warmth. Then there's the farrowing house—"

"The *what?*"

"Where they have baby piggies."

"Oh."

"And those are the grain silos, and the equipment barns—"

"What's that cute little cottage-looking thing, up there next to the house?" Devon asked, pointing.

"That? It used to be a bunkhouse—you know, for a hired hand? I had my darkroom in there when I was in high school, but I think it's probably used for storage, now. That's not the original—a tree fell on the old one during a thunderstorm. Happened the summer my dad first came here—long story." He brushed that aside with a gesture.

They were walking together, now, past the silos and down a slope toward open fields, following dirty hard-packed tracks in the snow, twin ribbons laid down by a tractor's tires. Far ahead, on a gently sloping hillside, the wind had scoured deeply enough to reveal the rough brown remnants of corn stubble. There, puffing out clouds of steam, grayish-white cattle were busily feeding on piles of hay the tractor had left in a long looping trail across the snowy landscape.

"Over there—see those trees?" Coming to a halt at a gate in a barbed wire fence, Eric pointed beyond the cattle and the hills and the stubbled field. "There's a little creek there that runs into the river. That's where the original homestead was—the one where my great-great—I don't know how many greats—grandmother outwitted a Sioux raiding party."

"The one who set fire to everything and tied her baby in her apron and climbed down the well?"

Eric threw her a grin. "You *were* paying attention."

"I always do."

In the next moment he'd caught his breath; his hand shot out to close on Devon's arm. "Wait—don't move."

"What?" Her whisper was hushed, breathless. He already had his camera lifted and was holding his breath, too, finding the focus. And then, following the line of the telephoto lens, she saw the reason why. Not twenty yards from where they stood, a little brown rabbit moved in tentative hops through the snow, weaving in and out among the tips of corn stubble.

It happened so quickly. Devon had just uttered a delighted and reverent "Ohh…" when something plummeted out of the sky with a screeching cry, in a fury of dark wings and curved talons. The rabbit uttered a thin, high-pitched squeal, and then was still. Devon watched in horror as the hawk began to tear savagely at the limp body with his hooked beak, holding it down with his talons. Bits of fluff floated into the air and caught the sunlight.

She became aware, then, of another sound—the rapid click and whir of Eric's camera. She whirled on him, trembling with shock. "How could you *do* that? How could you let that happen? Why didn't you stop it? You…you could have…shouted, scared it away…*something!*" Eric slowly lowered his camera. Unperturbed by the disturbance so nearby, the hawk went on methodically feeding. "How can you just stand there, clicking away, as if…as if…" Furious with herself and with him, Devon jerked away and began to plunge through the snow, back the way they'd come, brushing an angry tear from her cold cheek.

She hadn't gone far when she felt Eric beside her, but she pointedly ignored him. She was angrier than she'd had any idea she could be. He must have known that because he made no effort to talk to her then, just let her plow on up the hill until she ran out of breath and had to slow down.

They walked on together, then, plodding slowly in step, and after a while Eric surprised her by beginning to talk to her in a musing, reminiscent tone.

"Once, when I was just a kid, still in high school, my cousin Caitlyn and I were out exploring. There's this pond—it's over there, beyond the hill; you can't see it from here. We saw this mother duck, and she was trying to defend her babies from the drake—a drake'll try to kill baby ducklings, if he can. Anyway, I had my camera, as usual, and there I was, snapping away, and all of a sudden here comes Caitlyn just *flyin'* past me, screaming, '*Do* something!' She's throwing rocks and sticks, and she manages to drive the drake off, and then she turns on me. I'd never seen her so mad. She said almost the same thing to me you just did—how could I stand there and snap pictures, and why didn't I do something."

He glanced over at Devon. She couldn't help it—she lifted her head and looked back at him. Her heart gave that queer little bump again, when she saw the bleakness in his eyes. She'd almost forgotten that look—the one that made him seem older than eternity, the one that said those eyes had seen entirely too much.

"I never forgot that," he went on quietly, looking away again, his gaze focused on something Devon couldn't see. "It was years later, in Africa—that famine I told you about?—when I realized some things are just too big, there isn't a damn thing you can do." He paused. "It's terrible, you know? To feel so powerless. I guess that's why—"

He broke it off. "Why?" Devon prompted, almost against her will.

He threw her an angry glance. "Susan…I think it's why I got so involved. I thought here was a situation I *could* do something about—just one person, right? Turns out I was wrong then, too.'' Even in profile his smile was bitter.

He feels things... The thought had come to her, yesterday in the parlor, she remembered, the first time he'd told her about Africa. She'd felt the beginnings of a grudging respect for him, then. So why now did the same revelation make her feel bewildered, resentful and scared? Don't tell me these things, she wanted to shout at him. Damn you, I don't want to know what a great person you are. I don't want to admire you. *Most of all, I don't want to like you.*

Furious with himself, Eric trudged blindly ahead, not caring whether or not she kept up with him. Why do I keep telling her these things? he thought. Personal things, things he'd never told another soul. Things that had nothing to do with awakening *her* memories. Why did he find it so hard to remember who and what she was?

From the first moment he'd set eyes on Devon O'Rourke, he hadn't known what to make of her; his feelings where she was concerned had been confused, ambiguous, at best. So, that initial fear and dislike, even revulsion, had given way to sympathy and an undeniable physical attraction—fine. He had no real problem with that. But what the hell was he supposed to do with this...this strange sort of *tenderness* that kept coming over him when he least expected it? The bumpy rush of silent laughter he'd had to hold in check so he could snap her picture while she was floundering like a clumsy puppy in the snowdrifts, the urge to warm her hands, and smile at her cherry-red nose, and to pull her into his arms and kiss away the tears she'd wept for a damned *rabbit?*

What was he to do with the sore spot that took over the space where his heart was supposed to be every time he thought about Devon O'Rourke and what she meant to do to him and Emily once the Christmas truce was over?

''Hey, no fair.'' Something nudged him in the side.

Looking down, he saw green eyes glistening at him from below the rolled-up brim of the knitted ski cap, which had slipped down almost over her eyes. "I thought we had a truce."

"Yeah, so?"

"So, you're mad at me again."

"*Mad* at you?" There it was again—he couldn't help but smile. Did she know how childish that sounded? And how much she looked like one, shapeless in her layers, the cap low on her forehead...round, roly-poly and rosy-cheeked. And utterly adorable. "I'm not *mad* at you, for God's sake."

He stopped and looked up at the sky. *Ah, hell.* What did a man do with feelings like his? Only one thing left, Eric thought, since fighting them obviously wasn't working. *Give in.*

"Hey," he said, "did you ever make snow angels?" He grinned at her before she could reply. "Guess not, since you've hardly even seen snow, right? Where'd you go to college?"

"Berkeley—law school, too."

"Ah. Okay, then. Here's what you do..." He looked around. Next to the tractor tracks, the slope was pristine, and except for a few rabbit tracks, an untouched blanket of white. He turned his back to it, and catching hold of Devon's arm, made her do the same. "Now—do what I do." He let go of her arm and took two giant steps back. Then, first tucking his camera inside his ski-jacket for safekeeping, he held his arms straight out from his shoulders, took a deep breath and toppled over backward into the snow. "Your turn," he yelled.

A moment later he heard a squawk of alarm, followed by an "Oof!" and then a surprising cackle of laughter. "*Now* what?"

"Okay, now, move your arms up and down, and your

legs in and out—like this, see?'' His own ''angel'' completed, Eric levered himself upright and turned to look at his masterpiece. ''Hah—one of my best, if I do say so.''

''Is that *it?*'' Devon was still flat on her back.

''That's it—be careful climbing out, or you'll mess it up.''

A peculiar look flashed across her face. ''I don't think I can.''

''Oh, come on.''

''Eric, I'm serious. It's all these damn layers. I'm *stuck.* Give me your hand—oh, no—don't you dare. Eric, put that thing away. I swear, if you take—ooh, I'm going to kill you!''

He laughed and snapped pictures as fast as he could. He felt younger, lighter, more carefree than he had in more years than he could remember.

Threatening dire reprisals, Devon managed to turn herself over, then push up onto her knees. She had her back to him when she was finally standing upright, and his view was obstructed somewhat by the camera. So he didn't see that, when she turned, she wasn't empty-handed. He didn't see the snowball at all until it splatted him in the chest.

''Hey,'' he yelled, hurriedly stuffing his camera back inside his coat, ''for somebody with no snow experience, you sure do catch on quick!'' Pretending outrage when what he really felt was delighted—and surprised.

''I've always been a fast learner,'' she purred, dusting her gloved hands and looking smug—for about two seconds. Her dismayed ''Ack!'' and upraised arms were barely in time to deflect the worst of Eric's retaliation.

He had to say one thing for her: she wasn't a whiner. And she gave as good as she got. Eric hadn't been involved in a decent snowball fight since junior high, which was about when he'd finally gotten big enough and fast enough to get the best of his sister. Funny, though—he couldn't remember snowball fights with Ellie ever being like this. For one thing, Devon wasn't his sister. For another, they weren't either of them kids. And what a spectacle they must have made, he thought, two adults chasing each other around in the snow, firing snowballs as fast as they could make them, screaming and laughing until they were so out of breath neither of them could stand up.

If he'd taken a moment to think, he might have wondered why it didn't bother him to be acting like such an idiot. But he was caught up in it, his blood pumping, adrenaline flowing, and all he could think about was that he'd never had so much fun with a woman in his life—or desired one so much.

Later, when his blood had cooled and his heart resumed its normal pace, that was what stayed with him—the realization that what he'd wanted more than anything during that wild romp was to get them both to someplace warm and dry and peel her out of those layers of clothing, one by one, and make love to her every way he could think of until he couldn't anymore.

If things had been different, he knew, the morning might have ended that way, because unless his instincts were way off, he was pretty sure the same thought had occurred to Devon. In a perfect world, one with no abused and thrown away kids living on the streets, no Susans, no Emilys, no innocent baby girls in need of protection, making love might have been the most important thing on their minds, and anything that happened to develop from that, within the realm of possibility....

Of course, he reminded himself, in a perfect world, one with no Susans, he'd never have met her sister, Devon.

He could almost hear Gwen's lilting voice, the musical grace-note of her laughter: *Sometimes Providence works in mysterious ways, Eric.*

Maybe so, but Eric was well aware that, in his far-from-perfect world, desiring Devon was out of the question. He remembered that fact as he lay with her lumpy, snow-encrusted parka-padded body pinned beneath him, and her wet, cold-reddened cheeks between his gloved hands, and his mouth about two inches from kissing hers. He remembered it as her laughter died, and her eyes, gazing into his, were turning dark as forest pools.

And he knew that it was already too late. Like Pandora, having let those feelings out of the box, there was no way, now, that he could ever put them back.

It took all the willpower he possessed not to kiss her. Instead, with his mouth still hovering over hers he said, "You're shivering," in a voice so gruff and bumpy, it was obvious he was shivering, too.

"I guess I am," she said, sounding suffocated. "So are you."

He rolled away from her so she could breathe. "We'd better go in before you catch your death, as Mom would say. Shall we call it a draw?"

"I think you won, fair and square—well, maybe not *fair.*" She struggled to sit up, glaring at him. "You've had more experience than I have."

He held out his hand; she took it, and he hauled her to her feet. "What's experience got to do with it? A snow-ball's a snowball—you make 'em, you throw 'em. I'm just better than you—admit it."

"Better—hah! *Bigger,* maybe. Definitely louder—"

"And faster...plus, you do throw like a girl—"

"*What?* I do not—"

Bickering, Eric thought, was as good an escape valve as any. They managed to keep it up all the way to the house.

"Mike," Lucy whispered over the head of the sleeping baby in her arms, "come here. Quick."

"What?" He came to join her at the window of their

bedroom, moving in close so that her body brushed against his as she gently swayed. She tilted her head back to grin at him.

"Look—down there…"

He ducked his head so he could follow her line of sight. "Uh-huh…okay, I see them. What in the world are they doing?"

"Having a snowball fight." Lucy could hardly contain her glee.

"Funny," Mike mused, "I don't remember snowball fights involving that much body contact."

"Oh, hush." She jabbed him in the stomach with her elbow. "Don't you know what this means?"

He wrapped his arms around her and dropped a kiss onto the baby's downy head. "No, my little Machiavellian…tell me."

"My *plan*," Lucy said smugly. "It means it's working."

"Oh, God—I can't feel my feet. Does that mean they're frozen?" Devon asked as she clumped up the steps to the back porch. She felt as though she were walking on blocks of wood.

"Only if they're black," Eric said blandly, holding the door for her. "In which case, they'll have to be amputated."

She threw him a look to make sure he was teasing her, which of course he was. She looked quickly away again, but not before her heart had given that unnerving *bump;* she was beginning to expect, and in a strange way, look forward to that bump—and to dread it at the same time.

As cold as she was—and that was colder than she'd ever been in her life—there was a strange little core of heat deep inside her, a burning that was equal parts lust and shame. He'd almost kissed her; of that she was certain. What was worse—she'd wanted him to. Even now, cold to the point of pain and shivering uncontrollably, she was disappointed that the game, the time, those magical moments of fun and freedom and romping in the snow like a carefree child, had to end. And a profound sense of loss, because she'd never known such fun and freedom before in her life, and was afraid, was sure, she never would again.

Following Eric's example, she brushed and stomped away the worst of the snow there on the porch, then clomped after him into the service room where he was already shucking off his ski hat and gloves. She stood unmoving, then, and watched him unzip his jacket, peel it off and hang it on one of a row of hooks on the wall, then pull off his boots one by one, hopping comically on one foot. When he turned to her and with a ghost of a smile on his face, reached up to touch her cheek, brush it with the backs of his cold fingers, she still didn't move. Wrapped in a strange and unfamiliar lethargy, she stood and quietly watched him as he pulled her cap off, then her gloves, and finally unzipped even her jacket, as if she were a child.

No—not a child. There was nothing remotely childlike about the way her heart banged against her calm exterior shell, or the thirsty feeling at the back of her throat that wouldn't go away when she swallowed. Next, she thought when he had tugged off her jacket and hung it beside his, he will put his arms around me...hold me.

There was nothing childlike, either, in the disappointment she felt when he didn't.

"Come on in here—in the kitchen." His voice bewildered her. There was so much tenderness in it. It *felt* like arms around her, yet, except for that one small caress on her cheek, and the pulling and tugging as he helped her out of her wet clothes, he didn't touch her.

In the kitchen, he selected a chair and turned it half around, sideways to the table, then gruffly ordered her to sit. Incredibly, Devon did as she was told. *Devon*

O'Rourke—who never took orders from any man—unless he happened to have the words The Honorable in front of his name.

Silently, she watched Eric pull out another chair and set it facing hers. Then he sat down and, one by one, tugged off her boots. Numbness of another kind held her motionless and barely breathing as he lifted her feet into his lap, peeled away her layers of socks and began gently to massage them.

Pain made her gasp; reflexively, she pulled away. Eric brought her feet back to his lap. "They're gonna hurt a little." His voice was a growl. "But I think we'll let you keep 'em."

Devon tore her mesmerized gaze from his gaunt, beard-stubbled face and blinked her feet into focus. They looked ugly to her—bluish-white with purple toes—and unbelievably vulnerable, half swallowed by those lean, long-boned hands. The image wavered. Her memory overlaid it with another—those same big hands cradling an infant's tiny red-gold head.

Her stomach growled, and Eric chuckled—a sound like the one she'd heard his father make. "Should have listened to me," he said. Her eyes flicked upward almost guiltily to collide with his. Warm as brandy, they seemed much nearer to hers than they ought to have been. "Should have eaten breakfast."

Her lips parted to answer him, although she didn't know with what words. His eyes seemed to shimmer and move closer.

"Eric Lanagan!"

Devon straightened with a start. Lucy came bustling into the kitchen in her energetic way, the baby's head bobbing against her shoulder. She halted and glared over it at her son. "Did I just hear what I thought I heard? You've been out all morning without *breakfast?* Look at the both of you—soaking wet and half-frozen—it'll be a miracle if you don't catch pneumonia—and at Christmastime, too. I think the two of you lack good sense."

Eric's eyes found Devon's. They gleamed with amusement as he mouthed the words, "Treats me like I'm five."

"Well, sometimes you act like it," Lucy snapped.

Devon gasped in amazement and Eric exclaimed with a pained grimace, "Ma, how do you *do* that?"

"You think I can't read lips?" She gave her son a look of smugly maternal omniscience.

Devon's chest hummed with a warm little burr of amusement. She was beginning to look forward to the casual, sometimes bantering interplay between Eric and his parents, so different from the way things were in her own family.

"I'm going to heat up some soup," Lucy announced, expertly shifting Emily into the crook of one arm as she began to turn on burners and bang kettles. "Devon, you—" she paused to throw her a no-arguments look over one shoulder "—go upstairs and take a nice long hot shower and get into something warm. *You*—" she transferred the glare to Eric "—just as well go upstairs, too, and put on some dry clothes. No sense in *you* taking your shower until you've pulled Devon's car out of that ditch, which you'd better do today, before the snowplow comes by and buries it even deeper. But *after* you've got something hot in your stomach."

"You want me to take the baby while you—"

"Hah—I've fixed many a meal one-handed with a baby on my hip, young man. Go on, now—get." She jerked her head toward the door to the hallway and the stairs beyond, as a wing of nut-brown hair slid forward across her cheek to cover her smile.

Eric shot back a smart-mouthed "*Yes,* ma'am" as he placed Devon's feet on the floor. They exchanged looks as they both rose. Devon opened her mouth, but it was Eric who spoke.

"Oh—Mom. Devon says she'd like to take you up on your invitation to spend Christmas with us—if that's okay." His voice was bland, so devoid of expression, in fact, that she threw him a questioning look. His profile gave her no reply.

"I'm glad you decided to stay was all," Lucy said. Her smile was serene, as if, Devon thought, the decision had never been in doubt.

Chapter 11

"Your parents are something else," Devon said without turning from the window. She felt such a heaviness inside—strange that her voice should sound so light.

"Yeah, they are." And even above the sound of water running in the kitchen sink, she couldn't mistake the note of affection in Eric's voice.

It was the next morning—December 23, two days before Christmas—and she was standing with her arms folded across her waist, watching Mike and Lucy's early model four-wheel-drive SUV lumber down the lane, dragging a feathery plume of exhaust behind it. She watched it fishtail slightly—an almost jaunty little wiggle—as it turned onto the paved road. It was a beautiful, sparkly cold morning; the snowplow had been by earlier, and the sand truck after that. Mike and Lucy had gone shopping; the roads, they'd been told, were clear all the way to Sioux City.

Devon shifted her gaze to her rental car, which was parked in the driveway, still lumpy with snow and looking somehow forlorn, but otherwise none the worse for having spent a day and a half in a drift-filled ditch. Eric had checked it over and pronounced it driveable.

The roads are clear, she thought. *I have my car. I can leave if I want to.* Strangely, the realization failed to cheer her.

Yesterday afternoon while Eric was pulling the Town Car out of the snowdrifts, Devon had been on her cell phone to her office in sunny L.A., delegating and postponing meetings and other responsibilities—she was assured that her presence at her firm's annual Christmas party had been missed—and to her parents in Canoga Park, explaining to them why she wouldn't be spending Christmas Eve with them this year. They'd expressed regret, of course. Now, remembering her parents' voices, subdued, emotionless, she felt this heaviness inside.

I love my parents. I do.

But she knew they were only *words*. And though she pressed them into her mind as hard as she could, like a tongue probing a sensitive tooth, no matter how hard she tried, Devon could not find the *feelings* that went with the words. She tried to remember hugging her parents, or them hugging her. She couldn't. She couldn't remember the feel of her mother's arms around her. Couldn't remember the sound of her voice, comforting her after a nightmare. Couldn't remember cool hands stroking her forehead in a fever, or putting a bandage on her skinned knee. Couldn't remember sitting on her father's lap, having him read to her, or tuck her in at night.

Overcome with a terrible, panicky sadness, she turned from the window, already in full flight and thinking only of the stairs and the sanctuary of her room. Instead, she ran headlong into a solid object, one covered with a sweatshirt that was slightly damp. That smelled of baby powder, formula, dish soap and man.

"Hey," Eric exclaimed as his hands closed on her upper arms.

Her head snapped back and she stared at him. Whiskey eyes, startled and golden, gazed into hers. She opened her mouth to say something—to protest, to explain?—what, she never knew. Just that suddenly, she was in his arms, and his hands were tangled in her hair and his mouth was hard and hot on hers.

Hungry.

And, oh, God, she was hungry, too. How good he tasted—fresh and clean, like joy and hope and sunshine and snow. Famished, she opened her mouth to him, and he brought all those things inside.

And it wasn't nearly enough to satisfy her. Greedily, she clutched at his sweatshirt, filled her fists with it as she pressed her body against his, as if she were trying to soak him in, the very essence of all he was, trying to steal from him the warmth, the affection, the security and comfort, the gifts he'd been given in such abundance and hadn't begun to appreciate.

A sob rippled through her and burst from her mouth. He uttered a groan and stifled it with his as he caught her harder against him.

Something—a shock, like lightning—sliced through her chest. The fascinating little *bump* that had pestered her heart so often came again—and this time exploded. Her heartbeat resounded through her head like thunder. She trembled. And opened still more...

His mouth softened, persuaded. She felt the prick of his beard stubble on her lips. The delicious tingle of his fingertips stroking her scalp. She heard their breathing, the little groaning sounds he made, the soft whimpers that were hers. She felt the wiry strength of the muscles in his back against her palms, the thump of his heartbeat against her breasts. She felt melting weakness, the overwhelming ache of desire.

Dimly, she was aware of movement—clumsy, awkward, directionless. Blind and uncaring, she let it carry her where it would.

Then he was sitting in one of the kitchen chairs and she was astride his lap, her hands tangled in *his* hair as she arched above him, *her* mouth the aggressor now. His hands, free now to roam at will, pushed up her sweatshirt to knead the muscles of her back, reached between their bodies to nestle her breasts and chafe their hardened nipples with his palms, then thrust beneath the elastic of her sweats to grasp her bottom and pull the softest and most sensitive part of her hard and tight against him.

And that, without separating, standing, unzipping, undressing, was as far as they could go.

Devon acknowledged it first, with a tiny whimper of frustration. Eric's arms tightened in denial, his body tensed, and then his mouth withdrew from hers and his breath came in an exhalation that was more like a sigh.

"What the hell're we doing?" It was a whisper that grated like windblown sand. The only reply she could manage was the smallest shake of her head, before she let it come to rest against his forehead. She heard another soft, sandy sound and realized that he was laughing. "Whatever it is, I sure hope one of us has the good sense to stop it."

She cleared her throat, realized it was hopeless and whispered instead. "It seems to me, you just did."

"Then how come nobody's moving?"

"I don't know about you, but my legs are useless." She was shaking all over; some of it was laughter. She could feel her heartbeat and his, colliding in uneven rhythms.

"You're shaking," he said.

"No kidding!" Laughter gusted from her lungs. What she really wanted was to burst into tears.

And maybe it was fear that she might actually do that that gave her the strength, finally, to push herself away from him. To rise, jerky and uncoordinated, to her feet; to turn, hugging herself again, to the window. For a moment she stood blinking in the brilliance of sunshine on snow, and then in utter misery, closed her eyes and whispered, "I'm so sorry. I don't know what happened. God—we don't even *know* each other."

Behind her she heard the chair creak, and a gusty exhalation. Risking a glance, she saw that Eric was leaning forward with his elbows planted on his knees and his face buried in his hands, and for some reason she didn't add the rest: *Or like each other much, either.*

Instead, she said tightly, "There has to be a logical explanation for this."

Even muffled by his hands, the sound he made was replete with self-disgust. "Yeah, there is—I'm an idiot."

"For God's sake, it wasn't your fault. It was me. I was…I don't know, thinking about…*you* know—my parents, Christmas…"

He glanced up and his smile was almost painfully crooked. "Blame it on the holidays?"

This time the snort of self-derision was Devon's. "That's such a cliché."

"Darlin'," he said, stretching as if his bones ached, "clichés were meant for times like this." He'd managed to hold on to the smile, but the eyes that lingered for a moment on her face seemed a hundred years old.

When he pushed to his feet and turned away, she felt an irrational urge to call him back, beg him not to go. Her mind cast wildly about for reasons why he shouldn't leave her standing there, something that would justify continuing what they'd been doing before they'd both come to their senses. Her whole body felt hollow, empty.

Then, in the kitchen doorway he did pause, hesitate, and

for a moment turn back, and her heart jolted with an equally irrational stab of fear. Awash with prickles of adrenaline, she folded her arms tightly across her middle, and a pulse tap-tap-tapped against the wall of her belly.

"Look…Devon. I hate like hell to ask, but since she's asleep, and I shouldn't be long, would you mind keeping an ear out for Emily? There's…something I've got to do."

She was so shaken, she barely hesitated before she nodded. She heard herself say, "Yeah, sure. Okay. Where—"

"I'll be in the bunkhouse." He dodged into the service room long enough to snatch his jacket from its hook on the wall and was shrugging it on as he went out. A moment later she heard the back porch door close.

What I'm feeling is wrong, Devon thought. *It must be. Immoral and illegal, probably. Unethical, definitely.*

I should leave. Right now, this minute. Get in that big Lincoln, drive to Sioux City and hop the next flight to L.A.

And what would you do with Emily? Leave her here, or take her with you?

That was it—the million-dollar question. She clamped a hand to her forehead, gave a distraught whimper and raised her eyes to the ceiling. Even if she'd had the guts to try, she couldn't take Emily back to L.A. without Eric—until court-ordered tests and a judge said otherwise, he was the baby's father and legal guardian. She didn't dare go back alone, either; every instinct told her that would be a mistake.

No two ways about it, then, she was stuck—stuck on the horns of a dilemma, stuck in Iowa, stuck on a farm, stuck with strangers at Christmastime.

Worst of all was knowing that leaving here, even if she could have, was the last thing her heart wanted to do.

An hour later, Devon still had no idea what to do about a Christmas gift for Eric. She'd had no trouble finding something among the meager belongings she'd brought with her that would do for Mike and Lucy. The electronic pocket planner that had been last year's Christmas gift from her firm's senior partner, and which she almost never used, seemed perfect for Mike, and for Lucy she'd decided on a designer label silk scarf she'd brought along just in case she'd felt like dressing up a bit for that solitary hotel dinner. The brilliant shades of blue and green that complemented her own coloring so well would go just as nicely with Lucy's nut-brown hair and eyes and sun-freckled skin.

Mike and Lucy had both insisted, as they'd driven off on the freshly plowed road to finish up their own last minute holiday shopping, that under no circumstances was Devon to give them anything for Christmas. She was an invited guest, Lucy had reminded her, and a spur-of-the-moment one, at that. She was not to worry about gifts, period.

Fat chance, Devon had mentally responded, being possessed of a strong sense of propriety as well as a great deal of pride, the kind of person who wouldn't dream of showing up at a friend's home for dinner without bringing along a bottle of wine or a potted houseplant. As far as she was concerned, she was an *uninvited* guest in the Lanagan household, and the least she could do to repay them for their hospitality was to give them a Christmas gift.

That was fine, as far as her host and hostess went. But what about Eric? She had no real justification for giving him a gift—she wasn't *his* guest. She owed him nothing—except a trip back to L.A. and an appearance before a family court judge, as soon as that could possibly be arranged. But she couldn't keep her mind from chewing on possibilities.

What could I give him if things were different? What might he like?

The fruitlessness of that mental exercise only served to

remind her how little she really knew the man—Eric Lanagan, from Iowa. And how far apart they were. The gulf between them seemed enormous, unbridgeable.

How, then, to explain what had happened between them just now, down there in his mother's kitchen? The memory of that slammed into her like a physical blow; her stomach gave a lurch and her heart began to race.

Pure unadulterated lust?

Oh, no. Lust didn't begin to explain it—not as far as Devon was concerned. She hadn't come by her reputation for being one of Los Angeles's most unmeltable ice princesses by being lusty.

Not that she hadn't enjoyed her share of relationships—even sex, in her own way. It was just that in both circumstances she preferred to remain...perhaps the best word was the one used most often by her bed-partners, usually shortly before a dramatic departure: *Uninvolved.* Her most recent relationship, with a senior member of the D.A.'s staff, had ended late last summer when he'd complained that he needed a bit more from a woman than ''affectionate detachment, dammit.'' Or had it been ''detached affection''?

Either way, while Devon had been mildly distressed at his leaving, and in the months since had even thought of him once or twice with a fleeting sense of loneliness, frankly, she hadn't missed the sex at all.

So, what had happened this morning, with Eric? She'd never felt like that before in her life. Never.

That quickly she was feeling it again—the flip-flop in her belly, the pounding heart, the surging heat, the trembling legs. Oh, man, she thought, hugging and rocking herself. *Oh, man.*

For the first time in her memory, Devon was afraid.

That in itself was enough to propel her up from the bed where she'd been sitting surrounded by the contents of her briefcase and overnighter, to begin an agitated and jerky pacing—across to the window—where she could look down on Eric's "bunkhouse," which she thought looked more like a dollhouse, or a cookie house decorated with spun sugar frosting—then to the door, and back to the bed again.

What was he trying to do? What was he thinking of, to kiss me like that? What is he up to?

She asked herself those questions and was suddenly angry...*furious*. He had to have done it on purpose, to upset her. She told herself he could *not* have actual feelings for her. Given the circumstances, even the possibility of lust seemed remote.

He hadn't mentioned the court order or the mission that had brought her here since the first morning, but he had to have thought about it—how could he not? Just because they'd declared a Christmas truce, didn't mean they weren't still at war.

So, what was he up to? Could it be that— *Oh, God.* The truth hit her so hard she gasped and even buckled a little, as if from a blow to the belly. That was it—it had to be. Eric was deliberately trying to seduce her. Hoping she would then convince her parents—her *clients*—to drop their custody suit.

As if he could! (As if she would!)

If Eric Lanagan thinks he can get around me that way, he doesn't know Devon O'Rourke!

With that thought resounding like a bugle call in her mind, she all but lunged across the room, flung open the door and surged into the hallway, intent on setting the man straight, once and for all. She had actually reached the stairs—had one foot on the top step—when she remembered.

Emily. She was baby-sitting.

With a groan of frustration, Devon tiptoed back the way she'd come. She hesitated at her own open doorway, then went on past it and down the hallway to Eric's room. That door, too, stood open. No sound came from within—thank goodness Emily had slept through the racket she'd made, barging out of her room like that. Still, she supposed she ought to check, make sure everything was all right.

Holding her breath, she tiptoed closer and peeked into the room.

The smallest of movements caught her eye: a tiny pink fist, poking up from the mound of pastel-colored blankets. As Devon stared at it, the fist waved, jerked, punched the air like a miniature shadow boxer. Without a sound. Fascinated, she crept closer, until, by craning her neck, she could see into the nest of blankets. Her breath hiccupped, quivered, then stopped again.

Murky blue eyes gazed intently at the waving fist. The fist jerked, the eyes widened. Budlike lips drew together, forming a look of intense concentration on the round pink face.

Devon couldn't help it—she gave a squeak of laughter. And tried to hold it back with fingertips pressed against her lips. Too late—the eyes jerked toward the movement and the sound, and the look of concentration became one of expectation.

Busted, thought Devon with an inward sigh. "Hello, little one," she whispered aloud, and her heart did a stutter-step because that was what she'd heard Eric call her. "Hello, little girl," she amended as she bent closer still, and daringly touched the baby's chin with her forefinger.

It was startling to her—it seemed the most *miraculous* thing—when the baby's chin abruptly dropped and her mouth popped open, then widened...and just like that, became a smile.

"Ohh..." Devon breathed. Something inside her chest— her heart?—grew huge and began to ache. Her eyes misted over.

How it happened, she didn't know, but somehow, then, she was sitting on the bed in the midst of all those pink and yellow blankets, and the baby was nestled in her arms, instead. She was cooing to her and rocking, softly laughing, and didn't know or didn't care that there were tears running down her cheeks.

It was like stepping into a time capsule. From the moment Eric pushed open the door and switched on the light, he was fifteen years old again, coming home from school, getting off the bus and jogging up the lane, making straight for the bunkhouse. Throwing his backpack down on the narrow bed, reaching up to take the key to his inner sanctum, his darkroom, from its hiding place above the wall heater beside the door.

It had been his dad's idea to turn the back half of the bunkhouse into a darkroom, the part that included the bathroom with its water supply and drainage system to accommodate the mixing and disposal of chemicals. It had been years since they'd actually housed a hired hand in the bunkhouse, Mike had pointed out, and besides, it would be a whole lot more comfortable—and less expensive—than trying to convert the old root cellar and tornado shelter under the house, which had been Eric's initial plan.

Eric had insisted on paying for the renovations himself, out of the money he'd earned working summers for his mom and the sale of 4-H project animals, money that was supposed to have been saved for college. He'd been arrogant, he remembered, about the fact that he'd paid for it with his own money. It was only now, looking back, that he realized how much help on the project he'd gotten from his dad—and his mom, too. And that they hadn't said a word about him spending his college fund. Had he ever even thanked them, for any of that? Probably not. The thought made him feel itchy with guilt.

The bunkhouse was cold as a meat locker. He turned on the heater, and while the shoebox-shaped bed-sitting room was slowly filling up with warmth and the smell of burning dust, he felt above the heater, without much hope, for the key. Incredibly, it was still there. He felt a knot take hold in his chest as he fitted it into the lock, turned the knob, opened the door, flicked on the light. Sucking in a breath, he slipped the key into his pocket and stepped into the murky red gloom.

It was all there. Everything too large and bulky to take with him when he'd left home the summer he'd graduated high school, the drying racks and counters and shelves he and his dad had built out of scrap lumber and plywood from the local builder's supply store. There were even some packages of paper and chemicals, almost certainly long expired. And more than a few spiderwebs, not to mention dust, but not nearly as bad as he'd expected. Which made him wonder if his mom might have been keeping the place up all these years. That thought was another knot...another guilt.

Methodically then, he began to move among the racks and counters, waving away cobwebs, blowing off dust, sorting, counting, rearranging, setting to rights. And while he did that images paraded through his memory—mostly black-and-white; he hadn't been equipped, then, to process color—images taken with his old Pentax, his first SLR camera, given to him by his mom and dad on his thirteenth birthday. Images of Mom on her tractor, Ellie feeding baby calves, Dad at his computer, Aunt Gwen—well into her nineties and still wearing jeans—with her apron full of the eggs she'd gathered. Caitlyn on the swing, sticking her tongue out at the camera. School friends, wild geese flying, the tornado that had passed just to the north one spring. He saw the images the way he'd seen them for the very first time, floating in a pan of water, barely discernible shadings on white paper, gradually taking shape, becoming darker…clearer…sharper…while he held his breath and his heart trip-hammered in the excitement of each new discovery, each tiny moment in time now captured forever, each little miracle, like a birth happening right there in his developing trays. He thought it was the way he'd always seen the world—a series of images, flat, like photographs, composed, framed and developed in his mind, frozen and preserved and filed away forever in his memory.

Until Susan. Until he'd held her hand and watched the life fade from her eyes. Until they'd placed her baby in his arms, wet and covered with her mother's blood. And he'd known that this was *life*. Not a photograph, and not forever, but all the more precious for being so fragile and so fleeting.

The reality of that had hit him on that day, for the first time not in his head, but in his heart. In his guts. And he had known he would never be the same.

God knows, he wished he could be. God knows he'd been a much more carefree Eric, watching the world through the lens of a camera rather than feeling its pain in the pit of his stomach.

God knows he wouldn't be aching now for the damaged little girl he knew in his heart must be somewhere in the lost memories of a beautiful woman named Devon O'Rourke.

God knows he wouldn't be thinking of that woman every waking moment, thinking of her and remembering the feel of her heartbeat banging against his chest, the weight of her across his lap, the warmth and softness of her feminine places a delicious pressure on his masculine ones, and the taste of her still in his mouth….

He jumped, as something thumped against the bunkhouse door, as if he'd been guilty of the action itself rather than just the thought. He lunged for the darkroom doorway and got there as the outer door burst inward, and there was Devon, cheeks flushed, eyes wild and hair flying. She was holding in her arms what looked like a bundle of bedding.

His heart dove into his socks.

"I'm…sorry," she panted, "I…didn't know what else to do. I tried…everything. I fed her, and she didn't want any more, but she was still crying, and…I couldn't…" Her face crumpled. "I don't know what's the matter with her."

By this time Eric had relieved Devon of her burden and was peeling off the enormous comforter that completely engulfed the carrier-seat. "Let's hope you haven't smothered her," he muttered dryly, before he thought. He could have bitten off his tongue when he saw Devon's features freeze in a look of pure horror. He threw her a lopsided but reassuring smile as he tossed the comforter onto the bed. "Hey, I'm kidding. She's fine. Sound asleep."

"Really? Are you sure?" Her voice was cracked and fragile.

"See for yourself." He turned the carrier and edged it closer to her. They both gazed in silence at the baby's plump pink cheeks and delicately curled fingers, her mouth still making sucking motions as she slept.

Devon let out a long breath and closed her eyes. "Oh, God. I feel like such an idiot."

"Hey, it's okay." He glanced at his watch. "My fault, in fact. Didn't mean to desert you. Guess I lost track of time."

"Why do you suppose she was crying like that? Did I do something wrong?" Green eyes, bright with worry, searched his across the carrier seat.

Under that stark appeal, Eric's chest tightened. "Who knows why?" he said gruffly. "Babies cry." Then he asked, "Did you burp her?"

She clapped a hand to her forehead. "Oh, God—"

"Hey, look, it's no big deal. Obviously." He turned

abruptly and set the carrier on the floor beside the bed, then reached around Devon to close the door. In her haste to sidestep out of his way she lurched awkwardly, and he put a hand on her arm to steady her. He heard a sharp hiss of breath.

Heat engulfed him. His lungs felt sticky with his breath. He glared at her. "Forgot your hat and gloves again, I see."

She didn't answer, except to lift a hand to her head, as if to verify that what he'd said was true. When she lowered the hand again, somehow it came to rest on his arm.

Neither of them said anything. Both of them looked down at her hand, resting there on his arm. In the silence, Eric could feel his body rocking with the impact of his pulse. Just when he thought he would have to act or be suffocated by his own self-restraint, he felt the almost indiscernible lift of her shoulders, then a small sigh.

"It's still there, isn't it?" she said sadly.

Chapter 12

He couldn't pretend not to understand. He shook his head and breathed a soft affirmation.

"I was hoping…" she lifted her head and gave it a little shake, and he braced himself to meet her eyes "…it was, I don't know…some kind of crazy fluke."

"Temporary insanity."

"Yeah…"

He snorted. "It is, you know."

"Insanity?" Her lips quivered, and twisted when she tried to keep them from it. The look of utter desolation on her face tore at his heart. "It is—I know it. I don't know what else it could be." She would not meet his eyes. "I've never felt anything like it before. I know I can't let it happen. *I can't.* But, dammit…" She clamped a hand across her mouth, muffling the rest.

"But…what?" Something made him say it, lowering his face closer to hers.

He could barely hear her whisper, "But, I do so want it to."

His heart ached, trembled, thundered within him. He could remember experiencing such emotion only twice before in his life. Ironically, once for a birth and once for a death. Which, he wondered, was this?

"You want me—" he whispered, and could not go on.

"Yes—God knows why...beyond all reason." She said that angrily. "I want you—" her voice broke, then, and she tilted her face upward, defying her own resolve...tempting *his* beyond all reason "—to make love to me. Only—" with a hand covering her eyes she rushed to deny it "—only I *know* we can't. I know it. It's unthinkable. It's—"

"We can." He heard the words dimly, and the stirrings of excitement deep in his belly and groin told him they were his, though he felt them merely as a flow of breath over lush, warm lips, lips that were slightly parted and quivering in anticipation of the kiss they both already felt, and so badly wanted. Wanting made him believe the words were true. Overwhelming need made him nudge her chin with his and caress her lips once more. "We can...."

She gave an anguished moan. He closed his eyes so he wouldn't have to see the pain and confusion in hers as slowly, slowly they sank into each other, as their mouths melted together—though their bodies remained apart, swaying a little, touching only where his hand rested on her arm, and hers on his. All he thought about then was how hot and sweet her mouth was, the most intoxicating thing he'd ever tasted, like some enchanted elixir put in his way by a capricious god to tempt him. *One taste, and a man would be lost forever.*

And yet he could not make himself stop tasting. *Do it— yes,* everything in him shouted. *Do it. Sort it all out later.*

Breath drained from him as, in full surrender to the enchantment, he drew her arms around him and gently enfolded her in his. Deep inside her bulky jacket he could feel her body tremble. Galvanized by that, he lifted one hand and drove it into her hair, wove his fingers through the cold, slippery curls to cup her head in his palm, curled his fingers into a fist, tangling them in the vibrant mass of her hair as he held her against the deepening thrust of his kiss. Held her that way, kissed her that way, until he was trembling, too, and dizzy with the need for *more*.

With the hand not caught in the skein of her hair, he found the pull tab of her jacket zipper. It made a growling sound as he tore it down—a sound echoed a moment later, deep in Devon's throat, when she took her arms from around him long enough to shrug the jacket away. It slithered to their feet, and then her arms lifted, clearing the way, and her body was hard and taut against him. His hand was under her sweater, his fingers spread across the remembered, tender-soft skin of her back, and her hands were tangled in his hair, now, both of them—claiming and holding his neck and head as if they were precious treasures she'd found.

A strange, giddy happiness enfolded him, against all logic and reason, and his body, naive and feckless as an adolescent boy's, believed in it. He simmered with excitement, shivered with delight and smiled against her mouth as he picked her up in his arms.

What had he expected to do then? Who knew? He was in freefall, drifting on that strange, unwonted euphoria, conscious of and caring about nothing else but the woman in his arms, the soft-firm resilience of her body, the cool, damp smell of her hair, the hot brandy taste of her mouth. Had he intended this? He felt the bed bump against his knees, and he was laying them both down, still kissing her deeply and hungrily, filling his arms, hands and mouth with her. Was he thinking about causes, consequences and aftereffects? He was beyond thought.

And she, too, it seemed. She made no objection at all

when he measured her naked breasts in his hands, and gasped when he teased a taut nipple between forefinger and thumb. When his fingers discovered the button on her slacks, when he tore the zipper down, she only arched her body closer, turning...seeking...and her sounds were soft moans and tiny growls, every bit as famished as his. His knee slipped between her legs, urging them wider apart, and she moved them willingly, eagerly, inviting him to know the warm, pulsing, vulnerable softness hidden there. Her fingertips made frustrated forays beneath the waistband of his jeans.

He tore his mouth from hers and raised himself on one elbow, thinking to make the way easier for her. But she ducked her face into hiding against his chest and gasped out a muffled cry. "What are we doing?"

His tongue felt thick, his brain muddy and shocked. "I thought we were—"

"No." She reared back her head and glared at him. Dimly he registered the fact that her eyes were bright as diamonds, glittery with something that wasn't all desire. "What is it with *you*, Lanagan?" Though her voice was sharp and her words angry, her face was defenseless as a child's. Her hands clutched fistfuls of his sweater. "You can't possibly love me. I don't know how you can even *want* me. Why are you doing this?"

He felt his body go still. The hand still tangled in her hair relaxed its grip and opened to cradle the back of her neck. Accepting the sea change in her passion, he reluctantly gentled his, and with a stroking touch along the sides of his throat, said warily, "I don't know why. Any more than you do." He tilted away from her and gave her a crooked smile before he added, in a raspy growl that was meant to be sardonic, "It's not like I had this on my agenda."

"Are you sure?" She hadn't returned the smile. Eyes the impenetrable green of jungles gazed accusingly into his.

The movement of his fingertips over the velvety surface of her skin stopped abruptly. He caught his breath, held it a moment then let it go in a gust of incredulous laughter. "You mean, as in 'Plan B: If All Else Fails Get Devon into Bed?'"

"Something like that." Her gaze didn't waver.

He stared down at her for a long time before he answered, noticing the faint bluish shadows beneath the fine-textured skin around her eyes, the golden tips of her lashes, the faint, unexpected hint of freckles across her nose and cheekbones. Funny—he wasn't thinking at all about how beautiful she was then, only how terribly vulnerable she seemed. He could feel her trembling still, a fine, tight quivering deep down inside, and it was odd, too, how it affected him so differently now than a moment ago. Definitely not as a spur to his desire, but not to anger, either. He wasn't sure which he wanted to do most, in fact—turn away from her in utter defeat and thwarted passion, or gather her close and hold her in tenderness and protective care. *Like Susan...*

"You can believe me or not," he said in a voice that had become guttural with emotion—and it was odd, too, how much it mattered to him whether or not she did. "But until today it never occurred to me that I could. Get you into bed, I mean."

She believed him. And wished she didn't.

"It never occurred to me that you could, either. Until today." She couldn't believe she was actually laughing, but she was, in quiet gusts against his chest, but she knew it was the kind of laughter that can crumple into sobs in a heartbeat. Desperately afraid it might, she fought to stop it, drawing in a breath, holding it, parceling it out in little settling-down sighs as she lay back against his arm. "We can't possibly do this," she said in a low voice.

"Yeah, you're right." Eric gave a gusty sigh of his own and lay back on the cot's meager pillow, settling her subtly against him. "The bed's too damn small. Plus, if I have a condom at all, it sure as hell isn't *here*."

Was he joking? She didn't know him well enough to tell. She sniffed and said, "That's not what I meant."

"I know."

They lay together, side-by-side on the narrow, dusty cot, listening to the baby's gentle snores and staring up at the ceiling like children watching clouds. Devon's chest, her whole inside ached as if a tremendous weight was bearing down on her. Filling her lungs seemed a difficult task. She felt air-starved and exhausted when she said, "You could have me disbarred."

She felt his body flinch as though she'd struck him. "You think I'd do that?"

"I think you'd do whatever it takes to keep Emily." Listening to her own toneless voice, she felt a chill go through her. "To keep my parents—my clients—from getting her."

"You're right about that," Eric said softly, flatly. There was a pause, and then said, "Having you disbarred isn't going to accomplish that, though, is it? They'll just get themselves another lawyer."

She nodded, feeling her head move against his arm, and she thought how strange it was to be talking about such things as this, lying together like sated lovers. "They'll be doing that anyway." She hesitated, then added bleakly, "After this, at the very least I'll have to recuse myself."

"Would that be such a bad thing?"

She had no reply. As she tried to think of one, misery settled over her like a thick, musty shroud.

Silence came, then, too, until it was broken by a baby's

sleeping sigh. Devon felt Eric's body tense as he turned to check, then relax again beside her.

After a moment he said lightly, with an air of beginning, "Devon…tell me about your childhood."

The quiet words stirred through her and she held herself in a listening stillness, frightened at the emptiness she felt inside, thinking of images of dry husks blown away by cold autumn winds. The silence lengthened until finally she whispered, "I can't."

She felt his body sink as he exhaled. "Look, I'm trying to understand, okay? I just want to know how it was with you, with Susan. Make me understand."

"I said, I *can't.*" His hand, which had been a warm, strangely comforting weight across her ribs, now seemed like the bar to a cage. On the brink of panic, she pushed it away and struggled to sit up, scrambling over his legs and reaching with her feet for the edge of the cot. "I don't remember, okay?" She threw it over a shoulder, defiantly.

He raised himself on his elbows. "What do you mean, you don't remember? Your whole entire childhood? Not anything? Even a single memory? How's that possible?" He gave a disbelieving snort. "Everybody remembers *something.*"

Anger came, and she embraced it gladly. "What's with you? What's this…*thing* you have about memories? That's all you ever talk about, you know it? 'Remember when *this*? When I was a kid *that*?'" She was on her feet, now, turning jerkily, hugging herself between furious gestures. "What difference does it make?"

"What difference?" He swung his feet around and sat up on the edge of the cot, occupying the place she'd just left. "Hell, Devon, what are we without memories? Memories are…" He raked a hand through his hair, leaving it endearingly tousled while he searched for the thought. "Jeez—they make us who we are."

Endearingly? Confused and distressed, she looked away. "Well, I guess that's just who I am, then," she said, brittle and defiant. "A person who was never a child."

"Everyone was a child."

She wanted to hate him for the sorrow in his voice. She wanted to think of something sarcastic and clever to hurl back at him. Because she couldn't, she kept silent, while a pulse ticked crazily against her belt buckle, and the tension coiling inside her felt like a watch spring coming unwound.

"What about pictures?" Eric asked suddenly, straightening with inspiration brightening his eyes. "Your folks must have pictures...photo albums."

She shook her head and grimaced impatiently, not meaning to lie, really, just not wanting to explain that she never looked at the photographs in her parents' house. Except for the one on the shelf in the bookcase in the living room—she could hardly miss that one, the professional portrait of two little red-haired girls, one sitting tall and smiling with the gawky self-consciousness of adolescence, the other a chubby-cheeked baby in ruffles, propped on a pillow and clutching a stuffed Winnie the Pooh toy. A portrait of strangers. Devon felt no connection to the children in the picture whatsoever.

"What's your earliest memory, then?"

God, he was relentless. She wanted to stamp her feet, tear her hair, cry—ironically, all the sorts of things a child would do, and which she had no memory of ever having done. But in any case, she was an adult now, and all she could do was lift her hands to her head and give a tiny moan. "Oh—I don't know—jeez, I'd have to think—"

"You want to know what mine is?" She most definitely didn't, but of course he ignored her whimper of denial. "At least, I guess it's my earliest—I don't know how old I was, but I must have been maybe...two. I was sitting on my mom's lap...." His voice was gentle with remembering.

In spite of herself, she found herself turning toward it, then moving instinctively closer like a chilled animal seeking warmth in the darkness. And when she saw his face, not gaunt and full of shadows but lifted to her, smooth and light and young, her heart turned over and the anger in it drained away.

"And we were on this great big tractor. I had my hands on the steering wheel, pretending I was driving it—scared to death, you know? But so proud, too. And I know I must have been pretty small, because that steering wheel seemed huge. I had to stretch my arms wide to grip it on both sides. It felt warm in my hands…almost too warm…hot, actually."

"That's it?" She made her voice light, but there was a quiver of envy in it.

He spread his hands and smiled his lopsided smile. "That's it. Hey, memories don't have to be big, you know. They can be anything—a smell, a song, a certain food, a particular toy…a moment. Just one little moment in time, captured up here—" he tapped his temple "—forever. Like a photograph." And he grinned at her, cocky over the aptness of his analogy.

In capitulation, she sat beside him on the cot with her hands pressed tightly between her knees and drew a deep breath. "Okay…" she said on the exhalation, "I guess the earliest thing I remember is…I was packing, so I must have been getting ready to leave for college. Susan was watching me. She didn't want me to go."

Incredibly, she wished with all her heart that while she was telling him these things he would put his arms around her again, gather her in and hold her close and enfold her in warmth and safety. And prayed he wouldn't.

"Details?" Eric prompted softly.

Her mouth was dry. Her throat ached. She tried to swallow, and it felt like thorns. "The suitcase was open on the bed,'' she whispered. "She was leaning against it…crying.''

Please don't go. Don't leave me here, Devon…please don't leave me….

"That's all—I don't remember anymore—I'm sorry." And she was on her feet, heart thumping, racing. Yet she was cold. Cold clear through.

She jerked away from him, and as her gaze swept past the window, a movement caught her eye. A spurt of relief—and guilt and anguish—shot through her. "Oh, God—'' Bobbing to see past the tangle of a climbing rosebush heavily laden with red-gold hips, she managed a breathless, "Look—your mom and dad are back. I don't want them to see…." Snatching up her jacket, she ran from the cottage.

Shot through with guilt-adrenaline himself, heart pumping like a runaway freight train, Eric stood in the bunkhouse doorway and watched her make her way across the yard to the house, sliding a little on the trodden-down pathway through the snow. He felt jangled and shaken, but exhilarated, too, as if he'd just missed capturing a Pulitzer-winning shot, or a wild bird in his hands.

Coming up the lane in Lucy's old Ford 4X4, Mike and Lucy watched the stumbling red-haired figure in the unzipped ski-jacket half running through the well-trampled snow, accompanied and impeded by a pair of excited Border collies.

"Look, isn't that Devon?" said Mike. "Wonder where she's been."

"With Eric, I imagine." Lucy didn't even try to keep the satisfaction out of her voice.

Mike frowned at the windshield. "So who's minding the kid? Is that why she's in such a hurry to get back?"

Lucy was shaking her head emphatically. "They

wouldn't be so irresponsible. Look—there she is.'' She nodded toward the bunkhouse, where Eric was just coming out of the door with a comforter-swathed bundle tucked under one arm.

"Huh. What in the heck would they be doing out there in the bunkhouse?" Mike still looked puzzled as he pulled the Ford into its usual parking spot under the trees.

Lucy gave him an exasperated jab with her elbow. "Oh, Mike, don't be dense." He threw her a startled look, and she couldn't resist smirking at him. "I'm sure he was showing her his darkroom. What else?"

He let go of a gust of laughter. "Lucy, you are incorrigible."

"I love it when you talk writer to me," she purred, batting her lashes outrageously. She was feeling outrageously pleased. Her plan was working. She was sure of it.

"Hi, Mom…Dad." Eric paused beside the car as they were opening doors. "Need a hand unloading?"

"You get that baby in out of the cold. I can handle the unloading. Your mom's got to get ready for chores." Mike grinned. "Hey, how's the darkroom? Just like you left it?"

Eric grinned back at his dad, and Lucy's heart gave a little shiver of happiness. They didn't really resemble each other, those two, and yet, in the indefinable way of fathers and sons, they were so alike. "Pretty much. Need fresh chemicals, though." He turned to Lucy with a look of innocence she remembered well. "Hey, by the way, Mom— the photo albums? Where've you got 'em stashed?"

"Oh, heavens," she replied in pretended exasperation, "all over the place. Some in the parlor, some in your room…my sewing room. There's so many, I wouldn't begin to know where to…"

"That's okay, don't worry about it. I'll look." He turned back to Mike. "Dad, is it okay if I use your computer for a while this evening?"

Mike's eyebrows went up but all he said was, "Sure, go ahead. With all this yet to wrap, I can't imagine I'll be using it. Help yourself."

"Okay, thanks."

When their son had disappeared inside the house with his quilt-wrapped bundle, Mike said to Lucy out of the side of his mouth, "What d'you suppose he's up to now?"

"Who knows? It's Christmas," Lucy replied serenely. *At last....*

The rest of the day was devoted to preparations for the coming holiday—and, in Devon's case, avoiding Eric.

While Lucy and Mike were outside doing the evening chores, she stayed barricaded in her room like a hostage, listening to the intermittent sound of his footsteps going past her door. Up and down the stairs they went, in and out of his room, and her nerves jumped every time she heard his door click open or shut. Restless beyond bearing, she paced like a caged cat while the tension inside her tightened to screaming pitch.

When she finally heard the sound of banging doors, the clank of buckets and loud cheerful voices drifting up from the service room, she was so relieved she almost wept, and even though cooking had never been among her hobbies, went skipping down the stairs to volunteer to help with dinner.

Apparently delighted by Devon's offer, Lucy banished Mike, who—equally delighted to be relieved of kitchen duty—immediately went off to the parlor to help Eric with his mysterious computer project. She then handed Devon a knife and set her to cutting up vegetables for a salad to go with the beef stew that was already thawing in a Tupperware container in the microwave.

While she worked efficiently alongside Devon, Lucy chattered about all that had been and still remained to be done to get ready for the coming holiday. She sounded positively happy at the prospect of peeling and chopping the endless array of fruits, nuts and vegetables that would go into the various traditional family dishes—potato soup for Christmas Eve, corn bread and walnut stuffing, mashed potatoes, turkey giblet gravy, candied yams, creamed onions, cranberry Jell-O, fruit salad and pumpkin pies for Christmas dinner.

Devon had never heard of so much food. She asked, with twinges of alarm, how many people Lucy was expecting for dinner on Christmas Day.

Lucy smiled and explained that this year it was to be just her brother Earl, his wife Chris and their daughter, Caitlyn. "And you and Eric, of course," she added, and her smile was so radiant Devon had to look away, and wonder at the traitorous prickles that had come to the backs of her eyes.

Thus prompted, Lucy went on to talk about past Christmases when her children had been small and the household had included Great-aunt Gwen, and even farther back in the past when she and her brothers had been the children and their parents still alive. Boisterous Christmases, then, when the farmhouse had been crowded with children and noisy with laughter and music.

Listening to her, Devon felt a heaviness around her heart. Memories…everything here is memories, she thought.

What was it Eric had said about memories making people who they are? Who, then, am I? she wondered. The heaviness became an ache.

When the salad was finished, Lucy handed her a stack of plates and bowls and asked her to set the table. "That was always the children's job," she told Devon with an impish little smile. "First Ellie's, then Eric's."

Devon smiled back, but it felt bleak and fraudulent. *The children's job.* Did I do this when I was a child, in my own parents' house? she wondered as she arranged plates, bowls and napkins, knives, forks and spoons on the red plaid tablecloth. *I must have, and probably Susan, too.*

But if I did, why don't I remember?

She had no appetite for dinner, and had to force herself to choke down polite helpings of Lucy's delicious homemade beef stew and the fresh green salad she'd helped to make. There was no reason for it; the atmosphere in the kitchen was comfortable and welcoming, as always. In spite of the baby she insisted on holding in her lap, Lucy bounced up and down, back and forth between tending to Emily's needs and everyone else's, and ignored everyone's urgings to relax. Eric chatted with Mike about computer things and avoided Devon's eyes. They all reminisced—incessantly.

But Devon realized that, there in the midst of Eric's family, surrounded by unself-conscious love, easy conversation, affectionate teasing and warm remembering, she felt alienated…left out. And envious.

After dinner, Devon insisted on doing the dishes. "You must have other things you need to do," she told Lucy, nodding toward the baby she held casually cradled in the crook of one arm. "This is about the only way I know of to help. Please, it's the least I can do."

So, with twinkling eyes and secret smiles, Mike and Lucy vanished like co-conspirators behind the closed door of their bedroom, taking Emily with them. Eric went back to traipsing mysteriously up and down the stairs. Up to her elbows in soapy dishwater at the kitchen sink, Devon could hear him whistling tunelessly each time he whisked past the open doorway.

And each time he did, her heartbeat accelerated.

Dammit, she thought, staring into the froth of bubbles. *Dammit.* It felt like failure to her, this inability to forget the delicious warmth of his hand on her neck, the demanding weight of it on her belly, the tingling rush that lifted the fine hairs all over her body, the thumping ache of desire between her thighs. What irony, she thought bitterly. I'm a failure on the one hand because I can't remember, and on the other because I can't forget.

Devon wasn't accustomed to failure. She desperately wanted to blame someone else for it. Blame Eric, blame his parents, this farm, the entire cotton-pickin' Midwest, for that matter. One thing she knew for certain: she was sick to death of all of it. She couldn't wait to get away from these people and their old-fashioned corn-fed ways, their constant conversation and mushy Christmas songs, their house cluttered with holiday decorations, and a kitchen that always smelled of something cooking. Something fattening, naturally. She couldn't wait to be back in L.A., back at her job where she was almost never a failure, back in the solitude of her own cool, quiet apartment with its uncluttered serenity, everything in its place and classical music playing on the stereo.

She shivered. *I can't wait.*

Footsteps passed by in the hallway, and a rush of tuneless whistling, like a playful gust of wind. Her heart quickened, and her cheeks grew hot. "Dammit," she whispered to the sinkful of soap bubbles. "Dammit."

Later, still dodging Eric like a character in a French farce, Devon listened at her bedroom door until she heard him go downstairs, then quick-stepped down the hallway to knock on Lucy and Mike's door.

"It's me—sorry to bother you," she said in a low, urgent voice in answer to Mike's cautious "Who is it?"

The door opened halfway and Mike's face appeared, wearing a look of cordial inquiry. "Hey, Devon—what can I do for you?"

Behind him, Devon could see a bassinet beside the bed, and an overflow of pastel blankets, and Lucy sitting cross-legged on the floor in a sea of wrapping paper and stick-on bows.

"Could I trouble you for some of that paper?" She nodded toward the mess on the floor. "And a couple of bows, some tape and scissors... Oh—and if you have any to spare, a couple of boxes, about...yay-big?"

"Sure—help yourself," Mike said cheerfully, while Lucy was already scolding and absolutely forbidding Devon from even *thinking* about giving gifts to anyone.

But Devon stood her ground. And later, back in her own room with all the gift-wrapping supplies she needed, she had the strangest feeling Lucy had been pleased to find that Devon could be every bit as stubborn and strong-willed as she was.

It was late—by Iowa farm standards, not the L.A. life-style Devon was accustomed to—by the time she finished wrapping her gifts for Mike and Lucy. It took her longer than she'd expected, since she didn't normally do her own gift-wrapping, and it took her a few abortive tries before she got the hang of it. The finished product still lacked the professionalism and elegance she was used to, but under the circumstances, she thought it would do.

The house was quiet; it had been some time since she'd heard Eric's footsteps, and there wasn't so much as a peep coming from Lucy and Mike's room. What better time to play Santa's elf, Devon thought wryly as she tiptoed down the stairs to the parlor. While everyone was asleep, she'd slip her two small gifts among the growing pile under the tree....

In the parlor's near darkness, she felt for the twin light switches beside the door and chose one. And it was the Christmas tree that sprang to life, bathing the room in the soft glow of its multicolored lights. Her breath escaped in a tiny involuntary pleasure-sound, like that a child might make, as she stood in the doorway and gazed at the shimmering tree, tiny lights reflecting off a mishmash of ornaments accumulated through generations of a family's Christmases without regard to taste or style. And before she knew what was happening, she found herself blinking away tears.

Silly, she thought. *Really—it's just a tree.* She wasn't sentimental about Christmas—not even a little bit.

She dashed away the moisture on her cheek with a finger, but the ache in her throat remained.

Then, as she stood there alone in the doorway of that quiet, empty room, something came over her, a feeling so vivid it was more like memory than imagination. She saw the room no longer empty, but filled with people…adults in all the chairs, crowded together on the sofa—even perched on the arms—and children on the floor, all gathered around the tree. And no longer silent, but alive with laughter, and Christmas music playing on the stereo—something schmaltzy, Bing Crosby singing "White Christmas."

And Devon was no longer alone, as someone came behind her to slip his arms around her with the ease of someone who'd done the same thing countless times before. Someone whose touch and scent, though familiar to her as her own, never failed to make her heart bump, and beat with a new and faster rhythm. His arms enfolded her in their warmth and the lonely ache inside her vanished. A smile bloomed across her face as he whispered her name….

Devon…

Chapter 13

She drew in her breath with a shuddering gasp. The vision vanished, and the parlor was empty and silent again.

Cold and aching once more, Devon placed her gifts beneath the tree, turned off the lights and went back up the stairs.

At the door to her own room, she hesitated. She'd left it open; she could see the peace and privacy, the order and solitude she craved right there in front of her. The neatly made bed, the leftover wrapping materials in a tidy pile beside the dresser. But now for some reason the room seemed less peaceful to her than lonely. And suddenly she knew that, on this night, at least, it wasn't solitude she wanted.

A little farther down the hallway, she could see a narrow strip of light showing under Eric's bedroom door. There was no sound in the hallway; she could almost hear the pounding of her own heart. A shiver went through her, and she put a hand on the doorframe to steady herself. Drawing a slow, deep breath, she closed her eyes.

Devon...

She could feel his breath on her skin...smell his clean, wholesome scent. The longing to have his arms around her, the warmth and strength of his long, angular body against hers as it had been in her vision, was so acute she nearly whimpered aloud.

Her heart thumped against her breastbone as she pushed away from the doorframe. Her legs shook as she crossed the few yards of hallway to Eric's door. Her mouth was dry; her throat felt sticky when she tried to swallow. More nervous than she'd ever been in her life, she lifted her hand to knock.

And froze—just in time.

Above the pounding of her own pulse she could hear Eric's voice, not the low, crooning murmur he used when he spoke to Emily, but the recognizable cadences of adult conversation. Only one voice, though, with pauses between; he was obviously talking on the telephone. Devon couldn't make out words, but there was no mistaking the intimacy and affection in his tone.

Her skin prickled; chagrin washed through her in a cold flood. Stupid, she thought. *Stupid, stupid, stupid...* She'd never thought to ask him if he was involved with anyone. If he had a girlfriend. Had she just assumed, because he'd kissed her, because he'd been all too ready to jump into bed with her, that meant he was unattached? Why would she assume such a thing when she knew so well from personal experience that not even solemn vows and wedding rings were enough ''attachment'' to keep some men from taking advantage of any opportunity that came along. She knew better. Why was she so surprised?

Thank God I didn't knock.

Calmer now, her heart quiet and heavy inside her, Devon tiptoed back to her room and closed the door. She felt no less cold, no less lonely, but at least now she knew. She wouldn't be so stupid again.

"Eric, just one question—are you absolutely *sure* this is what you want to do?" Even on the bad cell phone connection, Caitlyn's voice sounded tense.

He gave a short, uneven laugh as he tried with one hand to rub the ache out of his eyes. "I wouldn't say it's what I want to do, no. But I think…I *know* it's what I have to do." He paused, then added, "I'm still hoping I won't, but I'm kind of running out of time, you know? This reprieve Mom engineered is only good through Christmas. Devon means to haul us both back to L.A. as soon after the holiday as she possibly can—the day after, probably—and at this point I think it'd take a miracle to change her mind."

"You really think she's got repressed memories of abuse?"

"I'm almost certain of it—yeah. She's got no memories of her childhood at all, and she gets tense and scared if you push her on it. But unless I can get her to remember and acknowledge what went on in that house, she's going to continue to do everything she can to get her clients—i.e., her parents—what they want. What they want is custody of their granddaughter, and…" His voice grew deeper with resolve. "I can't let that happen, Cait."

"No," she agreed softly. And after a pause. "Too bad Emily's not really yours."

"You can't fool DNA," said Eric dryly. "No, without Devon's testimony, I'm afraid the law's on their side." It was his turn to pause. "Cait, you know I wouldn't ask—"

"Hey," she interrupted in a brisker tone, "it's what we do. Now—it's kind of short notice…"

"I know—I'm sorry. I should have—"

"Never mind that. Let me get started on this—there's a lot to do. Where do you think you'll go, Canada?"

"For starters, yeah, it's the closest. After that...who knows? Someplace warm." His smile was wry, though she wouldn't see it. "I'm not used to these Midwestern winters anymore."

There was a little silence, and then Caitlyn's voice, sounding farther away than ever. "Eric? I'm sorry, but I have to ask. What about your mom and dad? They've missed you, you know. Your mom's so thrilled to have you here. I know you've been away a long time, but are you sure you're ready to give it all up? Forever? This is your home—"

Eric interrupted her with a pain-filled laugh. "If you'd asked me that a week ago, I'd have said, no problem. Now..." He took a breath. "Since I've been back it seems like everything—the place, my folks—somehow it all looks different to me."

In the gentle, attentive way that had made her not only his cousin but his best friend, as a kid, and in the years since, so often his confidante, Caitlyn prompted, "Different how?"

Sitting hunched over on the edge of his bed with his elbows propped on his knees, he tried again to rub away the ache behind his eyes. "You know how it was when I was growing up. All I could think about was getting away from this place, getting out into the world. I was scared to death I'd be trapped here for the rest of my life, like Mom. Now, maybe it's because I've seen the world, and I've seen how much misery there is out there, but I'm really beginning to realize for the first time, I think, how lucky I was— what a great childhood I had. I keep thinking how great my mom and dad are. Even thinking what a great place this would be to raise a kid." He smiled crookedly at the floor between his feet. "Ironic, isn't it? Now it's impossible...."

"Eric?" Caitlyn's laugh was gently teasing. "Is this you I'm hearing?"

He tried his best to erase it all with a snort. "Hell, maybe it's the holidays. Anyway, look—I know it's not much notice, but do what you can, okay? And I guess I'll see you here, Christmas Day?"

"You don't think I'd miss it, do you? Your first Christmas home in ten years? Sure, I'll be there—with bells on. I've even got a present for Emily. Thank you for the book gift certificate, by the way. It came in today's e-mail."

"You're welcome. Hey, don't think you have to— Wait—hold on a minute, Cait." He dropped his voice to a whisper. "I think I heard someone...."

Placing the cell phone on the bedspread, he crossed the room in two long, soundless strides, listened for a moment at the door, then carefully eased it open. There was no one in the hallway, but Devon's door was just closing with a soft *click.*

His heart gave a lurch and his skin shivered with a whole weird mix of emotions—curiosity and excitement, regret and alarm. Had she come to his door? If so, why? And why hadn't she knocked? How long had she been there? What had she heard?

He thought about going down the hall and knocking on her door to find out the answers to those questions. The pulse thumping in his belly urged him to. So did the not-so-well-banked embers of earlier fires simmering farther down. But both of those things also told him if he went knocking on Devon's door this late at night, in a sleeping house, it wouldn't be because he wanted questions answered. Who was he kidding?

And Caitlyn was waiting on the phone, her very presence there a reminder, and a warning. Getting involved with

Devon was a bad idea—for all sorts of reasons. Not the least of which was the fact that he was starting to care about her.

Oh, God. I'm starting to care about her.

He picked up the phone. "Cait? You still there?"

"Yeah, I'm here."

"Okay. False alarm. So, all right. You get everything together, and I'll call you first thing Christmas morning to let you know if it's a 'go' or not."

"Right. And meanwhile…Eric?" He waited, and his cousin said softly, "Keep hoping for that miracle, okay? 'Tis the season, after all."

He answered with a huff of laughter that gave him no comfort.

He broke the connection, but sat for a long time with the phone dangling between his knees, staring at nothing while his mind darted from one quandary to another, not knowing which to tackle first. No matter where he looked, his prospects seemed bleak.

I'm starting to care about Devon.

Oh, yeah, there was a happy thought. In fact, the realization that he was developing feelings for the woman who was trying her best to destroy his life had shaken him more than he'd thought possible.

Care about… What the hell did that mean? He'd cared about Susan, for sure, but it hadn't felt anything like this. His caring for Susan had been that of a friend, a big brother. His feelings for Devon weren't remotely brotherly, and they were a long way from being friends. He couldn't even chalk it all up to physical attraction, although he definitely had that. He couldn't say why or how, but he'd had physical attractions before, and all he knew was that this was different.

So, what are you saying, Eric? Are you trying to say you think you may be falling in love with her?

Oh, hell.

He hoped to God it wasn't true. Because even if it was, it didn't change a thing. Except to make it hurt a whole lot worse.

The day before Christmas—Christmas Eve Day, some people called it—dawned clear and cold. It would be a beautiful, sunny day. The snow was melting on exposed southern slopes and the livestock yards were a trampled, muddy mess, but it lay thick and crusty in the shady places, and there was plenty left with which to build a snowman. From her bedroom window, Devon watched Mike and Lucy assemble one in the front yard, working together to roll and lift the heavy parts and between times laughing and pelting each other with handfuls of snow, their chore-buckets abandoned in the driveway. The sight made her smile, even laugh a little. It also made her throat ache.

How happy they are. How is it that they—two middle-aged people—can laugh and play like this? Like children?

The answer came to her, sparkling clear as the day outside: *They love each other. Love their lives, their home, this place.*

But, she thought, I love my life, too. I love my home, my place. I could never live here—I couldn't.

The fact that she could even have such a thought shook her to her core.

The day that began on a note of whimsy continued the same way. After breakfast, Mike unearthed a long-handled pruning saw from somewhere in one of the sheds and cut mistletoe out of a tree in the front yard. Lucy tied sprigs together in bunches and hung them from every door casing and ceiling light fixture in the house, and she and Mike took turns "catching" each other standing under them.

Eric, who happened to be passing through the kitchen during the traditional consequence of one of those occasions, paused in the process of shrugging into his coat to roll his eyes at Devon. "Don't mind them. They get like this at Christmastime."

"Like what?" Lucy, roused and bristling, was struggling to free herself from Mike's rather theatrical embrace.

"Nuts," said Eric, and punctuated it with the growl of his ski jacket's zipper. Devon caught the grin he tried to hide.

"We'll have no 'Bah Humbug' in this house today," Mike warned his son's retreating back as the door banged shut behind him. He looked over at Devon and winked. "Don't mind him. He has a tendency to take things a tad too seriously."

"Eric always did have a hard time having fun," Lucy agreed, and her voice held a note of wistfulness. "I think he just needs for somebody to show him how." Then she looked at Devon, and for some reason her eyes seemed to warm, and then to sparkle, like embers kindling.

Devon murmured something ambiguous as she lifted her coffee cup to her lips, but as she looked away from Lucy's glowing eyes she was seeing another pair very much like them. Eric's eyes, going wide with surprise as her snowball plunked him in the chest, then suddenly igniting.

She remembered the thrill of excitement that had shot through her then, and her wildly pounding heart as she'd tried to escape inevitable reprisal. How they'd laughed, hurling and ducking snowballs, floundering and wallowing in the snow. She hadn't felt cold, only exhilarated, carefree. Like a child, she thought—and the realization came to her: *We were like them, Eric and I...like Mike and Lucy this morning.*

And then he'd come so very close to kissing her. She'd so very much wanted him to. And then...yesterday. And last night.

Tears came from nowhere to sting and blur her eyes, and

she plunked down the coffee cup and blinked them away in a panic. What would Mike and Lucy think?

But she heard their voices and laughter, now, moving on down the hallway. She was alone in the kitchen. For that one moment she could safely let her shoulders sag, close her aching eyes and lower her face into the cradle of her hand.

Ironic, she thought, that here in this house, surrounded by so much warmth, so much love, for the first Christmas in memory she should feel the desperate misery of loneliness.

It was like every day-before-Christmas he remembered—the whole household bustling with preparations for that evening and, of course, the Big Day, his sensible mom and dad behaving with uncharacteristic giddiness, and over everything a fog of suspense he could almost touch... smell...taste. Smelling and tasting being the operative words to describe the activity in the kitchen, from which cooking odors wafted through the house all day long in a confusing, ever-changing stew made up of everything from pungent onion and sage, to turkey giblets and cornbread, to pumpkin and cinnamon, chocolate, vanilla and rum.

All that cooking had always been Eric's cue to make himself scarce, and in that respect, too, this Christmas was like the others in his memory. He managed to spend most of the day in his darkroom putting together his gift for Devon, leaving Emily in his mom's care—although mostly it was his dad he'd spotted, during occasional forays into the house for food or some forgotten item, walking a fussy baby up and down the hallway. Which was definitely one thing about this Christmas that was different, the other being the presence of a redheaded stranger working side-by-side with his mother in the kitchen.

But while almost everything was the same, it felt different to him in *all* ways. What he couldn't decide was whether that had to do with, as he'd suggested to Caitlyn last night, some sort of epiphany he'd experienced "out there" in the big cruel world, or whether he'd just grown up.

One thing that was different was that today his reason for clearing out of the house had less to do with avoiding KP duty, and more to do with avoiding Devon. Developing feelings for the woman was a complication he hadn't counted on. And while there wasn't much he could do about that now, at least, he'd thought, if he didn't have to see her, be around her, maybe he could keep a bad situation from getting worse.

What he hadn't realized was that he didn't have to see her or be around her for that to happen. It happened anyway. It happened while he was working on her gift, or while he was looking at the snapshots he'd taken of her that day in the snow, and her red hair arresting as a single cardinal in all that white. It happened when he closed his eyes and memories invaded—sensory memories so keen he could feel her cool wet cheek against his skin, smell her hair, taste her mouth. See the confusion and accusation in her eyes.

It happened. Like an avalanche. A natural disaster. It was going to cause him grave damage and immeasurable pain, and there was nothing he could do to stop it.

Immeasurable pain. That was the second thing that was different this Christmas. Coloring everything, underlying the excitement and childish anticipation and feverish preparations, was the dull ache of knowing this would be the last time he'd ever be a part of it. While it was true he'd been away for a good many years, that he'd missed a decade's worth of these Christmases, the knowledge had always been in the back of his mind that he could come home any time he wanted to, that everything would still be here waiting for him—the warmth of this house, his parents, their love for him, all unchanged.

But after tomorrow… Once he'd embarked on the course Caitlyn was mapping for him even now, he could never come back. For the next eighteen years, at least, until Emily was legally an adult, they would be fugitives. If he saw his parents or any of his family again it would be brief visits in another place…another land.

That knowledge clutched at his insides like a cold hand. His heart, his throat, every part of him ached. But what could he do? Barring a miracle, it was the only choice he had.

When Devon's gift was finished and wrapped, Eric went down to the barn where he spent the rest of the day shoveling out stalls. He found no particular comfort in the solitude; it simply hurt too much to be around the people he loved.

Lucy was worried. Not that she'd ever admit it, but she was beginning to be afraid something had gone drastically wrong with her plan. And whatever it was, it had happened literally overnight. Yesterday, when she and Mike had gotten back from town to find Eric and Devon just leaving the bunkhouse and the tension in the air so thick you could cut it with a knife, she'd been certain everything was proceeding nicely, just as she'd intended. Now this morning, the two were barely speaking to one another, Devon drooping around like somebody with a bad case of Holiday Blues, and Eric looking so grim and purposeful, spending all afternoon in the barn….

Inwardly, Lucy shivered. It was Eric who worried her most. The way he was acting reminded her of that summer, the summer he'd graduated from high school, when he'd announced out of the clear blue sky that he wasn't going to Iowa State in the fall. He'd left not long after that, and they'd barely seen him since.

"I don't think I can stand it if he leaves again," Lucy told Mike on the way down to begin the evening chores. "We only just got him back, after so long.... And then there's Emily. I just hate to think of losing her, too."

"I'm afraid we won't have much to say about that," Mike said in the annoying way he had of saying out loud what Lucy already knew and didn't want to admit. "And the way it looks, I don't think Eric will, either."

Lucy sighed. "I wish I could hate Devon for trying to take Emily away from us—" she ignored Mike's smile at her use of the pronoun "—but you can hardly blame her for wanting to help her parents. She's a lovely girl, really— pretty and smart, and I think she's got a good heart, too. Oh, I know she's 'city' to the bone, but I don't think she's near as sophisticated as she pretends to be." She turned her head to look at her husband, and the cold December wind whipped a strand of her hair across her face. She fingered it back behind her ear and anchored it under the edge of her ski cap. "Mike, I know she likes Eric—I've seen the way she looks at him when she thinks no one's watching. And he likes her, too, in spite of everything. I know he does—a mother can tell. It would solve everything if they'd just…"

Mike looked down at her, then away. "What?" she demanded; Lucy knew that look.

He shook his head, grinning. "Nothing." The smile faded. "Except that it might not be that simple, Luce."

"Why not?" As far as Lucy was concerned, it certainly should be. That was the whole crux of her plan, actually; when two people were perfect for one another and didn't know it yet, all they ought to need was a push in the right direction.

Mike's head was up, his face, so familiar and beautiful

to her, golden in the last light of the rapidly sinking sun. "I just think there may be more to Devon than there appears to be. I told you that first day she reminded me of Chris, remember?" He paused to take a deep breath. "Well, she still does. More and more, in fact."

"Chris… *Chris?* Oh, Mike. You mean, you think—" She broke it off with a shake of her head, and walked a few steps in silence, thinking about all that might mean. Then she said, "Well. And look what happened to Chris—she met my brother, and he saved her life. Maybe Eric is meant to be Devon's—"

"Lucy," Mike said in a warning tone, "that's not for you to decide. If it's meant to happen, it will. Don't you try and manipulate Providence."

"That sounds like something Gwen would say."

"Yes, and think how often she was right."

Lucy tried her best to follow her husband's advice and stay out of Providence's way. Since Christmas Eve's activities were governed pretty much by tradition, that wasn't as hard as she'd thought it would be.

Potato soup for Christmas Eve supper had been the tradition in Lucy's family as far back as she could remember, though she couldn't have said whether it had actually begun then, during her childhood, with her own parents, or whether it went back farther than that. Gwen had said she thought it might have had something to do with the Great Depression, which certainly made sense to Lucy. She thought it a sensible tradition, and saw no reason to change it. The wholesome, everyday meal made a nice change from rich holiday food, and a simple preamble—rather like taking a deep breath—before the huge feast they'd all be consuming tomorrow.

It was Christmas Eve, and everything was just as she had hoped for, longed for. Prayed for. Here they were, she and

Mike, sitting down to the traditional supper with their family gathered around—half of it, anyway—with a precious grandbaby dozing in her lap and Eric home at last. And this year's batch of soup was especially good, if she did say so herself—just the right amount of pepper, perfect balance of potatoes, celery and onions—and the cornbread, Gwen's special recipe, was delicious, as always. So, why didn't it feel like a joyous occasion? Why didn't it feel like Christmas?

How could it, Lucy thought in exasperation, with Eric staring moodily into his soup and not saying a word to anyone, and Devon sitting so still and straight, her face pale as death, composed and beautiful as a statue of some ancient goddess. And yes, Mike was right, now that he'd mentioned it, she did remind Lucy of Chris, sitting right here at this same table that day so many years ago when Earl had brought her to visit for the first time…lovely Chris, with her desperate secrets and buried pain.

"Eric," Lucy said brightly, determined to lighten *his* mood, at least, "have you talked to Caitlyn since you've been back?" Eric cleared his throat, but before he could answer, Lucy turned to Devon to explain, "Caitlyn is Eric's cousin—my brother Earl's daughter. They were such good friends, growing up—the closest of all the cousins in age— Caitlyn's just a year younger. I hope you'll have a chance to meet her tomorrow. The last I talked to Chris—her mother—she still wasn't sure she was going to be able to get away. Caitlyn's a social worker in Kansas City, you know. Christmas is their busiest season…."

"She's coming," Eric said.

"Really? When did you talk to her? Did she say for sure?"

Eric shifted and once again cleared his throat. "I talked to her last night. She said she'd be here."

"Oh," Lucy breathed, "I'm so glad." Then she frowned. "Last night? When? I didn't hear—"

"It was late. You and Dad were already in bed."

"Oh. Well, then." Lucy subsided, but she was definitely losing faith in Providence.

On the one hand there was Eric, whose mood, far from being cheered by the prospect of a visit with his favorite cousin, now seemed blacker than ever. And on the other, well, what in the world had come over Devon? All of a sudden her pale-as-marble cheeks had warmed to a lovely shade of pink, and after not so much as glancing his way all evening long, now she was gazing at Eric with her eyes all aglow like Christmas stars.

Chapter 14

How did I get here? Devon wondered as she silently crumbled cornbread into dust and nodded, smiling, at whatever it was Lucy had just said.

How had Devon O'Rourke, up-and-coming L.A. lawyer with a reputation for being both hard-headed and cold-hearted, wound up in a farmhouse in Iowa, eating potato soup on Christmas Eve with the family of her adversary? Who was he, anyway, this man who had invaded her being like an alien life force and now acted as though she didn't exist?

It was her own fault that she'd walked into this mess unarmed and unprepared. She'd been so certain she had Eric Lanagan pegged, catalogued and pigeon-holed, only to find time and time again that she didn't know him at all. What did she know about him now, other than the fact that he was eons older than his chronological age—probably what New Agers would call an "old soul"? The fact that he was both kind and ruthless, a man of character and deep principles—even if those principles didn't always coincide with the law?

Those things alone would make him one of the most formidable opponents she'd ever faced. But what made her go cold and her stomach knot was the full and clear knowledge that she didn't want him to be her adversary.

What do you want him to be, Devon?

A wave of longing surged through her, like the roar of a powerful wind, and she clamped down on it with all the strength of her formidable will.

Impossible, she told herself with the harshness of hard-headed, cold-hearted reality. Even if the phone call she'd overheard last night hadn't been to a lover after all. *Impossible.*

Christmas Eve supper was finally over. It had seemed interminable to Eric, torn as he was between the anguish of knowing it would be the last one he'd ever enjoy here in his childhood home, and the desire to soak in and relish every moment, every detail, to imprint them forever in his memory. Torn, too, between an awareness of Devon that was a constant hum deep within him—a prickling just under his skin, and the knowledge that after tomorrow he'd never see her again.

After helping to clear the table, Eric relieved his mother of the baby and he and Mike retired to the parlor, leaving the women to dispose of the dishes and leftovers. While Eric introduced Emily to the wonder of Christmas tree lights, Mike carried in an armload of wood and set about building a fire. Other than his dad's running commentary on the progress he was making, neither of them said much. There seemed to be even more than the usual awkwardness between them, an odd kind of constraint. Almost, Eric thought, as if he knows.

"Okay, I think that's going pretty good," Mike said. He

rose and replaced the screen, then turned, dusting his hands. His smile as he came to join Eric beside the tree was tentative; regret tore at his heart. "What do you think? Should we make some popcorn to go with that eggnog your mom made?"

"I don't know, Dad, I'm pretty full."

"Yeah, okay. Maybe later." His father stood beside him in silence, thumbs hooked in the back pockets of his jeans. After a moment he said, "Nice tree this year, don't you think?"

"Yeah," said Eric, "it's a nice one."

Mike gave him a sideways look and cleared his throat. "Thanks for the book gift certificate, by the way. Came in yesterday's e-mail—your mother's, too. Forgot to mention it."

Eric lifted a shoulder and watched the tree lights reflected in the baby's eyes. "Yeah, well, I know you both always like books."

Mike rubbed the back of his neck and smiled ruefully as he surveyed the pile of presents under the tree. "With so few of us, I never can quite figure out how we always wind up with so many presents. Of course, some of 'em are for tomorrow—for Wood and Chris and Caity. And there're the ones Ellie and Quinn sent for everybody, too." He glanced over at Eric. "Where's the one you made for Devon? I don't see it here."

Eric brushed that aside with a quick shake of his head and muttered gruffly, "I'm going to give it to her later. I thought it might be kind of…" He coughed, knowing he couldn't explain.

"I understand," his dad said quietly.

Eric gave him a startled look, then a longer one. And he wondered if somehow his dad really did understand, though he couldn't think how that could be.

He thought about how it would be if he could put his

arms around his father and tell him…not so much that he loved him—he was sure both he and Mom already knew that—but how sorry he was that he'd been a rebellious, ungrateful pain-in-the-butt growing up. Tell him how much he appreciated the freedom he'd been given to leave and make his own way, and how deeply he regretted the years he'd stayed at a distance. Maybe try to explain that he'd kept that distance because he'd been afraid of the pull this place had on him—something he'd only just found out himself. He thought how it would be if he could tell his dad everything. About Devon, and why he had to leave again. Then, at least, he'd be able to say goodbye.

"Dad," he began. But he could hear his mother's voice in the hallway, now. He caught a breath and with an aching void where his heart should be, ducked his head and kissed his little girl's head to hide the brightness in his eyes.

Everyone was trying so hard to be kind. Devon didn't know how much more she'd be able to stand.

There was more food—popcorn and eggnog and those spicy molasses cookies—more reminiscences, and more schmaltzy Christmas music on the stereo. Lucy again begged "the young people" to sing, and this time—out of guilt, perhaps?—Devon allowed herself to be talked into joining Mike and Eric in singing "Silent Night." She sang the melody, since it was the only part she knew, joining her unspectacular soprano with Mike's pleasant baritone. As before, after the first few notes, Eric slipped into the harmony. Lucy sat sideways in the recliner and rocked Emily and beamed at them all, while her eyes grew shiny with happy tears.

After that, they opened gifts, taking their time about it, exclaiming, laughing…sometimes crying—over each and every one. Lucy's gift to Mike was a set of videos on the Vietnam War. Mike's gift to her was tickets for a February

Valentine's cruise to Hawaii, which Lucy loudly protested, though everyone in the room could see that she was surprised and deeply touched. Their daughter Rose Ellen and her husband had sent a videocam attachment for Mike's computer. "We got us one, too," they'd written on the card, "so we can see each other when we e-mail."

Mike and Lucy gave Eric a huge boxful of darkroom supplies. "You can take them with you," Lucy hastened to assure him, looking anxiously into her son's face "You don't have to use them here."

Eric leaned awkwardly across the space between them to hug her and murmur, "Thanks, Mom." Devon felt a lump in her throat.

In addition to gift certificates from an on-line bookstore, Eric gave each of his parents a framed photograph of himself holding Emily, small enough to sit on a desktop or dresser, or to join the collection on the mantelpiece. When she unwrapped hers, Lucy wiped away tears and blew her nose, and Devon, watching and doggedly smiling, felt her face would crack.

Lucy scolded as she accepted the small flat box wrapped in candy cane paper from Devon, but her face lit with a smile when she lifted the tissue paper and saw the scarf inside. "Oh, Devon, it's beautiful," she cried as she held the square of richly colored silk to her cheek. Then her eyes began to sparkle. "Great minds think alike," she murmured, handing Devon a small flat box decorated with Santa Clauses.

Inside, Devon found a scarf in a lovely shade of green, with an all-over print featuring tiny snowmen. "So you'll remember the Christmas you spent with us," Lucy said in her brisk, blunt way. Devon's eyes stung as she tied the scarf around her neck. Lucy put hers on, too, though it clashed gloriously with the poinsettia print on her sweater.

Mike gave Devon a pair of fur-lined leather gloves, because, he said, "The first thing Lucy noticed about you was that you didn't have any." He seemed pleased with the electronic pocket planner she gave him.

Devon was relieved that there was no gift for her from Eric, since she hadn't anything for him, either. But at the same time, when all the gifts had been distributed and opened—including way too many for Emily—she felt a kind of void, a sense of disappointment.

She thought of the mistletoe, and Mike sweeping Lucy into a classic Rhett Butler embrace. She thought of her vision of this same parlor filled with warmth and laughter and love, and of all those things embodied in a pair of arms wrapping themselves around her from behind...a whisper, sweet as music in her ear.

I have to talk to him, she thought—and remembered she'd had the very same thought at the beginning, that morning after she'd first met Eric. She'd told herself then that she needed to learn more about the man who was her clients' adversary—get to know him. Now—what was it?— four days later, he seemed more of a mystery to her than ever.

She almost wished they could go back to the way things had been then—even the open hostility of those first moments. Those had been honest, straightforward emotions, at least. Then had come confusion—the confrontation in the barn, Eric's terrible accusations, and finally, what had seemed like the beginnings of a grudging acceptance of her. And later, that first evening with his family in the parlor...Eric stringing tree lights with his father, sitting so close to Devon on the couch, challenging her, teasing, taunting her.

So much had happened since then. So much had changed. But what did I do, Devon wondered, to make him so distant? What did I do to make him hate me?

I have to talk to him about this, she thought. She had to.

But when? Tomorrow was Christmas; there would be company—Eric's cousin and her parents. It would almost have to be tonight.

She lingered, nervous with both resolve and dread, helping Lucy pick up wrapping paper and ribbon and tidy up the parlor, thinking she would catch Eric after his parents had gone to bed. But he excused himself, said good-night and went upstairs while Devon was carrying the popcorn and eggnog dishes and leftovers to the kitchen.

Later, she promised herself, dizzy and twanging with unspent tension. *I'll talk to him tonight…later.*

Eric sat on the edge of his bed and stared down at the large flat Christmas-wrapped package in his hands. It wasn't particularly pretty paper, now he really looked at it, kind of a muddy gold with sprays of evergreens and pinecones on it. But it had been that or Rudolph the Red-nosed Reindeer—the only pieces of wrapping paper left that were big enough to accommodate a 16 x 20 inch picture frame. What he was wondering now was why he'd bothered.

For the better part of two days, as he worked to put together the collage, searching through piles of photo albums, picking out scenes from his own childhood and his mother's and copying them on his dad's computer, he'd thought a lot about what he was doing, and why…daring to fantasize about what Devon might say when he gave it to her. *These are memories…memories of childhood,* he'd say to her. *Since you don't have any of your own, I wanted to give you some of mine….*

And she would say…what? What was he hoping for? Some kind of breakthrough? That Devon would take one look at the photographs and remember that her parents were monsters who'd molested and abused her and driven her sister out of their house and into a life of hell on the streets? Was he hoping for a miracle?

What had made him think he could bring about in a few days what could take trained therapists months or even years to accomplish? Or never.

Ah well, the collage had been a stupid idea, but he'd worked on the damn thing for two days, and if he didn't give it to Devon now, Dad—Mom, too, since it was a safe bet there weren't any secrets between those two—was going to wonder why. Devon was in her room now—he'd heard her door close a while ago—and his mom and dad were in theirs, and Emily asleep in there with them, in his old bassinet that his mom had hauled down from the attic. Tomorrow, Caitlyn and her folks would be here, and tomorrow night... Hell, who knew where he'd be tomorrow night?

It looked like, if he was ever going to give the collage to Devon, it would have to be now. He took a breath and stood up. Shifted the package under one arm and strode the three long paces to the door. Opened it—and froze in his tracks.

His heart catapulted through several layers of chest wall to lodge somewhere in his throat. "Devon—" he croaked. She was there in the doorway, almost nose-to-nose with him, one hand upraised to knock on his door.

"Hi." It was a whisper, hushed and hoarse. Her face was almost luminous in the dim hallway, her eyes lost in shadows. "I'm sorry—I didn't mean to startle you. Were you—?" She made a vague traveling gesture with her hand.

"No—no! In fact—" he hefted the package "—I was just—" Remembering where he was, he backed awkwardly out of the doorway and motioned her in. He closed the door as quietly as possible, then turned and looked at her and felt a strange and fleeting sense of unreality.

It struck him how out of place she looked—ludicrously so—standing there in his boyhood room with its faded denim curtains and horse-head lamp, his battered desk and worn paperback books. Slim and tall, elegant in black slacks and a sleeveless turtleneck shell—and on her even the green snowman scarf his mother had given her tonight seemed elegant—she made him think of the world she'd come from—a world of BMW's and valet parking, of Gucci shoes and Rolex watches and restaurants where famous people dined. A complicated woman, he thought—and as contradictory as the picture she presented now.

Looking at him the way she did now, with her chin up and her eyes green fire, she was all self-assurance, fearless and unyielding, beautiful yet untouchable—always in control, always in command. Yet, he'd seen her fearful. He'd touched her and felt her yield, at least to him. He'd felt her tremble on the brink of losing all control.

He knew that, if she were to turn just a bit, lower her head, just a little, he would see, below the sophisticated upswept hairdo she wore, caressed by a few errant tendrils of fiery red hair, the slender white column of a neck as fragile, as vulnerable as a child's.

"I was just on my way to see you," he said, and lifted the package, not thrusting it at her, just drawing her attention. "I wanted to give you this."

Her eyes flinched. She raised both hands in a small gesture of dismay, then clasped them together in front of her. "I didn't get you anything."

His smile dismissed that. "I never thought you would. Here—just as well open it." He nudged the package toward her.

"Oh, Eric..." She closed her eyes, then reluctantly took it from him. "Oh, God—" and she gave a light, unhappy laugh "—it feels like a picture frame. What did you do, blow up one of those horrible pictures you took of me floundering in the snow like a beached whale?"

He nodded toward the present. "Go ahead. Open it."

Devon's heart fluttered against her ribs. Her chest felt

tight, and the laugh she tried didn't do a thing to relieve it. She took a breath, summoned strength, then began to tear away the wrapping paper. As the pieces fluttered to the floor, she felt herself go still and cold. Her heart no longer pounded; she couldn't feel it beating at all.

From a distance she heard Eric say, "It's in there—the one you're worried about. That's it…right…*there*."

Oh, it was there, all right—funny that she'd focused on it first, even without his finger pointing it out to her—unmistakably Devon, even in all those layers that made her look like a pregnant penguin, with her hair shining like a beacon in all that snow. But not big, not blown up—oh no. Tiny. And not alone. There were others, so many others, some large and some small, square, oblong, round and oval, and except for hers, they were all of children. A little girl on a swing, pigtails flying, a plump little boy romping with puppies, children swimming in a pond, sleek as otters, children playing in mud, blowing bubbles in a bathtub, finger painting, making snowmen, eating watermelon, blowing out birthday candles, dressed up in costumes for Halloween, mugging for the camera with crossed eyes and stuck-out tongues, children in their Sunday best, grinning to show off missing teeth. There was even one of Emily, asleep with one hand curled against her cheek like flower petals.

"What is this?" Her voice was bumpy.

"They're memories," he said. "I thought, since you don't have any of your childhood…" He let it trail away.

She stared at him for a long, silent moment. His arms were folded on his chest, and his face was set—fierce and hawklike. Defensive, she thought. Defiant.

"Why?" she said in a tight, trembling voice. "Why did you do this? Because you wanted to give me *your* childhood? No—I'll tell you why. It's because you want me to remember mine. That's it, isn't it Eric? You want me to remember my childhood, but not a childhood like *this*—"

she turned the picture frame and thrust it toward him
"—all happy and sunshiny and bright. Oh, no. What you
want is for me to remember a nightmare. That my parents
were evil monsters—"

"Devon—" He reached toward her.

She jerked away from him just as his fingers were closing on her arm. Her hands lost their grip, and the picture
frame, with its collage of happy childhood memories,
slipped from them and fell to the floor with a cracking,
tinkling crash.

There was a gasp, a muffled oath; and for several heartbeats, deafening silence. Then Devon dropped to her knees,
and her hands darted here and there in quick, jerky forays,
snatching up shards of broken glass. She was saying, over
and over in a horrified whisper, "Oh, God—I'm so sorry—
I didn't mean to do that—I'm sorry...."

Eric had frozen, partly in shock, partly in dread, all
senses primed, ears cocked for the first sounds from down
the hall—a door opening, his mom's voice raised in question and alarm. When that failed to come, he didn't question the miracle, just let himself breathe again as he sank
to one knee beside Devon.

He didn't know what to do first, reach for her, rescue the
broken frame, or pull those unsteady hands away from the
perils of broken glass. He didn't know what to do, period.
He'd never been in such turmoil. He'd never been more
profoundly shaken, his heart pounding and his mouth dry,
clammy with adrenaline.

But at the same time his emotions had never been calmer
or more certain. In his heart, in his guts, in the deepest part
of himself, he knew he wanted to hold and soothe her, that
somehow he had to comfort and protect her. Seeing Devon
like this, with her customary self-confidence shattered, the
veneer of her composure and sophistication revealed for the
sham it was...the intensity of his feelings for her all but

overwhelmed him. Simple compassion, even protective tenderness couldn't account for this. This was something much more powerful, something primitive, possessive, life-changing.

His heart knew it, his gut knew it, but his head, his logical mind, caught somewhere between the turmoil and the certainty, refused to call it by name. His head, his reason, still insisted on telling him all the reasons it was impossible.

"Devon—" he said, reaching for her as he had before.

And again when he touched her she jerked, but toward him this time, not away. Magnified by a film of tears, her eyes locked with his, and this time the question was a plea. "Why are you doing this?"

His hand, instead of closing gently around her arm, dropped to his knee. He tried to smile. "Definitely not to hurt you."

"Oh, no?" Her voice was a thin, raspy whisper, as if she wanted to shout at him but was as conscious as he was of other ears just down the hall. "What, then?" She went back to grabbing up pieces of broken glass, her movements uncoordinated as she flung angry words at him over her shoulder. "I know what *you* want. You want me to tell you you're right, that the lies Susan told you are true. That our parents—" She gasped and jerked her hand back. Clutching it with the other, she began to swear in a low and furious whimper.

He reached for her, swearing himself; he'd caught a glimpse of telltale crimson, though she tried to shield it from him with her body. "Let me see. How bad is it?" She was on her feet, now, and so was he. "Come on, Devon—dammit—"

She twisted out of his grasp, stubbornly determined to evade him. Just as stubbornly he caught her by the arms and turned her to him. Her eyes blazed at him, more golden now than green. "Leave me alone. It's just a cut, for God's sake.'' She whispered it, desperate rather than angry. ''I just need some tissue—'' Her eyes darted past him in futile search.

He captured her hands in both of his and held them up so he could see the damage. A thin rivulet of blood spiraled down her left index finger in a candy cane design. His head spun; his heart thundered. ''You need a bandage on that,'' he said thickly, surprised at how calm he sounded. ''Some antiseptic. There's some in the bathroom.''

She tugged on her hands, trying again to pull away from him. ''No—your parents—they'll hear. Please. Just give me something to wrap it in. A handkerchief—*anything*.''

There was a plastic jar of baby wipe cloths on his nightstand, just out of reach. Afraid to let go of her, afraid she'd bolt if he did, he led her closer to the bed and holding her hands in one of his, reached to pluck several of the cloths from the jar. He wadded them around her bleeding finger, then folded it in and enfolded her hands in his. Held them close to him, close to his chest, close to his rapidly beating heart.

He didn't know how to help her. Leave me alone, she'd begged him. He couldn't do that, not until he'd given up all hope of ever getting from her what he so desperately needed. There was too much at stake—a little girl's future, not to mention his own. But she knew that—most of it.

What he hadn't anticipated, and what was complicating his life more than he'd thought possible, was that Devon's future had come to matter to him, too. *She* mattered. And he honestly didn't know whether forcing her to remember a nightmare past was going to help or hurt her in the long run. He thought it ought to help—like opening up a wound to allow it to heal. But what did he know about it, really? Sometimes, he knew, doctors might choose to leave a bullet or piece of shrapnel in someone because removing it would cause more damage than leaving it alone.

He didn't want to hurt her, or leave her alone—that much he knew. He wanted what he couldn't have. He wanted a miracle.

"Devon," he whispered, "I never wanted to hurt you."

"But you're willing to," she said, staring at their clasped hands, "to keep Emily."

He flinched inside but didn't try to evade the truth. "Yes." With eyes closed he bowed his head; his exhalation flowed like a caress over her fingers. "At first, believe me, it was just that simple. But it's not anymore. It's complicated. These past few days, Devon, I've come—dammit, I—"

She gave a cry, and her uninjured hand jerked from his grasp to press against his lips. Breathless and distraught, shaking her head rapidly, she whimpered, "No, no, no—" like a child denying the inevitable. "Don't you say it. You can't have feelings for me. You *can't*. I can't have feelings for you—"

"But you *do*," he said quietly. It wasn't a question.

She couldn't deny it, any more than he could. She didn't try. He felt her go still, still as death. Her mouth seemed to blur. The vulnerability of it tore at his heart.

Then his mouth was soft on hers...she whimpered, and he felt her lips quiver. The kiss grew urgent, hungry, and she was sobbing, the salt-sweet taste of her tears on his tongue. Her hands clutched at his shoulders, crept up the back of his neck. Her fingers burrowed into his hair. She gasped—or did he? He folded her close and held her hard against him, fearing his pounding heart would unbalance them both.

"I want you to make love to me," she whispered with her lips close to his ear. And she went on before he could answer. "I know it's insane. I know it's wrong. But I think I'll go crazy if we don't, just once."

He nodded. "I agree with everything you said. And it terrifies me." He gave a small, shaken laugh.

"I know. Me, too."

I never thought I could feel this way, Devon thought. That nothing else matters so much, that there is nothing more important than making love with this man, here and now. No matter the consequences. No matter the cost. The rest of my life will just have to work itself out somehow.

She drew back from him, but only a little. She held his face between her hands, and even the wad of baby wipe cloths on her finger failed to distract her as she said earnestly, breathless with resolve, "It's just this once…just for tonight. It has to be…"

"I know."

She felt a shock pass through his body, like a small seismic quake, and he held her harder against him. *Yes, this terrifies me, too,* she thought.

"It's all right if you don't have a condom." She whispered it, but her voice quivered with nervousness. "I think I can trust you. I know you can trust me. And I am on the pill."

He pulled back a little to look at her, his whiskey eyes warm and wry, half wary, half amused. "Will you think badly of me if I tell you I have one?"

"Why would I think badly of you? For being prepared—"

"I don't know, maybe you'd think I'm some sort of playboy—"

She laughed, and it felt warm and good deep down in her belly. "Eric, you're the last man I'd mistake for a playboy."

He laughed, too, a delicious quivering against her stomach. "I'm not sure whether that's a compliment or not."

"It is," she said, and added dryly, "Trust me." She lifted her face to him and he kissed her again, long and deeply this time. Exploring…inviting…promising. By the time he lifted his head again she was dizzy with longing, drunk with desire.

"Devon," he said in a thickened voice, "you're not going to change your mind again, are you?"

"No," she whispered, "are you?"

He lowered his mouth to hers. And that was his only answer.

Chapter 15

He drew her to the bed and they sat together on its edge, hands clasped, like children about to embark on a wondrous and terrifying adventure. Her eyes were brilliant, like emeralds, like diamonds, never leaving his as she picked up the edge of her black turtleneck and slowly drew it up and off.

As each slender inch of her body revealed itself to him, his hands touched her there, and he felt the soft skin of her belly and ribcage roughen with goose bumps. Her bra was black lace, stark against the ivory of her skin…translucent, like the insides of some shells. Reverently, he cradled the warm weight of her breasts in his hands, bent to kiss the sweet cleft between, the shadowy blush of her nipples—inhaling the citrus scent of her skin and tasting fabric and woman as he made both of them warm and wet in his mouth, then cold and shivering to hardness when he left them. He felt her gasp, and her breathing grow sharp and shallow.

He raised his head and looked at her. Her arms were still upraised and her hands fumbled, trembling, in the fastenings of her hair. Without saying anything, he gently pushed her hands away and usurped that task for himself. He plunged his fingers into the rich warm masses of her hair, letting them burrow without thought or plan to guide them, simply reveling in the sensual joy of touch. He kissed her the same way, and she him, in mindless, uncaring ways. The warmth, the feathery touch of mouths, the sharing of quick, rapturous breaths was enough for then. For the moment. He was in no hurry, and neither was she. He felt a sense of timelessness, of rarity, of awe, like being privileged to witness a comet that appears once in a millennium.

Though it was his first time making love to her, there wasn't the nervousness and fear, the excited urgency of other first times he remembered. He thought it was because it was also the first time he'd made love *with* love. He felt no need to be a virtuoso, no pressure to achieve a particular level of mastery or skill. It was enough for him just to love her, and everything he felt for her, give to her with his body, his eyes, his mouth, his hands.

And maybe also because, though it was his first time with her, the excitement and awe of that were tempered with sadness, and his joy with the aching awareness that it must also be the last time. He wanted to cherish and savor the moments he had with her now…as if he could somehow make them last forever.

She reached with her hands to lift the edge of his shirt, nudging it upward as her hands slid inside and rose along his ribs, fingertips finding deeper muscle where torso flared into back. He stopped kissing her in order to oblige her by pulling the shirt the rest of the way off, and when he would have resumed that breathless activity, she held him away with a hand, fingers spread wide across the middle of his chest while she drank in the perfection of his body with her eyes. It seemed perfection to her, the symmetry of his collarbones, the sweet way muscle clung to bone, the arrangement of hair in the center of his chest and around his nipples. Except for his arms and throat, his skin was fair, undamaged by sun, and blushed here and there with fever spots. Fascinated by them, she lowered her head and kissed each one, and felt his gasp, the thumping of his heartbeat against her lips. She felt his hands come to touch the sides of her head, lightly, as if he were bestowing a blessing, and he held his breath and shivered. She felt something inside herself rock with a strange quaking, somewhere between laughter and sobs.

Gently, so gently, he eased her down. Her eyes closed; rapture danced behind her eyelids when she felt his mouth, warm where she was cool, his hair a tickly coldness on her own fevered places. They undressed each other; what did it matter how, or in what order? She felt weightless, effervescent, her body no more hers to govern than if she'd been a kite riding on a storm wind. She had no purpose, no identity, no yesterday or tomorrow; her world was only in this moment; she existed only where he touched her.

But there was no part of her he did not touch! His touch was everywhere, first his hands—long, sensitive fingers guiding, stroking, boldly opening, preparing. Then his mouth—enticing, teasing, intoxicating, enthralling. His touch was stunning in its sensuality, rousing in her responses she'd never known herself to be capable of. Once reserved, now she was earthy and abandoned. She had no inhibitions, no shyness. She found herself opening to him without reserve, moving with and for him, and every part of her body his to touch, to kiss, to explore.

And there was such reverence in his touch, an almost worshipful awe. Everywhere he touched her body, touched her soul, her heart, her spirit, too, and when at last he sank himself into her body, she felt profound relief and overwhelming joy, as if until that moment she had never been whole.

She opened her eyes, and it was like seeing the sun for the very first time. His eyes gazed down at her, glowing with a rapturous light that warmed and softened his gaunt and craggy features, and it seemed to her the most beautiful face she had ever seen. She smiled, but didn't speak; she was too full of feeling for words.

He smiled, too, and for a long time they simply looked at each other, eyes filling with tears that were only emotions neither dared voice. Then Eric slowly lowered his mouth to hers; their fingers laced together as if from long and tender habit. Their bodies rocked slowly together as one body, without urgency or strain, and Devon felt herself softening, swelling, opening…like a bud ripening into a flower. The sensation was so exquisite, so beautiful, she smiled inside his smile, and tears squeezed beneath her eyelids. Her completion came, not like an explosion but like a blossoming, the unfolding of layers of petals, layer upon layer, growing and growing, until she clung to Eric, whimpering in fear and panic, sure her body couldn't contain so much sensation.

Afterward she wept, and he held her so tightly she could feel his own rapidly beating heart, and murmured broken assurances into her hair. But she couldn't tell him why she was crying. Couldn't tell him she was sure such exquisite joy and beauty were not humanly possible, and therefore could not have been real, that it must have been a dream. That she wept because she knew with utter certainty she would never know such happiness again.

She awoke in his arms. He felt her lashes tickle his cheek before she stirred, and slyly said, ''Good morning.'' And laughed at her dismayed gasp, her sudden stiffening. ''I'm teasing,'' he whispered against her temple, ''though it is morning—and Merry Christmas, by the way. You've only been asleep a few minutes. It's still a long time until daylight.''

"I still should go." Her voice was husky, her breath warm and humid against his shoulder.

"Not yet." His heart lurched in denial of the inevitable, and he tightened his arms around her and cuddled her closer. At what point—was it after the second, or the third time they'd made love?—had they actually made it into his bed? Now, inside the tumble of blankets, they lay twined together like puppies.

"What if we fall asleep? What would your parents think?"

He laughed again, with less humor this time. "Are you kidding? I think my mother planned this from the beginning."

She didn't reply, and the silence lengthened while they listened to their pulses ticking against each other, growing louder and louder, like unsynchronized clocks. At last she said very softly, "Eric...are you regretting this?"

His arms tightened reflexively around her. He uttered a garbled, "No—" then cleared his throat and repeated it. "No—of course not. What made you think that?"

"You're so quiet. I thought..."

He paused, feeling the ache come back into his heart, the sadness coming home to roost like the wintering sparrows in his mother's barn. "I guess I was just listening," he said.

"Listening to what?"

"The clock striking midnight."

"What clock? I don't hear—oh. Cinderella, right?" He felt her body relax with an exhalation, as if she were relieved to discover she knew the right answer to a question on a quiz. "You mean—"

"Back to the real world...."

She stirred restlessly, opening up space between them. The blankets seemed too warm, now—suffocating.

"Eric…" Her voice was so small he had to hold his breath to hear her. "I can't do what you want me to. I'm sorry." It broke, and she shored it up with a breath. "I can't remember what didn't happen."

"It's all right," he said, and discovered that it was true. He felt calm and quiet inside, now. His mind was clear, his course set, all decisions made. He had no more battles to fight.

"It didn't happen. What Susan told you—I don't know why she told you that, but it isn't true. It just isn't. I'd remember something like that."

He murmured reassurances to her, his hand moving on her back in long, gentle strokes, as if he were comforting someone waking from a bad dream. She lifted her head and looked at him; her eyes were jewel-like in the dim light, and luminous with hope. "She'll be all right, Eric. I want you to know that. My mom and dad will be good parents to her. She'll have a good home. You'll be able to visit her—your mom and dad, too, if they want to. We can work it out…"

"I know," he said gently, soothing her. "It's all right…it's going to be all right."

"Merry Christmas…Merry Christmas!"

The greetings flew back and forth across the yard like snowballs mixed with laughter, accompanied by cold-flushed cheeks and sparkling eyes and hugs, and dogs hovering, circling, darting everywhere with wiggles and excited yips.

Devon had watched it all from the kitchen window—Mike and Lucy hurrying down the steps and across the yard as a maroon SUV pulled to a stop beneath the leafless oaks, car doors opening, three people getting out—a tall, very attractive man with dark hair, graying at the temples, and two women, both also tall, both also very attractive. One, older but still slender and youthful, had long silver-blond hair worn in a ponytail, pulled straight back from a classic oval face and caught at the back of her neck with a red velvet bow that matched her red holiday sweater and red and green plaid skirt.

The other—and Devon caught her breath, because this could only be Eric's cousin, Caitlyn—defied such easy description. Even dressed in the nondescript casual, even scruffy way popular with Generation X-ers, with pale chin-length hair in spiky disarray, she was still breathtakingly beautiful. And there was something unconventional about that beauty—an ethereal, almost magical quality impossible to define. Her silvery eyes and full mouth seemed too large for her heartshaped face and delicate chin, and yet her smile was simply incandescent. Though thin to the point of appearing frail, she moved with such grace that her feet seemed barely to touch the ground, and when Eric swept her up in a hug and swung her around, Devon whimsically thought of gossamer wings shimmering, iridescent in the weak winter sun.

She felt a stab in the vicinity of her heart and pressed her hand against her chest, though she knew the pain wasn't physical. *It's jealousy. I'm jealous...* And how irrational is that, she thought, when I have neither right nor reason?

But she was. As she watched them talking together, heads leaning close, she knew that she was jealous of Eric's relationship with his cousin and childhood friend. Jealous of the easy intimacy between them, the familiarity that came of a lifetime of friendship, of shared memories.

Out in the yard, Caitlyn slipped an arm around Eric's waist; her face, lifted to his, was earnest, her beauty dampened now by the gravity of her features. Eric was smiling his crooked smile as he dropped his arm across her shoulders and gave her a quick, affectionate squeeze. And the pain in Devon's heart became an all-over ache of longing.

It's all right. It's going to be all right.

Eric's words, spoken in the quiet of night in the intimacy of his bed, came into her heart like a searching finger of sunshine, and she felt a small shiver of hope. When this is over, she thought. When the custody issue is settled, maybe then. Maybe it's still possible. Anything is possible, isn't it?

I hate this, she thought, with a momentary surge of anger. *I hate being like this. If this is what falling in love is about—so much doubt and uncertainty, so much vulnerability and fear—I don't want it. I want myself back!*

Just that quickly, the anger was replaced by fear. What if I never get the old Devon back, she thought. What if this is going to be me from now on? Her hand touched the cool glass of the window pane. *Oh, Eric. What have I…what have you done…to me?*

There was a clatter of stamping boots and slamming doors on the back porch, and a gust of cold, damp air swept into the warm kitchen. With a smile firmly in place, Devon turned to meet the newcomers, while outside Eric and Caitlyn walked on together, shoulder-to-shoulder, under the skeleton trees.

"Everything's in there," Caitlyn said. The envelope passed quickly from her hand to Eric's, and from there to the inside of his jacket. "Passports, social security cards, driver's license. It's an Arizona license, by the way—your hometown is Prescott. What about money?"

"I have enough," Eric said. "Enough to get us settled."

"What's your bank?" He told her, and she nodded. "They'll have branches everywhere. You'll need cash. As soon as the banks open tomorrow, stop at one and withdraw everything you can, then destroy your old IDs. When you get where you're going, you can open a new account with your new ID—okay?"

"Got it." His voice felt like gravel, like broken glass.

"You'll need to be ready. And watching. If the driver sees a light on in your bedroom window, he'll wait fifteen minutes, that's all. You'll have to take Emily and whatever else you can manage to carry and get yourself down to the road."

"Understood." He'd stopped walking to gaze over her head, frowning at nothing. She stopped, too, and put her hands on the front of his coat.

"Eric—if you change your mind, all you have to do is leave your light off. Don't keep the rendezvous. It's that simple."

He shook his head and grimaced in pain; his throat ached and his jaws felt cramped. "Don't have much choice, do I?"

"You always have choices," Caitlyn said softly.

He shifted his shoulders as if settling himself under a burden. "No—I'm doing the right thing. I know I am. It's just..." He took a breath and laughed with the pain. "I didn't know it was going to be this hard."

"Leaving here, you mean? Your folks?"

"Yeah, that, too..."

"You don't mean...*Devon?*"

He tried to smile. "It's ironic, isn't it? I've been all over the world and never found the right woman, and she goes and shows up here, of all places—on my mom and dad's doorstep."

"Oh, God, Eric..."

"It's like I said on the phone. I never really appreciated what I had here," he said quietly, squinting over her head. The day was turning overcast, but his eyes burned. "You know that—I couldn't wait to get away. Lately, though, I've actually been thinking about living here. Not full-time—maybe like a base between assignments, you know?" He threw Caitlyn a rueful, sideways grin. "I've even thought about living here with Devon—raising kids...Emily...a few more of our own." And he laughed at the incredulous look on her face. "Hey, it's a fantasy."

"Do you think she ever would?" Caitlyn's voice was hushed with astonished disbelief. "She seems so..."

Eric shrugged, and his smile slipped sideways. "Not that it matters now. Hey—come on." He dropped an arm across her shoulders and turned her back toward the house. "It's time you met the woman who's changed my life."

The family was gathered in the parlor again. The massive Christmas meal had been eaten—some of it; the rest, except for the desserts, left out to tempt and entice, had been packed in Tupperware containers and freezer bags and put away. The chores had been done early. The forecast was for snow, though not a blizzard this time, and no one seemed particularly concerned about the roads.

As evening came they all drifted, one by one, into the parlor, Mike and Lucy, with Emily in her arms, taking the recliner; Wood and Chris snugged up with Devon on the couch, friendly as family; Eric across the room on the piano bench and Caitlyn cross-legged nearby on the floor. They'd sung carols again—a great many of them, with Wood's and Chris's and Caitlyn's strong voices making a real chorus of it, and though she wasn't needed, Devon joined in when she knew the words.

Sleep in heavenly peace....

The last notes of "Silent Night" died away, along with Lucy's misty sniffles, and it occurred to Devon that there was a kind of quietness inside herself, now, that might be called peace. All things considered, it had been a good day, a pleasant day. She'd met Caitlyn, and wonder of wonders, found that she liked her. She liked Wood and Chris, too—they were all such warm, open-hearted people, these Lanagans and Browns, it would have been hard not to like them. The tension and turmoil of the past few days seemed to have disappeared, though outwardly Eric was as distant as before. But today she carried with her memories of the night they'd shared, and sometimes when she looked at him and found his eyes on her, glowing like warm brandy, she knew he was thinking of it, too.

It's going to be all right. He'd said those words to her with such calm, such certainty, as if he knew something she did not, and she clung to them now like a talisman.

Once again it was time for opening presents. Most were the gifts exchanged between the two families, of course, but to Devon's astonishment, there were two more for her, as well—a tiny gold angel on a chain from Chris and Wood, and a book of inspirational essays from Lucy and Mike. Chris and Wood and Caitlyn all thanked Eric for his e-mailed gift certificates to an on-line bookstore. Then Caitlyn held up a glossy gift bag decorated with teddy bears.

"This is for the wee one," she said, lifting it up to Eric.

He leaned to place the bag at Lucy's feet. "Here, Mom—you've got the kid."

But Lucy handed it on to Devon, saying, "Why don't you open it, dear? I've got so many...."

With an apologetic glance at Caitlyn, Devon placed the bag on the floor between her feet. Caitlyn smiled and nodded. Devon lifted the concealing pouf of tissue paper out of the bag. Slowly, then, she drew the plump yellow bear out of its tissue paper nest and placed it on her knees.

The room around her grew silent, the people in it faded to shadows. Of their own volition her fingers crept to the bear's back and found the small key they somehow knew was hidden there. She turned it and the tinkling notes of a familiar lullaby filled the room.

Someone in the happy babble of voices was saying, "Devon, what is it? Is something the matter?"

And from a great distance she heard her own voice reply, with a laugh as small and light as the notes from the music box, "My sister Susan used to have one just like this..."

Memories don't have to be big, you know. They can be anything—a smell, a song, a particular toy, a moment.

Devon lay awake in the last cold darkness before dawn with those words echoing in her mind and the tinkling notes of a music box lullaby all around her like ghost music. *A moment...*

Please, Devon, don't leave me...

She had woken from the nightmare, as so many times

before, with Susan's voice—the voice of the child Susan—ringing in her ears. Only this time, this time there were the images, too.

The suitcase, open on the bed, and Susan…eight years old, standing beside it…hugging her old scruffy yellow bear as if it were her last and only friend. Susan, with tears streaming down her face, sobbing, "Please, Devon, please don't leave me…"

And then the rest. The part she'd forgotten. The part she couldn't let herself remember. *"…don't leave me here with him. He hurts me, Devon. He hurts me…."*

She thought it strange, as she lay drained and heavy in the darkness, that she should feel so calm. It seemed to her it should happen more dramatically than this, remembering things so terrible, forgotten for so long. She thought of movies she'd seen—T.V. dramas involving shrinks and hypnotists and emotional trauma. *I should feel something.* But the memories were of things that had happened to someone else, some other little girl, some other life. All she felt was a cold and well-remembered self-loathing, an icy, crawling sense of shame.

I have to tell Eric, she thought, as the first gray light came to thin the darkness. *I have to tell him he was right…about Emily, about Susan… About everything.*

Part of her ached for the warm and comforting presence of his body, of his strong arms and gentle words. *It's going to be all right.* Another part of her—the biggest part—shrank from those memories, the memories of her uninhibited self, of her body so pliant and willing in his sensitive hands, his beautiful, incredible mouth, their bodies twined together as one being.

How can I face him now? She recoiled from the thought.

Somehow, though, she found the strength to rise, to walk to the door and open it. Her legs felt strange, wobbly, as if she were using them for the first time after a long illness. Her heart lumbered in her chest with such violence she wondered how she could even stand. She wondered if she would throw up.

Trailing her fingers along the wall to steady herself, she moved down the silent hallway. The floor was cold on her bare feet. At the door to Eric's room she closed her eyes...and summoning all her strength, raised her hand to knock. She knocked with one knuckle, then paused to listen. She knocked again, then quietly turned the knob and opened the door.

A moment later she was flying down the hallway, heart banging, pounding with the flat of her hand on Mike and Lucy's bedroom door, all thought of stealth forgotten.

The creaking of the stairs warned her. She spun around, trembling, both hands behind her gripping the doorknob for support as Mike and Lucy came toward her, close together, leaning on each other, looking years older, suddenly, and terribly sad.

"Is Emily with you?" she gasped, knowing the answer.

"They're gone," Mike said gently. He held something toward her—a folded sheet of paper, and she saw that Lucy was holding a similar one in her hands, this one unfolded. Her face was shiny wet with tears. "Eric's gone, Devon. He left this for you."

Chapter 16

"*"Don't* blame Devon...'?" Lucy read from the paper in her hands. Aroused and bristling with outrage, she reached for Devon's hand and gave it a squeeze. "As if we would. Our own son—how could he think such a thing?"

Mike's arm, lying in a comforting way across the back of Lucy's chair, tightened momentarily around her shoulders. "I don't think he knew the whole story," he told her in a private sort of way. "He was so young when he left, we hadn't told him." His face was gray with regret.

"You *should* blame me." Devon's voice was gray, too—flat and dull. "It's my fault—all of it. If I had only—"

"No." Mike's quiet eyes searched for hers, commanded their full attention, and for the first time she saw his son in them. Her throat filled again with the tears she hadn't been able to shed. "You're a victim, as much as anyone. More than anyone."

Devon stolidly shook her head. "You don't understand."

"No, dear," said Lucy, "it's *you* who doesn't under-stand."

They were sitting at the kitchen table, still cheery in its Christmas dressing, Lucy and Mike close together on one side, Devon at the end, coffee cups in front of them more for warming hands than drinking. Outside, a gloomy dawn was breaking. It had begun to snow again.

Lucy looked at Mike, who nodded. Her eyes came back to Devon's and she began to speak in a halting way that was most unlike her usual blunt and forthright manner. "Devon, this isn't the first time our family's had to deal with this kind of tragedy. Chris—my brother Earl's wife—you met her yesterday—had a childhood very similar to yours. Only she wasn't able to block it out, the way you did. Her way of escaping was to get married, when she was just sixteen, to an older man who abused her, too...in a different way. When she left him, he stalked her, and would have killed her if my brother hadn't gotten there in time." She paused, cast glistening eyes toward her husband and drew a breath. "So you see, dear, we *do* understand."

No, Devon thought as she gazed down at the small brown hand holding so tightly, so confidently to hers, you don't. *Devon, please don't leave me....* The truth was something that could never be understood, or forgiven.

Too exhausted to argue, she gently removed her hand from Lucy's and picked up her coffee mug. "I'd better get packed...."

"Oh, Devon," Lucy cried in dismay, "you don't have to go. Not so soon."

"I need to get back. There are some things I have to do."

"But, if Eric should contact us—"

"He won't—not for 'a while.' He says so in his letter." What did that mean, *a while?* Days, weeks, years? She pushed back from the table and stood up. "If he does, you can tell him there's not going to be any challenge to his custody of Emily. My parents will be withdrawing their suit." She added grimly, "I'll see to that."

She turned and walked out of the warm, bright kitchen for the last time, leaving behind a silence broken only by the sound of Lucy blowing her nose.

Snowflakes settled onto Devon's curls as she lifted her overnighter into the back seat of the Lincoln and slammed the door. It had been snowing all morning, not a howling blizzard, but fat, lovely flakes—Christmas card snow, Devon thought as she brushed the spun-sugar accumulation from the windshield—nothing the big Lincoln's all-weather tires couldn't handle.

Her hands, gloveless as usual, began to ache, and she stared down at her cold-reddened hand, at the bandage on her index finger. *"It's not a Christmas card. Don't you know it's cold out there?"* Is this what it's going to be like? she wondered. For the rest of my life, hearing his voice…remembering….

She turned from the car as the dogs came barking from their den under the porch. Shielding her eyes from drifting snowflakes, she watched a car, an unfamiliar dark SUV, churn its way up the lane in four-wheel-drive. It stopped a short distance away, its windows reflecting back a pale sky and the charcoal tracings of tree branches. The driver's door opened, and a man got out.

Devon put out a hand, groping blindly for support; finding none, she swayed, then steadied herself.

"Forgot your hat again, I see." His voice was nothing like the tender, gentle voice in her memory. It was harsh, and tortured her ears like sandpaper on raw nerves.

She didn't know what—or even *if* she answered him. As if in a dream she lifted a hand and touched her hair, and was surprised at the cold wetness of snow on her fingers.

She'd forgotten the cold. Her face burned with heat; her heart thundered, filling every part of her with its echoes.

His narrowed eyes shifted from her to the Lincoln and back again. One hand went out to grip the car's doorhandle, as if to physically prevent it from moving from that spot. "Thank God I got here in time." His voice, still a growl, held a different urgency now. "I couldn't go—I can't let you leave—"

"Where's Emily?" Devon found her voice at last.

"In a safe house. She's in good hands. Devon—I have to talk to you. There's something I have to tell—"

"Wait—I have to tell *you* something—" The rest caught in her throat as he grabbed her roughly by the arm.

"We can talk in the barn," he grated, walking rapidly through fresh-fallen snow, towing her like a broken tether.

"Eric, *wait.*" She pulled back, throwing all her weight and determination into resisting him, and he turned to look at her in scowling surprise. She jerked her arm from his grasp and gulped in cold, wet air as if it were an elixir to give her strength. Dry-mouthed and breathless anyway, she gasped, "Please listen to me—you don't have to run. You don't have to take her away. I'm not going to fight you, Eric. I'm going to make my parents give up their claim. Do you understand? You can keep her. Emily's yours...."

He'd gone utterly still. Even after her voice had run down and faded to nothing he didn't move, even to release the faint whisper of sound. *"You remembered...."*

"Yes." Her voice, tight with control, sounded clipped and hard. "Yes, Eric, I remembered. Everything. You were right—"

Suddenly, shockingly, his face seemed to crumple, and he threw up both hands to cover it, trying to hide it from her. After what seemed like forever, his hands moved out and upward to rake through his hair. He drew in air in a long sniff, then released it in a rush and a whispered,

"Ah…God." Bringing bright, red-rimmed eyes back to hers, he touched her arm and said thickly, "Come with me, Devon…please? We have to talk."

She didn't want to. More than anything, she wanted to run away, crawl into a hole, a dark quiet place, and hide. She was tired of emotions, tired of pain.

As she turned to go with Eric, Devon threw one brief look back toward the porch steps, where Mike and Lucy stood weeping with their arms wrapped tightly around each other—each, it appeared, keeping the other from following.

He didn't know how to begin, how to say to her what he'd come with such terrible urgency to say. What had seemed so simple and clear to him when he'd rehearsed it in the car now seemed neither, and the words themselves the most difficult he'd ever spoken.

As it turned out, he didn't have to begin. He'd barely got the barn door closed and latched before Devon whirled on him.

"How could you do that to them?" she demanded in a fury, whispering though there was no one but him to hear her. "Don't you know you almost broke their hearts?"

What about you? he wanted to ask. Did my going do anything to your heart?

What he said to her, turning from her so he wouldn't have to see her icy eyes and pale, frozen face, was an almost surly, "I came back, didn't I?"

"Why did you?" Her voice broke and he jerked back to her, but not before she had spun away, hiding her face from him. "You'd made it, free and clear. Your letter said you weren't coming back. So I'll ask you again." It was her courtroom lawyer's voice. *"Why did you?"*

"God, Devon, don't you know?" He flung it at her, in a voice like a shovelful of gravel. "I came back because of *you.*" She was backing away from him, shaking her head, her eyes dark and rejecting. Every part of him wanted to reach for her, haul her back and into his arms, his whole body ached with the need to hold her. It took all the self-control he possessed to make his body still, his voice quiet and calm. "Once I'd gotten Emily to that safe house, I realized I had to come back, even if it meant going to jail. I couldn't leave things the way they were between us."

"There's nothing between us!" She hurled it back at him like shards of broken glass. "It was *once*. We both said it."

"Once isn't enough for me, Devon." He made his voice warm, warm as rain. Moving closer, he saw the beginnings of her melting... "I want more nights like that one, a whole lot more. A lifetime of nights." He felt her face, cold and damp between his palms, and held it firm and fast when she tried to shake her head in frantic denial. "Yes—I'm going to fight you, Devon. That's why I came back. I'm going to fight you...for *us*." He paused to draw a knife-edged breath. "I guess what I'm trying to say is that I love you."

She uttered a cry as if he'd dealt her a mortal wound, and wrenched herself from his grasp. Crouched, she faced him like a wounded, cornered animal. "No—you don't. You couldn't possibly. If you think you do, you're wrong."

His crooked smile formed slowly. Was it more painful, he wondered, to have love rejected...or denied?

"Why can't I possibly love you?" he asked, stalking her relentlessly. Backed against a stall, she could only whimper and turn her face away when he pulled her into his arms.

"You don't know," she whispered. "You don't know...."

"I know you weren't to blame for anything that happened to you," he said, more roughly than he meant to. The pain in his throat, in his heart, was almost more than he could bear. Pain for her. "Don't you even think about blaming yourself."

But she was struggling against him again, pounding his chest with her fists and sobbing, great tearing sobs that must have hurt her throat…that hurt him to hear. "No—you don't understand—you don't know. You don't know *anything*. I left her, don't you understand? Susan…*I left her there*." She stared up at him, now, with dry eyes, the green of them swallowed in darkness. Her mouth twisted with self-loathing. "She begged me not to. She begged me…and I…left…her…with…him. My little sister. What kind of person would do such a thing?" Her voice was a desolate whisper. "What kind of person am I?"

He didn't know what to say to her. He tried to pull her close, to wrap her in his arms, but she shook her head and pressed her palms against his chest.

"I meant to go back—I did. I told her I'd come back for her, when I could. But I…I didn't…I…don't remember why…"

"You blocked it out," Eric murmured. "Your mind erased it for you. You didn't go back because you didn't remember why you should."

Her eyelids quivered down. He lifted her into his arms as her face crumpled.

He carried her into the stall and laid her down on the clean straw he'd put there only two days ago. He reached up and turned on the heat lamp and took off his jacket before he stretched himself out beside her. Then, carefully as he would have undressed Emily, he eased Devon out of her city coat. "Shall I tell you what kind of person I see?" he said as, gazing down into her hopeless eyes, he slipped his hand under her sweater and fanned his fingers wide across her stomach. "I see a woman who was once a little girl, a little girl who was horribly, terribly wounded by the very person she should have been able to trust to keep her safe.'' His voice was husky, his throat ached with tenderness. His eyes burned with unshed tears as they held on to hers, held them as if there were a line stretching between, and she dangled from it over a yawning chasm. ''And yet, she managed, that little girl, to grow up and make a life for herself in spite of her wounds. Managed to grow into a beautiful, successful woman, capable of warmth and kindness, capable of giving and receiving love—''

''How do you know that?'' she asked him, breathless and disbelieving.

''I've seen you,'' he told her softly. ''With Emily...''

''I ran away from her! I was afraid to even hold her.'' But he saw her eyes kindle with the beginning of hope.

Eric thought about what his dad had said and smiled. ''I know,'' he murmured, and leaned down and slowly, deeply kissed her. And kissed her, and kissed her, and while he kissed her he slowly, slowly undressed her, and himself as well. ''I know,'' he whispered, caressing her lips with the words, ''that you are beautiful in all ways. And I intend to spend the rest of my life showing you how beautiful you are—as beautiful in your soul as you are here, and here, and here.'' And with his mouth he showed her just where she was beautiful—her throat, her breasts, her belly and thighs, and all the sweet soft womanly places between....

When she was honeyed and wet and trembling on the edge of breaking, he surged up and over her and grafted her to him with one tremendous thrust, and in that union was all the power of his love for her and faith in her, all the strength of his will and conviction. He felt what resistance and doubt there was left in her melt away, felt her shatter, and then himself, too. Felt himself come apart with her, then form again, both of them whole, and at the same time, forever and ever a part of each other.

Afterward, she wept at last. ''That's right, cry, my love,'' Eric whispered, kissing the tear-pools on each eyelid. *Let the healing begin.*

Epilogue

"Mr. and Mrs. Lanagan, say hello to your daughter. As of this moment, Emily is one hundred percent officially yours." The family court judge beamed like a happy elf as he brought the gavel down. "Congratulations. Oh—and Merry Christmas. Now…let's see. Who's next?"

Mike and Lucy rose from their seats farther back in the courtroom as Eric and Devon turned from the judge's bench, faces flushed with happiness and love, Emily squirming in her daddy's arms, loudly demanding to be put down. She'd only recently mastered walking, and was eager to put her new skill to good use. Lucy watched with a grandmother's indulgent smile as the baby swayed, found her balance, then took off—only to fall on her diapered bottom three steps later.

"Oh, Mike," Lucy whispered as Eric swept his daughter

up and settled her on his shoulders, then put an arm around his wife's shoulders, "it's going to be such a wonderful Christmas."

"Even in L.A.?" Mike whispered back, raising an eyebrow.

Lucy jabbed him in the ribs with her elbow. "Christmas with our son and daughter-in-law and brand-new grandbaby—doesn't matter where. Oh, Mike—what a wonderful gift Eric's given us. The greatest gift a child can ever give his parents."

"You mean...a grandchild?"

With glistening eyes Lucy shook her head. "He's made us *proud*."

* * * * *

CODE NAME: **DANGER**

The action continues with the men—and women—of the Omega Agency in Merline Lovelace's *Code Name: Danger* series.

This August, in TEXAS HERO (IM #1165) a renegade is assigned to guard his former love, a historian whose controversial theories are making her sorely in need of protection. But who's going to protect *him*—from her? A couple struggles with their past as they hope for a future....

And coming soon, more *Code Name: Danger* stories from Merline Lovelace....

Code Name: Danger Because love is a risky business...

If you enjoyed what you just read,
then we've got an offer you can't resist!

Take 2 bestselling
love stories FREE!

Plus get a FREE surprise gift!

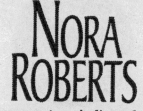

**Where royalty and romance
go hand in hand...**

The series continues in Silhouette Romance
with these unforgettable novels:

HER ROYAL HUSBAND
by Cara Colter
on sale July 2002 (SR #1600)

THE PRINCESS HAS AMNESIA!
by Patricia Thayer
on sale August 2002 (SR #1606)

SEARCHING FOR HER PRINCE
by Karen Rose Smith
on sale September 2002 (SR #1612)

And look for more Crown and Glory stories in
SILHOUETTE DESIRE starting in October 2002!

Available at your favorite retail outlet.

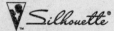

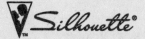

COMING NEXT MONTH